Sometimes the healing

Sometimes the healing

SallyAnne Clark

Copyright © 2017 SallyAnne Clark

The moral right of the author has been asserted.

Apart from any fair dealing for the purposes of research or private study, or criticism or review, as permitted under the Copyright, Designs and Patents Act 1988, this publication may only be reproduced, stored or transmitted, in any form or by any means, with the prior permission in writing of the publishers, or in the case of reprographic reproduction in accordance with the terms of licences issued by the Copyright Licensing Agency. Enquiries concerning reproduction outside those terms should be sent to the publishers.

This is a work of fiction. Names, characters, businesses, places, events and incidents are either the products of the author's imagination or used in a fictitious manner. Any resemblance to actual persons, living or dead, or actual events is purely coincidental.

Matador
9 Priory Business Park,
Wistow Road, Kibworth Beauchamp,
Leicestershire. LE8 0RX
Tel: 0116 279 2299
Email: books@troubador.co.uk
Web: www.troubador.co.uk/matador
Twitter: @matadorbooks

ISBN 978 1788036 603

British Library Cataloguing in Publication Data.
A catalogue record for this book is available from the British Library.

Printed and bound in the UK by TJ International, Padstow, Cornwall
Typeset in 11pt Aldine401 BT by Troubador Publishing Ltd, Leicester, UK

Matador is an imprint of Troubador Publishing Ltd

*This book is dedicated to the memory of my
beloved sister Lorraine, because during all
the chats, and the advice to each other on
improving our health, it was in the love and care
that sometimes the healing was found.*

Acknowledgements

Firstly, thanks are due to my father, who brought me home from his printing works a perfectly bound but very old (1952) dictionary when I was about ten years old. Mysteriously, it contained a select list of characters from Greek mythology, and my interest in the topic was sparked.

Thank you also to Tina, for my knowledge of kinesiology, to Hilary, for my knowledge of the Alexander Technique, and to Charlie, for his 'home planet' idea.

Particular thanks go to Beth, Wendy and Joy, for being so supportive and helpful in a very practical way.

Contents

1. Stephanie Harman, Clinic Director   1
2. The Clinic fails Ivy Lennox   21
3. Andy's Alexander Lesson   34
4. Fun in the Book Centre with Jane   54
5. Jon and Amy in the Real World   76
6. Sasha's Story   85
7. Lizzie's Lucky Day   96
8. Coffee Break Conversation   115
9. Tom's Troubles with the Young People   126
10. Sir Galahad and His Lady of the Overalls 142

11.	Michelle finds her Voice	165
12.	Malcolm's Harbes	179
13.	Man, Waiting	195
14.	Teresa's tired, but wait a bit: She just needs her coffee hit	203
15.	The Revenge of Typhon	218
16.	Friends, Enemies, and Lovers	232
17.	The Fall	255
18.	Telos	259

Chapter One

Stephanie Harman, Clinic Director

"I'm sorry, Mrs Harman, I didn't mean to imply – "

"In which case you might have chosen a better form of words, Mr Gilbert." There was silence for a moment while I considered my options. I had invited him here to try and get a balanced account of the Yatross clinic on public record, instead of the wild speculation that had been growing recently. I could hardly expect a reporter not to raise that same issue of public speculation. It was time for an olive branch.

"Would you like some coffee before we start the interview?" That cheered him up. "Yes, that would be great; er, you really have *coffee* here?"

"What did you think, that I'd force you to drink a vegetable extract drink or something?" He grinned at that, and I was aware that the atmosphere had warmed a little as I walked to the door and called to Sharon for some coffee. He isn't so bad, I thought, and turned round just in time to see him expertly scanning the file I'd left open on the desk. Naturally there was nothing of any use to him in there, but I would have to be more careful.

Oh, well, attack is the best form of defence, or so they say. "Your editor told you, I hope, that I want to see your article before it goes to press?"

"No, he didn't, actually. That could be rather difficult. In fact, probably impossible."

That arrogance!

"Why, were you intending to write something I probably wouldn't approve of?"

He smiled so superciliously I was tempted to throw the paperweight at him. What was it about this man? I usually had much better control of my emotions than this.

"You see: it's really a question of timing, Mrs. Harman. If I have to write an article in time for you to give your approval before the print deadline – "

"Mr Gilbert, I'm not going to do a critical appraisal on it and give you marks out of 100. It will either give a true picture of the clinic or it won't, in which case I shall tear it up. If you can't agree to me seeing copy then we should stop wasting each other's time."

Bob Gilbert swallowed, shrugged slightly, and then the coffee arrived. While he helped himself to milk and sugar (lots of sugar – mental note – he has sweet tooth) I wondered how he would describe me for his article: 'a tall woman with a cap of silver hair, and sharp features,'? or would he be kinder? Then, seeing he had his digital recorder set up and ready, I began speaking, hoping we wouldn't have another false start.

"I set up an alternative health clinic, and named it 'Yatross,' more than ten years ago. We started in a small way, with just a few practitioners, and about seven years ago moved to this building, so that we could expand."

"It's beautiful here – the gardens are amazing," put in the journalist. I gave him credit for not asking what 'Yatross' meant, as this meant he had already taken the trouble to find out.

"Yes, the gardens are part of the treatment, on several levels – I'll come on to that. I chose here because of the amount of land that came with the building – it meant we could stay here for a long time, and provide continuity for our patients."

"You call them 'patients'. You started as a GP, I gather?"

"That's right. I believe in the NHS, and worked for the benefit of patients within it for many years. But whereas it met many people's needs well, there was a large section of my practice for whom standard medical practice just didn't work, or wasn't what they needed or wanted to get totally well. I had friends who consulted various alternative health practitioners, and they seemed to thrive, and eventually I came to the conclusion that for some people, alternative medicine really was the answer. And holistic therapy is even more effective, I discovered."

"But you can get acupuncture and that on the NHS anyway, can't you?"

"Yes, but we offer so much more than that. We assess patients over several appointments to find out what would work best for them, and they then have access to herbal medicine, homeopathy, kinesiology, Alexander technique, shiatsu, and so on. We also provide various forms of counselling and cognitive behaviour therapy; also mindfulness training. I won't go into what all these are now, as it will take up too much time, but I'll give you an information pack before you go."

"Tell me about this charging policy you have – is nothing here free?" I shifted in my chair and looked out of the window, as I did dozens of times every day when I wanted to think, and then immediately realised the recorder would not pick up my voice, so reluctantly I turned back to the desk.

"The initial assessment is free – how can you be expected to pay for something when you don't understand why you need it? But then patients pay for their treatments."

"What if you can't afford it?"

"Then," I smiled, "as I'm sure you've heard, we find a way for you to contribute, in an alternative way. Everyone contributes something: that too is part of the healing process. I have, for example, several people who work in the gardens under the supervision of my Head Gardener, who will proudly tell you that he too was once a patient here. I have young mums working in the crèche and the café, there are patients running the library, and some of the day and evening activities. One patient in her 80's asked me what she could possibly have to offer, but after talking with our bursar, she now regularly brings in cuttings from her garden, and argues with the gardeners about where they should go. I'm sorry, strike that out, please, *chats* with the gardeners, I should have said."

"Mrs Harman, if you make this article too bloodless, no-one will want to read it. Come on, that's a lovely human touch that surely your old lady could not be offended by, and which our readers will enjoy immensely!" I focussed on the view out of the window for a moment. Would Brenda mind? I decided not.

"As long as you don't make a caricature out of her." He nodded, but I didn't entirely trust him. We'll see. He's starting to look fidgety though. "Shall we go for a look round, then, Mr Gilbert?"

I might as well have said 'Walk' to my cousin's retriever. He grabbed the recorder and flicked a switch with a practised movement, bounded up from the chair, shook his hair back and looked eagerly at the door. I mentally picked up his lead from the hook by the door (this one needs to be kept under close control) and led the way through into the corridor.

"There are a few interview rooms on this side of the courtyard, and some administration offices – do you want to see an interview room, if one is empty?" I opened one door which had the 'not in use' sign showing, and we looked in. I expected to see the usual set-up: chairs, table, tissues, flowers, but instead every surface was draped in white sheeting.

"Decorating?" he queried, a dry tone evident in his voice. I wasn't quite sure what to say. I was aware we had a new patient who needed to protect every surface he sat on with sheets, as his fear of contamination was so overwhelming, but if this was his therapy session, where was the patient, where was the therapist, and why did the door sign indicate the room wasn't in use? I would not let this patient be the subject of a newspaper article.

"I'm sorry about that; I'd forgotten about this room being out of use – let's find another one for you." I closed the door and slid the sign to 'in use,' taking care not to seem hurried. Bob Gilbert had missed nothing, however. As we moved away down the corridor, he casually said:

"I suppose some of your patients have very great needs? Do you ever feel they should be in hospital instead? Or in a psychiatric ward?" I stopped to look at him in feigned surprise, as if his question had come out of the blue, rather than being prompted by the carefully draped sheets in the room behind us.

"Perhaps that question might be more easily answered after you have seen more of the clinic, Mr Gilbert. Is it ok with you if we leave it until the end? You may find you can even answer it yourself." I was quite pleased with that and swept on down the corridor, but I was beginning to feel quite weary, and it was only half-past ten. Was the whole morning going to be like this, with the journalist and I circling each other warily and landing the occasional wounding blow? I realised that Bob Gilbert had ranged in persona from Sherlock Holmes through Golden Retriever to Medieval Knight, and I wondered who or what else would emerge before the tour was completed.

Another room, apparently free. I listened carefully. No doubt about it, quiet sobs from inside. For goodness sake, why couldn't they remember to put the signs across when they went in? I shook my head to Bob's interrogative eyebrow lift, and tried the room next door. Here, at last, all was as it should be, clean and quiet and tranquil, ready for any journalist that might be visiting. Bob nodded, and moved away as there was nothing of any interest here for him.

"The male toilet is just here, should you need it,' I pointed it out, looking at him. I couldn't actually see the calculation being made: 'If I go in here, what are the chances of an off-the-cuff interview with a patient?' but I felt sure something like that was going on behind those eyes. He shook his head, obviously deciding against it, and then soon we were at the kitchen door. Inside, we were hit by warm cake smells, and hot sausage smells, with onion, garlic and spices; and somewhere in that mix, a lovely citrusy waft of orange. Time to have some fun.

"I'm afraid you'll need a white hat in here, Mr Gilbert." I pulled one out from the dispenser and handed it to him, carefully avoiding his eyes, and pulled a second one out for myself, immediately putting it on and tucking my hair inside. He quickly scanned the room.

"Not everyone here is wearing one, Mrs. Harman? The young people over there, for example." It was true: there were a few young boys who had been persuaded into the kitchen to learn about food and how it was prepared. Oh dear, the damage to his dignity was going to be great.

"All the more reason for us to set a good example. Come on, if we ask Mariella nicely, she'll let us try some of that marmalade cake cooling over there." The lure of cake was too much. He pulled on the hat, tucking in his long hair, and reverted to retriever mode as he bolted towards the smiling Mariella.

Stephanie waved goodbye to Bob Gilbert just before lunchtime, with a rather more fixed smile than the one she had welcomed him with earlier this morning. 'That is the last time – no more reporters, ever,' she told herself firmly. 'I only agreed to this one to try and quash the rumours going round about the clinic, but now I wonder if I'm going to regret it.' The journalist had spent the rest of the morning as Sherlock: probing, questioning, eyes darting everywhere. As she walked back through the clinic, Stephanie hoped he hadn't noticed the fracas going on in the library as they passed, or that the fish tank badly needed cleaning. He had definitely noticed Suki in the crèche, though, smiling and laughing with the children. She watched them chatting together and thought he was going to ask her out on a date, he was so obviously smitten. Suki was friendly and charming and Bob Gilbert would not have been the first man to make the mistake of thinking it was all directed at him.

Stephanie shut the door of her office, leaned against the door, and let the tranquillity ease into her. She always felt at peace here, on her own. The apricot coloured walls and the birch desk felt warm and light and easeful, and her Magritte prints added an individual touch. She liked Magritte because she found him quirky, but she never understood what his paintings meant. The never-ending puzzle was stimulating, in a low-key way. She sank into her chair, stared up at 'The Blank Signature,' and wondered for the ten thousandth time what connection a blank signature could have with a lady riding in the woods. The perspective was all mixed up, with a tree that was clearly behind the lady somehow rising up in front of her right arm, and managing to also be both behind and in front of the horse's rear left leg. She had never worked out how he had done it. He had defied the laws of perspective, but it also looked normal at first glance.

A bit like Yatross. It too had defied normal laws and normal health settings and had survived despite taking quite a different perspective on people's health needs. But what had struck Stephanie as she walked round with the journalist this morning was how normal it all looked on the surface. Apart from the lack of white coats and blue uniforms, it could have been any health clinic, any group practice, if you looked at it superficially.

A knock on the door brought the thoughts to a halt. "Come in. Oh, hello, Kirsty, how are things?" Kirsty was a fairly new counsellor, recently out of training, and very young. A few practitioners had shook their heads meaningfully when Stephanie took her on, but Stephanie had found her gut instinct about people too reliable too often to worry. Kirsty had the right attitude, she thought, and most importantly, was never too proud to ask for guidance or suggestions. This meant that Stephanie felt she always knew what Kirsty was doing, what direction she was taking, the way her brain was working. Supervision was a breeze with Kirsty.

"Sorry to bother you, Stephanie, but this afternoon I've got Trevor Browning coming for his appointment, and I wanted to have a chat with you first. Last time he was here he wouldn't talk, as you know, and if he does turn up this afternoon, which I'm only half-expecting, to be honest, well, I want to be prepared. I mean: he will possibly still refuse to talk to us." Kirsty shifted about from foot to foot like a schoolgirl in front of the headmistress, and Stephanie belatedly waved her into a chair. Kirsty continued:

"I know that if he arrives for an appointment, but won't talk, that must be telling us something, but I'm not sure what that something is."

"What strategies have you already considered, Kirsty?" Kirsty lifted her chin and took a breath. "Well, I'm not going to get impatient, or angry, or try to trick him into saying something. And I'm not going to go off and leave him. I'll stay with it, whatever happens. But all this is what I'm *not* going to do – all negatives. What positive things can I do?"

"Actually, I think they are positive things. We don't know what happened to him before, what other people have done that makes him so reluctant to trust. So all those things you said, they may well feel very encouraging to him. But one of the problems of patients who won't talk is that we have no idea of what is going on in their heads. You will keep the panic button close by you, yes? And make sure he sits on the far side of the room, so that you can reach the door first?"

"Yes, of course, I'll do all the usual security things. But he obviously needs our help?" For the first time, Stephanie wished Kirsty wasn't quite so young and idealistic. 'Let's hope he doesn't break her spirit with another two hour marathon of silence. And that he doesn't have a knife or something.' However, Stephanie kept these thoughts to herself.

"You might be surprised at how many people come to us for help but are then not able to accept that help for one reason or another. But let's think about your Mr. Trevor…"

Fifteen minutes later, Kirsty shut the door on her way out of Stephanie's office. The bounce was back in her walk: she knew now what she had to do. She hadn't really needed to talk to Stephanie; the ideas had flowed as they were speaking, and she could have done it without bothering her boss and showing herself up. Well, not that exactly, but she knew how some of the others thought about her. It didn't help, being blond and pretty, with a good figure and baby blue eyes: she might as well have had 'bimbo' tattooed on her forehead. She was quite pleased to have such a difficult client; when she finally got Mr Strong and Silent to talk, perhaps she would get a bit more respect from the other counsellors. Everyone thought it must be idyllic to work here…*Yatross, how romantic… Greek isn't it?.....and all working on holistic principles…I wish I had a job like that…so worthwhile…* 'But Yatross is still made up of humans,' thought Kirsty, 'and humans will be humans, with the same jealousies, and spite, and apathy, and manipulation – in fact all the same traits that the patients come in with.'

In the kitchen, she thanked Mariella for the milkshake she'd asked for earlier, and drank it down in one gulp while Mariella looked on indulgently. 'Kirsty, you really don't help yourself, do you? *Milkshakes,* for the love of God – whatever next? Crayons? Oh, focus, do, please!'

Kirsty was relieved to see Trevor Browning in reception (at least he had turned up) and she smiled, said: 'Good afternoon, how are you?' and waited for a response. He looked at her in the same way as last time, slightly bemused, as if still waiting for his people to come and get him and take him home to his own planet, and wondering where they could possibly be. It was no more and no less than she had expected, and she led the way to the interview room located nearest to reception. This room had a glass panel half way up the wall, and staff going by had a very good view of what was happening, but could hear nothing. They settled down into their seats, and Kirsty made a point of getting comfortable, and letting Trevor see that she was getting comfortable, thus sending the message: 'We're in it for the long haul, my friend.'

After about ten minutes, Kirsty embarked on the first of her strategies. "It seems as if you may not have decided yet whether you want to be here or not, Trevor, or if you want to speak or not. I understand that you may be cautious. It may be that I can help you a bit with that decision, if I tell you a little about the sort of things that happen in counselling. I can also tell you about what I do and what I say when people come to talk to me about the things that are happening to them in their lives at that time."

Meanwhile, Stephanie had tracked down the counsellor who was dealing with Mr No-Germs, as he had been tagged. Sarah was very happy to go along with Stephanie's suggestion that they get some fresh air and have a chat while walking round the grounds.

"I saw the fact that he was willing to use the clinic toilets as a really positive move forward," said Sarah, with emphasis. She was walking faster than Stephanie, who had to ignore the ever-present twinges in her knee in order to speed up to Sarah's pace. "He had always left the clinic before he needed to use the loo, as he only trusts his home facilities, and I just felt I had to seize the opportunity and help him. Sorry about the sign – it didn't seem very important in the scheme of things."

"Hold on one second, Sarah – what do you mean, 'help him'? You went in there with him?" Sarah, seventy-two next birthday, drew herself up to her full five feet in height and somehow managed to look down on the much taller Stephanie.

"You're old, Stephanie Harman, but you're not old enough to be my mother. In fact, I could almost be yours… yes, of course I had to go in with him – I had to open doors, cover over handles and taps with paper towels, and God knows what else. Luckily he decided he could – "

"Yes, all right, I get the picture; thank you for the detail, mother. So what happened after that?" Stephanie was thanking fate for whatever impulse prevented Bob Gilbert from going in there when they had been passing by the facilities earlier – he would have had more material for his article than in his wildest dreams.

"Well, your water rates will go up next year, I'm sure of that – I've never seen washing hands like it – he took the practice to a whole new level. He was somewhat traumatised by the experience, and I didn't get much more out of him for the rest of the session. One of two things will happen: he will realise that he can encounter germs and he won't die, and be in a position to move forward in his therapy; or he will think: 'I can't go through that again,' and never come back. You're quiet – what is it?" Stephanie grimaced, and told her about the journalist and the near-miss.

Sarah laughed heartily. " What a shame he didn't join us – I could have done with some help!"

"So, will you be here for a while tonight, then, Steph?" Lizzie was one of the few people who felt quite comfortable around the Director, and certainly comfortable enough to abbreviate her name.

"Yes, I'm debriefing Kirsty after her meeting with Trevor Browning this afternoon."

Denece, another of the clinic counsellors, looked up from the journal she was reading.

"I heard about that – it didn't go too well for poor

Kirsty, I understand?" Stephanie studied her for a moment. 'Nothing wrong with the words, but is it my imagination, or was her tone a bit too avid, perhaps?' she thought wryly. 'I know the counsellors give Kirsty a hard time in many ways and some would be delighted to see her fail. No point in hiding what has happened, though.'

"Trevor just got up and left in the middle of the session," said Stephanie flatly. "He had never said anything, and I suppose he got to the point where he knew he didn't want to communicate with us. We may never know why." Denece looked as if *she* knew why, should anyone want to ask her, but Stephanie had no intention of letting Denece provide ammunition for the anti-Kirsty faction, and changed the subject.

"Denece, did you manage to get to the bottom of why Dina Richards was so miserable last week? I remember her telling you that she was so much better, her skin problems had cleared up, she felt more on top of things and so on, but at the same time she seemed more unhappy than ever. What was all that about?" Denece was pleased to tell the story, particularly as she felt it gave her own image a boost.

"After talking with her a while, I found out it was the husband: he was grumpy and was moaning all the time. It seems he didn't like the new stronger Dina who wasn't so dependent on him, and how many times have we heard that story? It makes me so mad. Anyway, I told her she would have to choose – she could go back to being the old Dina if she wanted; he would be happy, but her health would likely suffer again."

"You can't entirely blame the husband," put in Lizzie,

reasonably, "as she has willingly played victim all these years. It is going to take him a while to adjust." Denece wasn't happy that her black and white scenario was being overlaid with shades of grey, and suddenly found a need to check her watch.

"Oh, Mercy, but I'm going to be late, see you all tomorrow," and in a moment, she was gone.

Lizzie and Stephanie carried on working at their screens, peacefully. After a few minutes, Lizzie suddenly said:

"Did you ever think it would turn out like this?" Stephanie glanced at Lizzie's calm face, which was still studying the screen in front of her.

'Like what?' thought Stephanie. 'Like having to deal with people like Denece every day? Like watching people suffer unnecessarily, no matter how much you tried to help them? Like getting exasperated with journalists like Bob Gilbert?' She got up, walked to the window and assessed the view. The lovely gardens were starting to look quite murky now the light was going, the lines of shrubs and bushes indistinct.

"When I was eighteen, I went to Greece on holiday with my boyfriend. First time on holiday without my family, first time in Greece, first time on a motorbike. Sean had some bike experience, but not on roads like Greek island roads were in those days. The inevitable happened, we came off the bike. I got away with a few grazes but Sean got a nasty burn from the bike exhaust, which wouldn't heal. I looked up the word for 'doctor' in my phrase book – it was the first time it had come out of my bag as neither of us could be bothered to learn any

Greek – and pointed to it in front of the little Greek lady who looked after our studio.

"'Yatross? Yatross?' She shouted a lot, and waved her arms about a lot, but the upshot of it all was that we didn't need a doctor as she had some herbs that she mashed and warmed up on her stove and then applied to the burn. Of course, after a couple of treatments, it healed beautifully. Kids that we were, we just thought: 'Cool,' and went on our own selfish way. I went on to university and medical school, as I had always planned, and Sean became a barrister."

Lizzie's large dark eyes were wide. Stephanie rarely talked like this. "I don't understand – why 'selfish' – what else could you have done?" Stephanie turned back from the window and sat back in the chair.

"Perhaps 'self-absorbed' is what I meant. But several times in the last ten years I've thought: imagine if I had started learning about alternative medicine at that point – how much better a practitioner would I be now? If I had taken that incident as a cue to go down a different path, would I have had a totally different life? The Ancient Greeks had a word – 'eudaimonia,' which means doing and living well – having a meaningful and well-lived life. Something about happiness through virtue – I might not have got that quite right but you get the idea. Would I be more eudaimonic if I had realised what fate was trying to tell me?"

Lizzie burst out laughing, and her dark ponytail skipped about her head. "Never mind about eudaimonia – I think you're suffering from overdo-mania, or just possibly megalomania. You can't do everything, Steph.

The experience you had in the NHS is invaluable to you now – you can make good judgements about whether people are going to benefit from alternative or conventional medicine. There is no way you could have done that if you hadn't been a GP first. So Doctor Lizzie's prescription is: Go home! And get some sleep, eh?"

"I can't," said Stephanie, moving reluctantly to the door. "I need to see Kirsty first. Thanks anyway, Lizzie – I'll see you tomorrow." Stephanie only had a few moments to cover the distance to her office, which was probably just as well, as she had limited time to ponder what her much loved bursar had meant by megalomania...another Greek word ...she opened the door, and just as she had feared, Kirsty was crying. No, she was facing away from her: not crying, but shaking with laughter. What on earth – Kirsty handed her a scrap of paper on which was written just two words:

'NICE TITS'

"This was left at reception in an envelope with my name on it," said Kirsty, "and when I asked Beatrice who left it, she was quite sure it was Trevor Browning. I've been sitting here puzzling over why he would do that, but I was laughing then because it just seemed so funny."

Stephanie examined the paper as if it might provide a further clue. After her introspection of the previous half-hour the blunt comment was especially bewildering. What did it mean? Other than that Kirsty had nice tits, of course.

She and Kirsty discussed Trevor for the next ten minutes and came up with three possibilities:

- Trevor had sat through two long counselling sessions in silence because he had no problems to speak of but enjoyed looking at Kirsty's breasts;
- Trevor had decided he didn't want to talk to anyone but felt sorry for Kirsty, and this was his way of making amends for the lost time;
- Trevor fancied her but didn't know how to ask her out on a date, and could only use this method to communicate.

They were fairly sure he wasn't suicidal, as this didn't seem to be the act of a man driven to desperate measures. Stephanie explained, with her mouth quivering but held under fairly good control, that at no time in the history of the world had a man written the words 'nice tits' and then gone on to take his own life.

"I'm going to come out with you to your car, though, just in case he is hanging around. Are you ready to go?"

"There's no need, Stephanie, honestly, I'll be fine."

"No, no, I insist. I'm a megalomaniac, apparently, so I can insist on whatever I like. Come on, let's go and see if he's left a picture of himself naked on your windscreen or something."

'She's in a funny mood,' thought Kirsty, as she was almost marched to the front door. 'Control issues, I bet. I don't think she likes the idea of things going on in Yatross that she is not the instigator of in some way. Never mind, she cares about us, I know that much.' She suddenly stopped, struck by an idea.

"You go and check the coast is clear, I just need to do something before I go," and she hurried back to what in every other workplace she'd known had been called a staff room, but here had the sign 'Agora' on the door. She pulled out Trevor's message and pinned it up on the corkboard, next to a picture of Beatrice's cat, whose tits were nothing compared to hers. 'There,' she said to herself, 'just a little reminder. For me, to stop me thinking that I can solve every problem a patient presents with, and for everyone, to remind us not to take ourselves so bloody *seriously.*'

Chapter Two

The Clinic Fails Ivy Lennox

The following week's edition of the Herald was read with interest by many in the local community, and with particular attention by everyone at Yatross. The staff and Helpers knew that the public would believe what was written. This was a judgement on them, whether they liked it or not.

Jim Stafford worked as a handyman and cleaner for the clinic. He had never been a patient there, but was fiercely loyal to Stephanie Harman and her team. He settled his round bulk into an armchair in Agora, as soon as the newspaper appeared, and poured over the details.

" 'After seven years in the same building, some of the décor looks a little tired'? What is the man on about? I'm sure I don't know of anywhere that needs more cleaning or painting than it already gets. Bloomin' cheek."

"Talking to yourself again, Jim?" It was Denece's sly voice, with her trademark implication of something derogatory. Jim was too incensed to notice, and he peered over his wire-framed spectacles at her.

"Have you seen this piece of twaddle?" he said, his incredulity evident. Denece let the door shut and came to peer over his shoulder. She wasn't too interested in what the journalist thought about the building, but the section on the crèche caught her eye.

> 'The crèche is used for children of staff, patients and Helpers, and is led by a well-qualified and enthusiastic team. Whatever the efficacy of the treatments delivered to the adults, they can be confident that their children are safe and happy at the Yatross crèche.'

There was more in this vein, and Denece thought how pleased Sue was going to be. At that point, Suki, another crèche worker, came to Agora in search of Denece.

"Dominic says you've still got his brontosaurus, Denece." Denece fished out a green plastic dinosaur from her handbag and handed it to Suki.

"Thanks, pet. Was he making a fuss? I'd forgotten it had fallen out of his back-pack as we got in the car."

Suki smiled and shook her head, her sleek hair falling back into its perfect shape. "Not yet, but I thought we'd try to prevent one."

Denece waved her arm in the direction of Jim, who was still reading. "Have you seen the article on Yatross? That journalist was very complimentary about the crèche: you obviously made a good impression! Sue should ask Stephanie for a raise for you all."

Suki lowered her chin in embarrassment at the unusual praise from Denece, but before she could reply, another head poked round the door opening. It was Anna from reception.

"Sue says has Lucy developed any allergy to sticking plaster? Her record says no, but she was very young when she first came and no-one knew one way or the other."

Denece's face became mildly anxious. "Plaster is fine. Has she hurt herself already?"

"A tiny cut: don't worry, Denece," reassured Anna, and paused only to exchange a warm glance with Suki before disappearing again.

Jim launched himself out of the chair and the small coffee table fell over with a bang. "Right then! I'm sure I know what I'll be doing today," and with that pronouncement he thrust the paper at Suki and stomped off out of Agora and down the corridor. Neither Suki nor Denece were too worried about what Jim was up to, and Suki took the newspaper for Sue to see, while Denece got ready for her first patient.

Meanwhile, Stephanie Harman was reading another copy of the same article. Her demand to see copy had been met. 'There shouldn't be any surprises, but you never know,' she thought, eternally suspicious of anyone connected with the media. In the event it was a fair account, with little in the way of negativity, and a reasonable amount of praise for their commitment to holistic health. She put the newspaper aside for Lizzie to see later.

In another part of Yatross, Jim was turning out cupboards, looking for the paint he used when he last decorated the reception area. "A bit tired, eh? Well,

I'm sure it won't be tired by the time I'm finished," he mumbled as he pushed aside paint cans and assorted equipment.

Thirty minutes later, Jim had cordoned off an area of reception and was rolling fresh paint on to the walls. His guarding was perfectly adequate for the grown-ups, but not for four-year-old Lucy, who wandered out to reception to show any passing adult her special plastered finger. Before Jim could get down his ladder, she had slapped her hands on the wall. Finding that they were then wet, she tried to dry her hands on her clothes. Anna was busy with a patient at reception, and by the time Suki came out in search of her, Lucy's dress had gained an entirely new pattern.

While the fall-out from this everyday incident was being dealt with, (finding clean clothes for Lucy, bigger barriers in reception, re-rolling walls) a new prospective patient had arrived at the Yatross' main gate, having been dropped off at the bus stop a short distance away.

Ivy Lennox stopped at the entrance and hung on to a gate support while she rested.

The road inside swept away to the left, and she couldn't see where it went, but ahead and to the right she could see a large building with a sloping roof. Between her and the building were lawns, flower beds, shrubs and trees; also a cycle path and a pedestrian walkway, both helpfully labelled with their respective images.

Ivy sighed. 'Perhaps I should have accepted Joan's offer to drive me here after all.' That path stretched ahead such a horribly long way and Ivy winced in anticipation of pain. She set off slowly, leaning heavily on two sticks. The flowers nodded a welcome in the light breeze, but her returning stare was sour.

'Yes, very nice, I'm sure,' she said to herself. 'This must have cost a king's ransom to set up – shame they didn't plough some money into setting up a little bus or something to get us there in the first place. I wish I hadn't listened to Joan.'

There were even a couple of gardeners, and one studied her painful progress for a moment. He had a wheelbarrow next to where he was working, and for a moment Ivy had the wild thought that he was going to sweep her up with the weeds and whisk her to the front door, legs waving and sticks everywhere. The thought made her increase her pace a little, and by the time she reached the entrance she was out of breath, and stood under the verandah for a few minutes, watching two squirrels run round a nearby tree.

'I wouldn't mind being able to move like that,' she thought enviously, and remembering that that was why she was here in the first place, pushed the button for the automatic door. Once inside a double door entry system, she was taken aback by the number of people milling about, and she instinctively moved back to a wall, fearing being knocked over.

On one side a round man with sandy coloured hair was rolling paint on to the walls. The smell of paint wasn't unpleasant, and reminded her of her husband

Colin. There was a kind of reception desk, if she ever managed to reach it, but the man and the woman behind it were both talking to several different people, apparently at the same time. The next thing to draw her eye was an enormous fish tank in the corner, with three children standing in front of the glass, mesmerised by the darting fish. People of various ages ('am I the oldest one here?') were moving towards the café on her left, and the faint smell of coffee now reached her as the door opened to admit them. She looked to the right and saw a range of seats – some soft chairs, some upright chairs, a couple of bean bags, and a few with no backs and sloping seats that she couldn't work out at all.

'That straight chair in the corner – that's the one to go for, if I'm going to have any chance of getting up again this side of Christmas,' and with that thought she started to make her way through the human traffic to her goal. At one point she hesitated when a young boy climbed on to her chair in his attempt to keep a mobile phone away from a younger child ('what was his mother doing letting him play with her telephone?') but he soon decided there were better defensive positions elsewhere, and ran off just before she reached it. Ivy sank into the chair, put her bag and sticks on a table, and looked around once more. 'Were all these people ill, then?' She thought they looked like a real mixture. Some were even laughing.

'It's all right for you: you want to try living with this for a while, that'll show you what pain is. We wouldn't see you laughing then, would we?'

Ivy started to take in more of her surroundings as the

pain from her long walk started to dull, and she could concentrate again. There were posters and pictures on the walls, leaflets and books on the tables, and off to her right she could see signs for 'Book Centre' and 'Children's Area' and 'Toilets'. The painter man glared at two children standing at the barrier to his work area, and they ran away.

'And what about the doctors, where are they?' she wondered. She had seen no-one yet that looked like a doctor. A smiling young woman entered through another automatic door at the back of the reception area, and walked straight up to a middle-aged man reading a magazine in a comfy chair. Ivy watched his easy move to a standing position as he greeted the young woman ('that would have taken me the best part of half an hour,') and followed their progress back out through the door.

'She was a bit young to be a proper doctor,' thought Ivy, and looked around for someone a bit more mature. Several minutes went by and then Ivy became aware of a book on the table in front of her. On the cover it had some strange symbols that sort of looked like words, followed by some English that she did recognise:

Ναςτε καλα

May you be well !

'So is this place run by foreigners, then?' wondered Ivy. She had heard that it was a bit odd, that people got better but didn't know why or how, and she knew there were lots of rumours about witchcraft and unnatural practices. But Joan had given such a good account of how her son-in-law had got better from a chronic back problem, and how the clinic had helped her neighbour's rheumatism, that Ivy, desperate after many years of pain in her joints, had decided to come and see for herself. But it all seemed so different to what she had expected, that now she didn't know what to think. She had read the Herald that morning, although her plan to visit Yatross had been made weeks ago; it was interesting to read all about the different approaches they had to making people well again. 'But you still need doctors,' she said to herself. 'So where are they?' Not quite ready to tackle the reception desk, she opened the book. The first page began:

Welcome to Yatross! And may you indeed be well.

This book contains messages and stories from our patients.

The book was their idea – they wanted to record what had happened to them, and tell others about some of their truly astounding recoveries from serious (and not–so-serious) health problems.

It may be that you recognise your story here. In which case the well person going out of the door in due course could be you.

Trust us, and try to be open to what for many of you may be new ways of combatting illness and disease.

Most of all, trust yourself, and trust that one day, you will be well.

Naste Kala!
With all good wishes from
Stephanie Harman
Clinic Director

Ivy was a bit puzzled by who Nasty Karla might be, but she could always recognise a sales pitch when she heard it. Her first thought was: 'Yes, and how much is all that new stuff going to cost me?' It seemed to Ivy that you couldn't go anywhere, not even in your own home, and be safe from someone trying to sell you something. Men on the TV, women on the telephone, leaflets came in the door, her magazine was full of adverts, and it all made her feel anxious and panicky. What if she succumbed and bought all those things? Suppose she spent all her money and had none left? She wouldn't be able to pay the electric or the gas, or shop for food. Ivy found she was getting breathless, and tried to take some deep breaths.

The little boy who had relinquished the chair suddenly reappeared in front of her, pointing a toy pistol to her forehead. Nevertheless, she felt some of the anxiety seep away. He could be her grandson Rob, he was about the same sort of age… 'Ivy, Ivy, no-one is holding a gun to your head. You don't have to pay for any treatment if you don't want to. Let's read a bit of this book and see what the patients say about it all.' Having given herself that little lecture, she turned to the next page.

The first story didn't take long to read, as it went:

I wos ere
I got better

Sooki nice
Cak nice
　Tom

'I bet they even charge children,' she thought, before turning the page to the next one. This one might have been written by a grown-up, but she couldn't be certain, as he had added little cartoon pictures all round the edges of his story:

Hi, hope you get better soon! I'm Si, and I'm an artist.

I used to suffer from depression so bad I couldn't get out of bed in the morning. But the good people here, they worked out what was wrong with me – it happened that the food I was eating just didn't suit my body. Now I'm eating different things, and feel great!

And best of all, I'm painting again. When I've paid my dues – I'm working on a really amazing painting for the reception you're sitting in now – then I'll be off to Italy, which is heaven for painters.

Ciao! From Si Bevan

Ivy really didn't know what to make of this one. 'Yet more foreign words I don't understand. 'Ciao'? How do you say that? And could the food you eat really make a difference to depression? Joan had been on those Prozac for years, but she'd never said anything about food. Mind you, Joan hasn't actually been here yet. Now, where did he say?

Italy. I know people who have visited Italy on holiday, and they gave very good accounts of it, in the main.'

Ivy thought back to the last holiday she'd had, many years ago. A woman friend had organised a long weekend in Hastings. 'Very nice, it was, not like Bracklesham Bay of course, but very nice in its way…when Colin was alive it was different, of course…' Ivy sat for a while, remembering, and then came to herself again, the book still in her hands.

Hoping that the next letter might be a bit more helpful, Ivy turned another page.

Dear Anyone,
Anyone can benefit from homoeopathic medicine, but many people think it can't possibly work.

I am living proof that it does.

I had been told by my doctor that I had been on HRT for too long and had to stop taking it. I soon went back to hot flushes and mood swings – all the symptoms I dreaded.

I started to avoid people in groups, as I got anxious that I would go red and start perspiring, and the anxiety made it worse.

The homoeopathic practitioner took a long time to decide what I needed – she asked me lots of questions about my symptoms and a whole lot of other things that didn't seem connected, and then gave me two different lots of pills to take.

After a couple of months the hot flushes eased, and then gradually I started to feel normal again.
Thank you to all the helpful people at Yatross.

Yours sincerely
Mary Barton

Ivy read Mary's account and sat back to think for a bit. Mary seemed like a woman of sense, but Ivy wondered if she would have adjusted in time anyway. She had heard of that homoeopathic medicine, but didn't set much store by it. And menopause wasn't her problem – if only it were. Still, at least it was a sensible, logical account – unlike the next entry:

Aeroplane?
I used to think that all I needed to do was to become a pilot. How I was going to do that I had no idea, but if I was a pilot, I could take the aeroplane of my life up through the clouds to that layer of sky where the space above is a deep clear blue, the sun always shines, and all the shitty cloud stuff would be below me, out of sight.

Really out of sight.

What Michael has taught me is that the clouds are not the problem. You can dream on clouds. You can wrap one right around you. Clouds protect you against the fierce sunlight.

What I needed was a different way of looking at the clouds.

Thank you Michael
Barti

Ivy felt very tired. She was not used to interpreting nonsense, and this was the most nonsensical so far.

Aeroplanes, clouds – what did they have to do with being ill or in pain? And Ivy deeply disapproved of the swearing. Suppose a child found this book and read that word?

Perhaps the people here didn't have very high moral standards. They published this weird letter from 'Barti' so they must have read it.

Suddenly the whole enterprise didn't seem to be a good idea. Ivy had no faith that anyone here could help her. Fish, coffee, Italy, painters, food, aeroplanes, cuddly clouds – they all jumbled together in her mind. Ivy thought: 'How can these things help me? I've come to the wrong place. This is no good to me. I'm not going to get any help here. And I don't plan on spending good money just to get ripped off by a bunch of nutcases.'

She spent another couple of minutes looking round, hoping to see someone she could have faith in, someone who looked even a little bit like a doctor. With a deep sigh of resignation, she took her sticks and struggled to her feet again. She put her bag across her shoulder and started to make for the door.

'At the least the NHS is free and you know where you are with Doctor Patterson. I'll go back to him and tell him I need to change my pills. I'll ask him to increase the dose – that might help. I'll have to tell Joan that this place is not what she thought. Weird, that's what it is. I'm not having anything to do with it. I should have listened to my insides – I always knew there was something wrong with this place…'

Chapter Three

Andy's Alexander Lesson

It was cool and pleasant here, next to the trees in the smokers' garden. Andy was relieved to find there was such a place here at Yatross, as he had been convinced he was going to have to have his last roll-up outside the gates. Instead, he sat on the bench and lit his cigarette, and settled back to enjoy the peace and quiet.

After a minute or two, he started to pace the small area, as the initial relief gave way to anxiety about the evening ahead of him. His brain then veered from that uncertainty to his more familiar workplace concerns.

'...that new bricklayer is a right piece of work; not sure how long we'll keep him... thinks he's too good for our small outfit...well, we'll see. Dave reckons he used to work for Wacky Billy, which would explain a lot. When my back starts behaving itself we won't be so dependent on outsiders, and no-one will be happier than me...when, though?' Andy replayed his conversation with the ponytailed bursar:

"So how many sessions do you think I'll need, then?"

"How long would it take you to learn Spanish? It really

depends on how much work you're prepared to put in, Andy."

'And that,' he now thought wryly, 'is a fat lot of good to me as an answer.'

He'd imagined that he could come to the clinic, get worked on by some therapist for a few sessions, and then be better. But Ponytail had said that his assessment had shown he had longstanding bad habits of body use ('bad habits? you'd want to see some of my others, love,') and that learning the Alexander Technique was the best long-term solution for him. Andy wasn't sure that he had the motivation to come back week after week, in the hope that one day he would be better, but had agreed to give it a try. He knew he was impatient, but the therapist who had assessed him pointed out that that was half the problem – he needed to stop and learn better ways of standing, walking and lifting, to avoid pain.

'I'm 32 years old, and I don't relish some bloke telling me things I learned 30 years ago, especially if there are other people watching – oh hell, suppose I know them?' He had rolled a second cigarette without knowing, and he paced and smoked some more, imagining the next couple of hours as an exercise in humiliation and embarrassment.

Eventually, he checked his watch, stubbed the end of his cigarette out on the container provided, and strode back through the trees towards the front of the clinic. He paused outside to take an automatic inventory of the building: '…good design…about ten years old… interesting roof detail – those long eaves are great for keeping a place cool…looks like there might be an internal space – some sort of courtyard, maybe?' But then the embarrassment of being late loomed, and he pressed the 'door open' panel, half expecting to have to wait for someone to unlock it. But it slid open immediately, and he ducked under the doorframe, with the usual accompanying jab of pain to his lower back.

Had Andy looked back, he would have seen that the height of the door frame was a good chunk of space higher than his head, but he was so used to ducking under things to avoid hitting his head that he had moved automatically. Inside the reception, there was no-one around, but then it was 6.00 p.m., after all. After a minute or two an older bloke with dark curly hair appeared from an opening to the left of the welcome desk.

"Hello, Andy, is it? Good to meet you. I'm Daniel, and I'm your Alexander teacher. Come through here and join the others." Andy shook his hand, and followed him back through the doorway, while cursing himself for not arriving earlier. Everyone else was obviously already here, and would have started getting to know each other, and he would be the odd one out. It would be just like going into that party that Mira had dragged him to, where they were late, and he spent most of the night in the kitchen, trying to catch up to the alcohol consumption levels of everyone else.

In no time, Dan the Man had glided (did he have feet? Andy found himself taking a quick look, just to be sure) down the corridor and into a large studio. Sure enough, five other people in a group of chairs were chatting together, and a burst of laughter carried across to where Dan and Andy were walking across a large expanse of floor. 'Christ, I could use a fag,' went through

Andy's head, closely followed by: 'Bloody hell, they look like normal people!' and then he was being introduced.

"This is Andy," said Daniel warmly. 'Andy, meet Jonathan, Tosca, Amy, Siobhan, and Sheila. Please, join us and take a seat." All eyes were on him as he painfully lowered himself to the chair, but Andy took comfort from the empathy in Daniel's eyes. 'He knows,' Andy realised. 'He's been here, and he knows exactly what it's like.' Then Daniel was addressing them all.

"Have you ever watched how a toddler gets up and moves towards a toy? Have you seen a cat unfurl itself and stretch, before moving off? These are examples of how our bodies were designed to work: head leading the rest of the body into movement: smooth and aligned, with head, neck and back in perfect harmony. That is what you need to get back from your childhood, and that is what I am going to teach you, so that your bodies work the way they are supposed to. You may not lose all pain, but you will definitely have less pain, providing you take what I show you and use it in your daily life. Use the Alexander Technique when you sit, stand, walk, brush your teeth, reach for your sandwich, and yes, even when you reach for your partner. Now, let's go round the group and hear what you want to improve in your life. Amy, you start, please."

The last bit of Daniel's introduction had perked them all up a bit, with 'does he mean sex?' flashing through five of the six heads in front of him. Amy obediently explained her motivation for being there.

"I am a nursery school teacher, and I have to bend over to help the little ones all day long. It is getting more and more difficult, because of the pain in my back, and I am hoping to find some way of alleviating the pain."

Amy was very young to have back pain, thought Andy. She was sweet-faced, and earnest, and Andy warmed to her instantly. Siobhan, it seemed, had a stiff neck, Jonathan was an IT teacher and had a chronically painful shoulder. Andy was not a natural listener, and already bored, tuned out for Sheila's story, but he came back again when Tosca started talking. She had a deep resonant voice, and explained that she wanted to learn the Alexander Technique to improve her performance as a hurdler. If she could shave some seconds off her time, she was in with a chance at the county championships. Andy looked at Tosca with respect, but then it was his turn. Performance: yes, that would be a good angle.

"Hi, I work in construction, and speed and quality of work is essential to us to get the jobs, and to keep customers satisfied. If I could get rid of this pain in my back then I can work faster and better and not let the other workers down." There, that sounded good, not too self-pitying, and an emphasis on customer service. Only Amy looked truly impressed; Andy had the unkind thought that she was probably impressed at everything.

Daniel was talking again. "Thank you, everyone, that was helpful. Now, Sheila, I'm aware you've had Alexander lessons before. I'm going to ask you if you would please lay down on the couch so that I can carry out a demonstration."

While Sheila moved to the couch, Andy took a quick look round the studio: the first chance he'd had to absorb his surroundings. There was a mirror taking up all of one wall and large posters on two of the others. *'Don't be an Alexandroid!'* exhorted one. *'Keep free and relaxed. Focus, not try – trying brings in tension.'* One corner of the studio appeared to be set up as a room, with chairs of several types, bookshelves and a low coffee table.

"I am putting a book under Sheila's head that will allow her head to be in good alignment with her back when she is lying down," continued Daniel. "You need to do the same when you practice this at home. I will guide each of you as to the right size of book." Andy thought this was a joke and smirked. But everyone else was listening carefully and he realised that Dan meant width, not large or small; already he had changed Sheila's book for a narrower one so that the angle was better. Bloody uncomfortable-looking, but Sheila seemed cool and relaxed.

"What Sheila is now doing, and what I'd like you to do for at least two sessions a day between now and next week, is giving her body directions. I must emphasise that this is a *mental* activity, not a physical one. Daniel's eyes flickered over Tosca and Andy for a second and Andy wondered if he was thinking that they were both going to struggle with that idea. 'It's all right, mate; I do have a brain as well as muscles, you know, and if I couldn't picture how a building was going to look when it was finished then I'd be crap at my job, so don't you worry about a little thing like thinking.'

"'Let my neck be free,' is always the first direction, and it is a matter of 'allowing' the neck to be in its correct place in relation to the head and back, not trying to make your neck do anything. 'Place' could be a misleading word – perhaps it is better to think of the right direction." Daniel had his hands cupped around Sheila's head, his fingers gently under her neck, and he moved her head very slightly as some tension was released.

"'Let my neck be free, let my head go forward and up, let my torso lengthen and widen, let my legs move away from my body and my shoulders widen.' These are your basic directions, though we can add others as necessary. I'm going to continue to help Sheila as she thinks these thoughts, but remember: it is a focussed mental instruction, with no muscle movement and therefore no added tension. Tension is nearly always unwanted."

Andy watched in fascination as Daniel worked on Sheila's legs and arms. At one point he put one hand under her shoulder and other under her arm, and just stood there, waiting. Sheila, eyes closed and obviously concentrating, finally managed to do whatever he was waiting for and Daniel seemed to glide her arm out to an apparently longer length. Andy had a vision of walking out of here looking like a monkey, but Daniel had already anticipated what his students might be thinking.

"It is not uncommon for people to change shape over a series of Alexander lessons, as their bodies are no longer held in tightly and can settle into their proper shape. You may become taller," Daniel continued, as Andy winced. He had enough trouble dealing with the size of his frame as it was. "Your feet may get wider, your rib-cage expand, and your back may get wider. This is all as a result of mental activity, as you will see. Now we're going to do some work all together, and during the evening, each of you will spend some time with me individually, practising your directions while lying down."

Daniel went on to show them a skeleton of the human body, and gave them some tricky names to call some of the bits that hurt. He explained about how easy it was to be in a pattern of chronic misuse, but that it was possible to change. They went on to work on standing, walking and reaching for small objects. Andy watched with amusement as Jonathan manoeuvred himself next to Amy in order to work with her on the exercises.

"We're both about the same height – shall we work together?" he asked her, blithely ignoring Sheila and Siobhan, neither of whom were that different in height to himself. Tosca was the only one even approaching Andy in height and he was content to work with the dark, serious girl. Andy wondered aloud why they hadn't done any work on sitting, which was the activity that gave him the greatest pain. Daniel heard and explained that sitting was an advanced activity, and would begin next week. He must have noticed Andy's disbelief, because he added:

"The human body is only designed to carry out certain ranges of movements. Standing, lying down and squatting are all ok, but sitting in a chair does a lot of damage. It is just not what we are designed for. But I will help you limit that damage.

"Andy, it is time for you and Tosca to practice your directions. The rest of you, try putting those books a little higher on the shelves before attempting to reach for them. Remember to direct the movement from your lower back, rather than from your arms and shoulders."

Andy lay down first ('let's get this over with,') and Tosca watched, her solemn eyes taking everything in. Her seriousness was infectious, and Andy found himself able to concentrate on what Daniel was asking him to do, or as he put it: "to allow to happen." It was deeply unfamiliar territory, but he got an inkling of what might be possible when he realised his lower back had just dropped to the couch as the tension released. That feeling of widening across the lower back was amazing, but it was gone in an instant, and he felt the anti-climax of it.

Daniel, as always alert to what was happening, reassured him: "Andy, that was good, and as you get more practiced at this it will happen more often. It is perfectly normal to feel things go right, and then for the feeling to go – you just get better at getting it back as time goes on. The same thing happens to me and I've been practising Alexander technique for sixteen years.

"Now, let's see how you can release those legs out of their sockets – imagine they are made of elastic, and you are just going to allow them to release away from your body the way they've been wanting to…" Daniel held his ankle while Andy attempted to imagine elastic legs, but the only clear image that came to him was his Great Aunt Ruth's elastic stockings, on varicose veined legs. "Let my legs move away from my body," encouraged Daniel. Andy desperately wanted to keep his legs close to his body, and was generally less successful with this idea, but Daniel seemed unfazed. After working round the rest of his body, Andy was 'done' and it was Tosca's turn.

Andy's eyes skimmed the room, taking the same

automatic inventory of its features as he had done with the external structure, but then he found his wandering attention caught by another poster.

> 'Try not to 'launch' yourself out of the sofa – this adds tension to the movement.
> You can relax when sitting, but consciously re-energise before getting up – get the bubbles fizzing at the base of your spine!'

'Back to drink again,' thought Andy. 'That's great. Now, not only have I not got a gnat's arse's idea of what that means, but I want a drink as well as a fag.' Moving from foot to foot, his restlessness was picked up by Daniel.

"Andy, we're going to take a break in a minute. Would you mind putting the kettle on over there before you go outside? We'll take about fifteen minutes. Remember to use your lower back to fill the kettle."

Andy nodded, glad that Daniel had recognised that a visit to the smokers' garden would be necessary, but struggled with the concept of not using his hands to do a task which, let's face it, cried out for that particular part of the body to be used. The lounge area he'd noticed earlier had, he now saw, a nice little kitchen set up in one part of it, and Andy calculated that it served the dual purpose of providing a break-out area for groups using the studio, and props for practicing Alexander. He felt stiff and unnatural, reaching for the kettle and holding it under the tap, and knew that this wasn't what Daniel meant, but it would have to do – he had an urgent appointment outside with his tobacco tin.

Where he was joined, a few minutes later, by a slightly sheepish Jonathan.

"Trying to give up," he waved his cigarette at Andy, "but not tonight." Andy appreciated his honesty, his acknowledgement that what they were trying to do was bloody hard work, and not to be attempted without nicotine support. So he gave him an opportunity to talk about Amy.

"I think she likes you, mate: you'll be all right there," and Jonathan didn't pretend not to know what he was talking about.

"I want to ask her out, but wondered if I should wait until next week?" Andy studied the end of his cigarette, and considered this in his new role of wise elder brother.

"I'd get on with it, before someone else does." He added, in case Jonathan misunderstood: "Not me, I've got someone; but when you think about it, it's amazing she hasn't got snapped up already."

"Maybe she has," said Jonathan gloomily.

"I don't reckon that's true, not from the way she was sizing you up back there. Come on, let's go and see if she's had enough sense to make you a cuppa. If she has, then you're in." They stubbed out the cigarettes and went back to the clinic, where they found that tea had indeed been made, but by Sheila. However, the seat next to Amy was empty, and Jonathan grabbed a mug and claimed it quickly. Andy entertained himself while he drank his tea by watching their animated conversation, and the slightly less animated chat between Daniel, Siobhan and Sheila. He noticed that Daniel was sitting in the lowest, softest seat available, and he was looking forward to watching him get out of it.

'Let's see you fizz your way out of that one, Danny boy,' thought Andy, fully expecting to watch a degree of manoeuvring. He himself had picked an upright chair, so as to not look like too much of a cripple when he got up.

When the end of break came, though, Andy was stunned to see Daniel rise up out of the sofa as if he had already been standing; one second he was lounging back at ease, the next he was upright and walking towards the sink with his mug.

'That was unbelievable – I've got to learn how to do that,' and Andy's motivation to persevere with this Alexander business received an unexpected boost. The group moved back into the studio, and Andy, fuelled up on nicotine and caffeine, together with a large dose of self-interest, found he was volunteering to be the dummy in the next activity. He called them dummies, because as far as he could see, any volunteer would end up looking like a dummy in front of the group – you were bound to do something stupid, however encouraging and supportive Daniel might be. Still, there he was, putting himself in the limelight, an unusual spot for him.

'Ok, thanks, Andy. Now, we're going to do some work on choice and inhibition. I'm going to set up a few obstacles here," and Daniel swiftly moved a few pieces of furniture into various positions in front of Andy, "and now I'll ask you to walk between and around them for a minute. Remember the walking principles we covered earlier." Feeling a bit like a performing dog, Andy did as he'd been asked. Then as Andy was about to turn to move past a chair, Daniel said:

"Stop a minute. Which way were you going to go – right or left?"

"Er, left," said Andy, hoping it was the right answer.

"So, go right instead. And the next time you come to an obstacle, whichever way you were going to go, do the opposite instead. And in the gap where you change your intention, give your directions, if you can." Andy proceeded in a more halting fashion, until Daniel told him to stop.

"Thanks, Andy, that was just what I wanted. What you saw Andy do was inhibit his instinctive movement. This inhibition is what you will all need to learn, in order to stop doing things the way you are used to. Your normal way of carrying out activities feels right, but it may not be the best way for your body.

"Let's set up two more obstacle courses, so you can all practice this. Why not go backwards at some point? Or spin round? Do something your body is not expecting, so that you get used to the idea of inhibition and choice." As Daniel stopped speaking, the group were released into movement, and Andy watched in amusement as the other five set up obstacle courses with the enthusiasm of a parent and toddler group. After a few minutes of wandering round one of the courses, Tosca spoke up unexpectedly.

"It's very freeing, this."

"Yes?" Andy felt obliged to say. He had felt like one sandwich short of a picnic, himself.

"In hurdling, I am used to focussing on the next

hurdle, and the next. There is no choice. I have to leap the next obstacle and each one I approach in the same way. But there is a lot of tension in that. This freedom is new and unexpected. I need to see if it is a help or not."

Andy could not help but admire her attitude. Single-minded, focussed, but willing to consider another way of doing things if it improved her performance. He thought of himself, if he were to wander round the building site and debate whether to go up a ladder or not, whether to pick up a panel or not. 'Chaos, mate, utter bloody chaos. They'd be getting the men in white coats for me, no doubt at all.'

"Ok, guys, good work; can we put everything back to where it came from, apart from three standard chairs – Siobhan – those ones you've got there will be fine – could you bring them over here? I'll grab this one, and we'll set them up in a row like this. I know I said sitting is for next week, but this is a different exercise." Everyone was getting weary now, and drifted over to the chairs with varying degrees of enthusiasm. Siobhan said to Daniel:

"I'm amazed at how tired I feel – I expected my poor old body to be tired, but it is a real mental activity too, isn't it?" Andy didn't hear Daniel's reply as just then Amy gave a peal of laughter at a comment made by Jonathan, who was grinning and looking very pleased with himself. When they were all quiet, and gathered round, Daniel sat in one of the chairs.

"Siobhan: would you help me get up, please?" and he held out an arm in front of him. Siobhan put out her own arm, then used her other arm, then fixed her feet and hauled at Daniel with all her strength, but he did not budge. 'Funny, he didn't look that heavy,' thought Andy. Jonathan had a go, with the same lack of success. Next, Daniel asked Amy. She approached with obvious reluctance, but the moment her hand started to pull on his, he was upright, with that smooth flowing movement they all envied.

"The only difference," Daniel explained, "between what Amy was trying to lift and what Siobhan and Jonathan were trying to lift, was my focussed intention. I thought myself into a heavy, immovable state, and then into a light, free-flowing one, using Alexander directions.

"I wanted to show you the power of your minds. You can do exactly the same thing. Before you leave, I'd like to see each of you individually for a few minutes, while the rest of you practice that exercise. Amy, would you like to come over first?"

Tosca went to sit in a chair, saying to Andy: "Let me think myself into a heavy state for a moment, please." Such a serious girl. Andy watched Jonathan and Siobhan, one on each arm, try to pull an apparently lead-weighted Sheila out of the other chair. Andy suddenly wondered if he would actually be able to move Tosca. Surely the girl, as strong and muscular as she was, wasn't going to beat him?

She didn't, as it turned out, but he was impressed by how much effort he was forced to use to shift her. He wasn't so used to focussing as Tosca, and so she was also able to move him from his perch, despite his larger frame and weight.

When it was his turn to see Daniel, he wondered

what he would say. ' *"Forget it, you'll never make the grade?"* I doubt it, though – they want the money, don't they?'

"I've been impressed by how much you've felt able to contribute to the group, Andy," began Daniel, "and I know it hasn't been easy. But it will get easier, particularly if you practice your directions as I've explained: formally for 5 – 10 minutes at the beginning and end of the day, lying on the floor, but also when you have an opportunity to apply them during your normal activities. I'm giving everyone one of these," and Daniel handed him a small laminated card with the standard mantra for directions. "I've also got a card for everyone with something I'd like them to practice, that is individual to them. For you," and he handed Andy a postcard-sized note, "I'm suggesting you stop at intervals through the day and concentrate on what is happening with your body. Where is the tension? What can you feel? It will be helpful for you to get to know your body better, so that your focussed intention to allow a certain part of the body to be free, will be more productive. On that card there is also a link to a web-site where you can go if you have any difficulty, but I don't think you will. You've decided that you are going to succeed at this, haven't you? And you are very determined. I think you'll do well."

Andy didn't know that he had, or that he was, but it sounded good, and he was nodding, and shaking Daniel's hand, and going back to the others feeling as if the evening had gone well. It didn't last, of course, and as they finished the session, said goodbyes all round, and left the clinic, Andy thought: 'You've been conned, Andy, you know that, don't you?' but he recognised it was all in a good cause, and was feeling fairly content as he walked back to the car park.

Sheila's car was parked next to his, and he nodded to her. "See you next week then," he said, getting out his tobacco tin, ready to roll up a much-needed cigarette.

"Well, I'm not sure, actually," was the surprising answer. Andy looked at her head, bent over her handbag, searching for keys.

"Why not? You were doing ok?" Andy wasn't sure why he was so disconcerted by the idea of someone leaving already. In the space of two hours, they had formed a fledgling family, and he instinctively rebelled at the idea that one of the family might leave.

"I've had Alexander lessons before, but one-to-one, and I don't know if I really like being part of a group instead – no offence, Andy – I like you all, but I find it hard to concentrate when so much is going on." Andy didn't know what to say. He tried to imagine what it would be like to have an Alexander teacher all to himself.

"Bit heavy, isn't it, just you and them?"

"Well, the sessions only last fifty to sixty minutes, but yes, it is hard work. I don't know what to do at the moment. I'll see." Sheila wasn't really his type: 'posh sort of bird,' but Andy felt he had to say something to encourage her to stay.

"I think it's a good group. Shame to break it up, so hope to see you next week anyway. Gotta go: bye, Sheila," and he jumped into his car and started to roll his cigarette. 'Funny sort of evening, and now I've got bloody homework to do,' he thought, starting the engine, and with a last nod to Sheila, he sped out of the car park, looking forward to a late date with Mira.

In another part of the car park, Jonathan and Amy were still chatting, reluctant to end the evening. Jonathan finally said:

"Perhaps we could go out for a drink one night, either after Alexander, or another night?" Amy smiled and looked pleased, Jonathan was glad to see.

"I'd like that, but not tonight. I've got my mother staying for a bit. Can we organise something after next Monday? I think she'll have gone home by then and I'll know what nights I've got free."

"Wednesday and Thursday are out," put in Jonathan quickly, anxious to show that he too had friends and commitments. "Wednesday is evening class and Thursday is pub quiz night."

"Oh, what are you doing at evening class?"

"Italian," replied Jonathan casually, and suddenly this pleasant, but unremarkable young man gained an unexpected dimension. Amy looked at him, eyes shining in what was left of the sunlight.

"I love listening to Italian!"

"In that case I'll come up with some phrases for next week," promised Jonathan, and with that he lightly touched her arm as they went to their respective cars.

In fact, everyone bar Sheila was fairly pleased with how the evening had turned out, including Daniel, sitting in the clinic writing up his notes from the class. Next week he would do some more work with the mirrors. Unlike some Alexander teachers, Daniel waited until after the first class before doing any in-depth mirror work. Introduced too early, he felt, seeing exactly how they looked and comparing themselves to each other could be very discouraging for the students.

He was aware of Sheila's uncertainty, but was philosophical about the outcome: she would either go or stay, and the rest of the group would just deal with it.

No, the one that concerned him most was Andy. He knew so well the type: physically strong, furious that his body had let him down, but would rather be in pain than lose face in front of his peers. Andy could so easily be lost: all it would take would be a humiliation in class, a problem on his building site that resulted in him missing a week or two, a row with his girlfriend about him not being there for her – and that would be it. No more Alexander. Added to these pitfalls was the very real difficulty Daniel knew Andy would have in trying to change long-standing poor posture and use, and his lack of awareness of what caused the pain in the first place.

Still, he had seen worse cases, and he would do everything he could to help him. 'Look on the bright side, Daniel,' he told himself cheerfully, and he whistled softly as he started to switch off equipment and lights. On his way out, he hesitated by the back door, but then remembered that Jim the handyman was coming back later to set the alarms.

In the car park, he wasn't entirely surprised to see Sheila, waiting by her car.

"Daniel!" There was a wealth of feeling in her voice, and he sighed heavily. He had hoped she had finally understood that he was not interested in her other than as a teacher, but that one spoken word told him his error.

He raised his hand. It could have been the beginnings of a wave. It could have been saying: "Stop, don't say any more." Either way, the hand stayed in the air, becoming a barrier to conversation. Daniel slid into his car and drove away, nearly as quickly as Andy had done.

Sheila watched him go. 'So, he is not yet ready. But I can wait. I can wait for as long as it takes.'

∽

Chapter Four

Fun in the Book Centre with Jane

The lady with her hair in a sort of doughnut on top of her head looked over the top of her glasses at the man standing in front of the counter.

"Well? Can you confirm that no aliens have had access to these books?" The man's eight-year-old daughter reached out for her father's hand, and held tight, while her eyes grew into saucers. "I am especially concerned that the three-eyed Gorillons from the planet Wen have not been able to access this knowledge," the woman continued sternly. "Can you confirm that for me?"

"Hmm, well, we can't entirely vouch for what happened during the times we were out of the house, of course, but I think we would have noticed a three-eyed alien when we were there, wouldn't we, Darcey?" The girl nodded vigorously and the doughnut-hair lady continued:

"In that case, my mind is at rest. The Gorillons can only activate when humans are present, as they use our energy fields. So all is well. Thank you Mr Benfield, you may go." The man smiled and turned to the door, and Darcey began the inevitable questions.

"Daddy, why did that lady ask about the aliens? Have we got aliens in our house? Why mustn't they read your books? Why was she cross, Daddy? Daddy, can I have a Gorillon? With three eyes?"

Jane watched them go, smiling while listening to the child's chatter. She swiftly stacked the returned books and turned to her next customer. "Good morning, may I help you?"

"I hope so – I'm looking for a book on the Gorillons from the planet Wen – do you have anything?" Jane studied the grinning man in front of her. She didn't smile back, though he obviously thought he was hilarious.

"Let me check the catalogue." She started keying into the book centre's computer system, and the man stopped grinning. Not sure where to go next with this, he shifted restlessly. "I'm afraid everything we have on the Gorillons is out on loan at the moment. Did you want to reserve something?" Jane continued briskly.

"Er, no, probably not, but there is something else you could help me with. There's a book called: 'Be excellent at anything,' but I don't know who wrote – "

"Tony Schwartz," Jane interrupted decidedly. She gave him that stare over the top of her glasses. "You know it's not true, don't you? You can't be excellent at absolutely anything. We'd all be astronauts and nuclear scientists if that really were the case."

The man started to marshal his arguments as to why he thought it was worth trying anyway, but Jane had swept off towards a corner of the room and he reluctantly followed her. She put her hand straight on a copy and thrust it at him.

"Fiftypenceperweekloanmaximumoffourweekscover priceifyouwanttopurchase," she rattled off without a breath. She turned away, and the man stood for a moment feeling bewildered. He looked at the book in his hands.

'Could I be excellent at anything?' he wondered. 'I could certainly have a go at serving someone in a book centre, and do better than that nutcase. Let's get out of here.' He went back to the counter, fishing for coins in his pocket, and handing Jane the form with his details on.

"I'll take it for four weeks then," and he watched Jane attach a loan sticker to the inside cover of the book, write a date on it and put the book on the counter in front of him.

"You realise I can't be held responsible for what you might achieve as a result of reading this?" She looked at him seriously. He decided he no longer wanted to play.

"It's all right, dear: I wouldn't make you responsible for anything," and then, insult delivered, he strode out of the centre, telling himself he had definitely won that round.

Jane watched him go, committing his details to memory. She didn't mark his card. She had no need to. Jane never forgot a customer.

The next person to approach the counter was a young woman. Jane had her back to her, and the woman took in her sturdy shoes, the calf-length pleated skirt, plain jumper and hair in a bun. When Jane turned round, the customer was startled to see that she had the face of a young woman her own age, behind the old-fashioned spectacles.

"Can I help you?" Jane noted the necklace bearing her name: 'Harriet'.

"Yes, I hope so. I've just come out of a session with Sarah, you know, the – "

"Yes, I know Sarah. And what did she recommend for you?" For a brief moment Harriet thought the librarian was seeking to know the content of her therapy session, but then realised what she meant.

"She said you had some books I might be interested in." Harriet quickly looked round to see who might be listening, and then, even though no-one was in earshot, lowered her voice. "She said you would have some books by Dorothy Rowe."

"Yes, of course – great choice – come this way, please," and Jane led her immediately to the relevant shelves, wondering why the woman was being so secretive. 'You're lucky,' thought Jane wryly. 'Sarah's last patient had to come in and ask for something much more embarrassing…'

"We have them all; fifty pence per week loan, maximum four weeks, cover price if you want to purchase," Jane repeated her mantra and Harriet smiled her thanks and turned her attention to the shelves. Jane suddenly pounced on a paperback and pushed it at the woman.

"This is my favourite: 'The Successful Self' – have you read it?" and as Harriet started to shake her head, "Try it, I recommend it." Harriet felt the force of Jane's strong personality and tried to assert herself, just a little.

"Is it ok if I have a look – ?"

"Of course. I have no problem with that. They are all worth reading. I'll leave you to it." And with that, Jane turned away and strode back to the battlements, ready to deal with the next insurgent.

The insurgent turned out to be Ben, a sixteen-year-old boy Jane had met before. Her impatience with and superiority over the majority of the human race extended to teenagers too, but she did have a slightly softer spot for rebellious, stroppy young men.

"Hiya, Jane, how you doing?" Ben was slightly wary of Jane, particularly as she appeared to be a different person to the bouncy, smiley, short-skirted young woman who had entertained him with stories of Greek myths when he was here before. Gone was the long, scarf-draped hair, the make-up, the high boots, and in its place – what was she wearing? And that hair! But the warm smile was the same.

"Hello Ben: I'm doing fine, thank you. How about you?"

"I'm cool, thanks." Jane registered with amusement the simple mind of a sixteen – year-old. He had come to the book centre, had met one person, had come back to the same place, therefore this must be the same person, even though the differences were to a degree that most other customers assumed they were different members of staff. But not Ben.

"Did you find it, then?" he asked abruptly. Jane looked at the queue of people waiting and none of them looked as if they would provide as much interest as Ben, so she turned back to him, saying:

"Yes, I'll show you what I found – come and see what you think," and off they went to the bookshelves.

A few sighs and mutters went up along the queue. When Jane was busy with a reader there could sometimes be a long wait, but one of the customers knew what to do, and slipped next door to the crèche.

"Excuse me, could someone come and help? Jane is tied up with a customer."

Sue's face twisted with anxiety and her eyes widened.

"Oh, no, not again! Stephanie's told her about that before – she can't just go tying people up because they won't pay their fines; there are other ways…oh, you didn't mean that, did you? Ok, I'll pop through."

Sue wrote out loan stickers and sold some books to the waiting customers, but the last one took some time as she was particularly dithery.

"Now, the problem is, you see, when I last came in, I explained to the young lady here what I was looking for, and we looked all over for it – very helpful she was – but you know we couldn't find it anywhere, and the young lady – you may know her – I remember she had long hair right down to her waist; I remember when my hair was just like that! That's why I remember her, you see. Oh yes, and she had stripy tights – now they were very lairy indeed – I wouldn't have worn those in my day – " Sue thought she had better interrupt or they would be here till midnight.

"Yes, that was Jane."

"Was it, my dear? Well I did come in again, but that time, the time when I actually reserved it, you see, I spoke to another young woman: all in black, dark hair, with strange sort of spikes in it."

"That was Jane as well, Mrs. Nicholls." Gothic Jane, in fact.

"Oh, you have two staff called Jane? That must be very confusing for you all!"

"Actually we've got about twelve, but that's another story. You were saying the name of the book you reserved?" Mrs. Nicholls tried, and failed, to imagine twelve library ladies called Jane, and gave up.

"Well, yes, now, let me see – something about friends, and influencing people?"

Sue found it under the counter immediately and asked her whether she wanted to borrow it or buy it, preparing herself for more dithering.

"I think I'll just take it for a week, thank you, dear. And would you thank Jane for me? Whichever one it was that ordered it for me?" Sue agreed to do this and despatched her out of the centre with a feeling of relief.

The queue dealt with, and Jane still in deep conversation with Ben, Sue hovered at the counter, and looked around the room. There were neat, well-stocked bookshelves, some comfortable chairs and a few tables, all looking exactly like a small library – all very normal. It was just the custodian that was off the wall. Sue remembered that Jane was an ex-patient of the clinic. 'What was it – OCD, I think, though she is allegedly cured. Not much point, is there, if she's just going to swap one personality disorder for another? What would they call this one?' Sue had no name for what Jane was like.

Then Jane was moving back to the counter while the

young lad she had been talking to was walking out with a book in his hands. Sue's sharp eyes recognised the cover.

"Isn't that the Greek mythology book that came in with the new children's books?" she demanded.

"Ssh, he'll hear you, he thinks it's from the Adult section," hissed Jane, who had carefully planted it there for Ben's benefit.

"But Jane, he hasn't booked it out – he's just walking off with it!"

"I know," Jane snapped. She had no intention of telling Sue that Ben did not read and write very well and she had decided not to humiliate him by asking him to complete a form he wouldn't understand. She just hoped – no, believed – that he would bring it back.

Sue was still going on.

"That book was for the children's library – "

"No, I ordered it," cut in Jane. "Now, thanks for helping, but can I get on?" Jane concentrated on her computer screen while aware that Sue was staring at her. Jane knew that Sue would give up first – she had no stamina. And so it was Sue that flounced off, back to the crèche, leaving Jane in the peace and quiet of a suddenly deserted book centre.

Jane realised she had an opportunity to reorganise the books, and after the altercation with Sue, felt an overpowering need to do so. She thought for a moment about what it should be for tomorrow, and then set to work.

Jane regularly re-ordered the books in the centre. It was small enough, and she knew the stock so well, that it wasn't an impossible task. To be fair to the customers, she always provided a neat sign on the table by the entrance: 'Today the books are ordered by author' or: 'Today the books are ordered by subject'. Occasionally it would be: 'Today the books are ordered by size' and one day it was: 'Today the books are ordered by colour'. The most memorable reorganisation was when she decided to shelve them by ISBN number. It took her three days to do, and every other task went by the wayside. The customers were generally pretty tolerant of Jane's eccentricities, and some were openly amused by the variety of persona she chose to adopt. The regulars were a bit put out by their books turning up in a variety of places, and grumbled a bit, but they had to admit she knew everything there was to know about not only the books in the centre, but also any other book they asked her about.

The staff in Yatross were probably the most wary of Jane, mainly because they never knew which Jane they were going to get next. Stephanie gave her quite a lot of rope, but did get annoyed when Jane used it to tie up the customers. This was really beyond what was acceptable, Stephanie thought.

While Jane was quickly moving books around so that they were in order (of publisher this time, she decided) Sue had lost no time in alerting Lizzie to the latest developments. Sue had chosen Lizzie as she thought the bursar would be upset at the idea of losing books to young yobs – it all meant loss of income to Yatross, she reasoned.

"You might want to suggest that they up her medication," sneered Sue, gesturing to her head. Lizzie, calm and pleasant as always, assured Sue she would deal with it, and waited for Sue to leave for the day before entering the book centre. She guessed Jane would still be here, and had also guessed a reorganisation would be underway, as this was always what Jane did when she was upset. Lizzie wondered, not for the first time since she started this job: could they really heal someone completely? Or under stress, would they always revert back to a version of what they had been?

"Hi, Jane, I've brought you some grapes, as – "

"I'm not ill!" cried out Jane, in a much louder voice than she had intended. She took a deep breath. Lizzie wasn't the enemy. "I'm sorry, I just need to be left in peace, that's all."

"Then that's exactly what you shall have. I only brought the grapes because a grateful patient brought in a great bagful, and they were sitting in Agora, waiting to be eaten. Goodnight, Jane."

After Lizzie had left, Jane looked at the grapes. She remembered she hadn't eaten all day and she also remembered what they had told her about what happens to the brain when it doesn't get the fuel it needs. She sighed, pulled a couple of grapes from the bunch, and popped them in her mouth, although she didn't really feel hungry. Chewing slowly, she looked round her domain.

'Mine, and they are *not* going to take it away from me – I'm not going to let that happen: I don't care what I have to do.'

When Lizzie left Yatross about half an hour later, she decided to do what she occasionally did, which was to leave by the front door and check out what it was like for patients on their route out of the clinic. Sometimes she found a light not working en route to the car park, or that someone had thrown up across the path, and she was able to organise repairs or cleaning as necessary. Tonight she wasn't entirely surprised to find the book that Sue had described thrown down to one side of the path, and she halted, looking around, but of course the boy had long gone. Stooping, she picked it up, used a tissue to wipe off the soil clinging to the cover, and straightened the dust jacket. Now was not the time to go back and destroy Jane's faith in the young lad, and Lizzie put it in her bag and walked on round to where she had left her car. She felt sad for Jane, but thought the best way of preventing the boy being strung from the rooftop was to find some way of slipping it back into the book centre without Jane's knowledge…

∽

'Classic Librarian' had been only a partially successful venture yesterday, Jane decided the next morning. She couldn't decide whether the costume brought out the worst in her or the customers, but she discarded the clothes to the back of the wardrobe and looked for something completely different. She remembered that Stephanie was bringing a group of VIP's to see Yatross today, so that called for something really special. Jane pulled open the wardrobe door in her spare room and exclaimed with glee as her eyes lit upon something that hadn't been used in a long while. It was time to get dressed.

∽

Jim strode through reception, whistling happily. He was pulled up short, though, by the white feathers on the floor. 'Bloody pigeons in the loft, I'll bet. I'll ask Simon if he can see where they're nesting.' Continuing to mutter about the birds, he picked up the feathers and went on his way.

Ten minutes later, Lizzie arrived. She went to her office as usual, collected two teas from Agora and took them to the book centre. She hoped Jane hadn't been here all night, rearranging the books into order of number of full stops or something. Jane was nowhere to be seen, so Lizzie left one of the teas on the counter and turned to leave. Jane was always in early, so she wouldn't be far away. Then she stopped. On the floor was a large white feather. That was odd, because Jim would have only just cleaned in here early this morning. She picked it up and took it thoughtfully into reception. Coming the other way was Daniel, also holding a white feather, and studying it with interest. Daniel, seeing her, immediately folded his arms.

"Me Big Chief of Tribe White Feather. Who you? You my squaw?"

"Me confused of Yatross, I think," responded Lizzie. "Where are they coming from?" At this point, Jim appeared.

"Don't worry, it's pigeons: I'm on to it," he assured

them, and all three dispersed through the clinic, to start their daily tasks.

Meanwhile, Jane was in the book stockroom, trying to repair her costume. One of the feathered strips had got caught in the car door, but with some staples and a bit of careful rearranging of top feathers, it would look all right. She padded back to the counter in her special flexible rubber running shoes, which looked satisfyingly like webbed feet. A white baseball cap with painted eyes and a black beak completed the costume, and Jane contently unpacked a new batch of books and made them ready for the shelves, as she waited for her first customer.

Teresa Tapley was the first patient to arrive at Yatross that morning. Her therapist had suggested she read a book called 'Blink' but she had been too busy, and she thought she could at least slip into the book centre before her next appointment and see if it was there. To have a copy in her hand, albeit unread, would look better than having done nothing. She turned away from the temptation of the coffee shop on one side of reception, and walked into the book centre opposite. At first glance there was no-one around, apart from the large bird shelving the books…What!! What on earth was that? Oh my God! It was a real human being! It even spoke:

"Good morning, can I help you?" The black beak came up, and underneath was a normal human face, thank goodness. Teresa swallowed hard. If the creature was going to behave as if it was normal to be dressed up as a bird, who was she to behave as if it wasn't?

"Do you have a book called 'Blink,' please? I'm sorry, I don't remember the author."

"Malcolm Gladwell," responded the bird. "Loan or buy?"

"Oh, loan I think, please," and Teresa watched the bird put the books down, go to a nearby shelf and pick up a copy of 'Blink.' It padded over to the counter on webbed feet, and attached a loan sticker.

"Can I have it for three beaks – I mean weeks," spluttered Teresa in great confusion. She thought she could pull this off, acting normally while a bird pretended to be a librarian, but it was too hard. The bird calmly wrote in a date for her.

"One pound fifty, please," it said. At least it seemed friendly and polite, and unlikely to peck her eyes out. And Teresa had her book. There was a small problem when Teresa put some coins down on the counter and a feathered hand swooped up to collect them, as the feathers got caught in the strap of Teresa's handbag, but after a bit of tugging, and apologies on both sides, Teresa was free to go and the bird had only lost a couple of feathers. Teresa escaped out to reception and wondered if she had time for that cup of coffee. Sadly not, though she could surely do with it.

Customers continued to arrive in the book centre through the morning, and Jane was thoroughly entertained by the variety of reactions she received. There were several like Teresa, who just carried on as if everything was normal. Several more felt the need to make bird jokes, and by lunchtime, Jane thought she had probably had more than enough of those.

"Fancy you tracking down that book for me! No-one could call you bird-brained…er, well, maybe they can," and "I had a bird once, looked like you, only difference was: I kept her in a cage!" and "Daphne Du Maurier's got a lot to answer for," and so on. One customer tried to recruit her to be a member of the RSPB; another asked her if he could count her as one of the birds he'd seen today for a bird-spotting survey:

"I might get extra points for a large one like you!"

Two customers actually entered the book centre at a time when Jane was standing just inside the door, and the effect of all those feathers and beak was overwhelming – they turned right round and went out again. On the other hand, two different customers went over to the coffee shop and brought her back seed and cereal bars to eat.

Sue, in the children's crèche next door, kept sending in children to see 'The Big Bird.' The constant intrusion of noisy children irritated Jane, and she started frightening them away by swooping down on them until they ran, screaming, back to the safety of the crèche.

Several people thought it was a stunt to advertise something, like people you see in the High Street sometimes, and looked in vain for some bird-related product.

Book-lovers got quite inventive with the titles they managed to conjure up and Jane was tolerant of these, as some showed real creativity. Jane treated with disdain the man who could only come up with:

"Have you got a book called 'Large Birds of England'?" but she smiled at the one who said gently:

"As I've always been one to put my head in the sand, I'd like to read something about ostriches. I believe they cannot fly?"

Sue relieved Jane in the book centre at lunchtime so she could take a break, and she fluttered off to Agora with one of her seed bars. She was settling into a comfy chair with a coffee, when Kirsty came in and studied her for a moment.

"Jane, you're moulting, did you know?"

"Yes, all right, I've heard everything now. I'll pick them up on my way back, ok?"

Kirsty smiled at Jane's grumpiness. 'I guess it's not easy,' thought Kirsty, 'being a bird in the cage of the book centre.'

"Where did it come from, anyway?" and Kirsty gestured at the costume. Jane finished chewing a few more seeds and grimaced.

"These are like cardboard – have you ever tried to eat one? The costume? I had a boyfriend once who kept referring to me as his 'bird.' I got so fed up with it that one day I made this costume, and answered the door when he arrived, all dressed up for our date. His face was just wonderful. 'Where are we going?' I trilled, and made as if to come out of the door. 'You've got to be kidding me!' was the response, but when I made it clear we either went out with me dressed like this, or we didn't go out at all, he got really annoyed. That was the end of it, really. It was a shame, because he was quite good company, apart from the 'bird' business."

Kirsty had sometimes wondered what kind of man would suit Jane. Someone very special, she'd decided. She couldn't think of anyone quite special enough just at the moment, though.

The next person to enter Agora was Steve Ellis, the

acupuncturist. He was singing 'My Guy,' which both Kirsty and Jane thought was a pretty innocent choice, until they realised he had timed the verses perfectly in that he was pouring himself a coffee, standing right next to Jane's chair, when he got to:

"'…like birds of a feather, we'll stick together, and there's nothing you can do that will take me away from My Guy.'" Jane's eyes glinted as she smiled up at Steve.

"I'm sorry, Steve, you're the third one to come up with that song today."

"No, I'm not, I'm the first, I know I am! Yes!" and Steve punched the air in triumph.

He was right, of course, but Jane was loath to let him have the last word. Kirsty, shaking her head at Steve's lack of caution when dealing with someone like Jane, left them to it.

Jane let him drink half his coffee before saying: "Steve, come here a minute." Steve was understandably wary. Jane sounded very reasonable and calm – almost normal, in fact, but she was sitting in a bird costume. Just how reasonable and normal could she be? He approached the chair carefully, not taking his eyes off her.

"What are you going to do to me?"

"Nothing, come closer." Steve, all senses alert, leant over the chair, at which point Jane gave him a big hug. Steve backed off fast.

"Whoa there, big bird, no-one said anything about hugs! I'm off – I've got a patient in five minutes," and he whirled round and was gone.

Jane smiled to herself. It was very fortunate that Kirsty had already left, as she would have felt compelled to tell

Steve that there was a half-eaten seed bar hanging out of his back pocket. Jane didn't kid herself that Kirsty would feel any sort of sisterly solidarity with her – she knew she wasn't the type to inspire loyalty in others. With a sigh, she got up and left Agora without a backward glance to where she had been sitting, which now looked rather more like a nest than a chair.

As she approached the book centre, she thought she could hear screaming. It wasn't entirely unheard of, but usually she was the cause, so what was going on this time? The panel slid open and Jane was aware of people moving about swiftly: some rushed towards her, and on past her to reception. There was a flutter of wings, and Jane was astonished to see that a real bird, a pigeon, was flying about the book centre. Sue was standing helplessly by the children's crèche door, to try to prevent any children coming in, so no-one was actually dealing with the bird. Jane thought: 'Steve hasn't had time to set this up as revenge, so how has it got in here? How to get it out, though?' Jane was happy to scare the customers herself, but she had no intention of allowing a mere pigeon to do the same.

The pigeon settled on top of a bookcase in the corner, and cocked its head on one side, one beady eye fixed on Jane. She thought she was probably going to need some help from Jim. She halted one fleeing customer by reaching out a feathered arm (not the best method, in the circumstances) and said:

"Could you ask at reception for them to find Jim, please?"

The book centre was now empty apart from Jane,

Sue and the pigeon. Jane padded over to the stockroom and carried out a stepladder. She opened it up, keeping an eye on the bird, so didn't notice that one of her feathered strips had got caught in the latch that she clicked firmly into place. Meanwhile, the bird had continued to trot up and down the bookcase, but then thought he would have another go at flying through glass. It was as unsuccessful as his first attempt, but this time he hit his head and fell to the floor, stunned.

'Thank goodness,' thought Jane. 'Now all I've got to do is scoop him up in something and get him outside,' and she started to move towards the window.

Only a few yards away, Stephanie was explaining about the ethos of the book centre to her visiting doctors, as she led a group of seven NHS practitioners along the corridor towards it.

"We have a wide range of titles, and not all are self-help books," she explained. "Many fiction titles can help our patients just as much; also technical books, and even some biographies. We rely on the therapists and patients to suggest titles, and we also have a highly qualified librarian in charge." At this point the group swept into the book centre, where a scene of considerable chaos met them. There were books dropped by customers who had been startled by the (real) bird, newspapers open on seats and pages scattered. A large number of feathers littered the floor – some were even from the pigeon.

There also appeared to be a large bird wrestling with a stepladder. Not quite what any of them had expected, least of all Stephanie. Her composure, however, remained unruffled, unlike Jane's feathers, which were now in a very sorry state.

"In a moment I'll introduce you to Jane, our librarian in charge of the book centre, but meanwhile perhaps you'd like to have a look at some of the titles?"

One of the doctors, more gallant than the rest, went immediately to Jane's aid, and extricated her from the stepladder faster than he had removed a skin tag from his last patient. Jane was too cross to say 'thank you' but shook herself down and padded over to meet the group, who hadn't dispersed at all, but were studying Jane with various degrees of surprise and amusement. The real bird chose that moment to reawaken from its stunned state, and started to flutter against the window. Stephanie glared at Jane. It was obvious she thought Jane had gone too far. Jane defended herself:

"I'm not sure how that one got in here – I've been trying to remove it – does anyone have any ideas?" Sir Galahad immediately removed his jacket and moved swiftly to cover the still fluttering bird. Jane opened the door to the patio area, and within seconds the bird was despatched. Relieved, Jane smiled her thanks at her gallant knight, who grinned back at her, and made a quick check of the state of his jacket before slipping it back on.

"Thank you, David," said Stephanie frostily (this wasn't how the visit to the book centre was supposed to go *at all*,) "now, does anyone have any questions for Jane before we move on?" One doctor said bluntly, gesturing to Jane:

"Is this normal?" There was a burst of nervous

laughter through the group. Jane decided to take the comment at face value.

"No, I have other costumes I choose to wear. As many of our patients struggle with the idea of choice, that they can choose one course of action over another, I provide a living example of the possibilities for them. If I can choose to be different people in a very obvious way, so can they choose to be different people, in a more subtle way. It brings the message home, you see." Which was all a complete load of balderdash, but as an attempt to redeem herself with Stephanie, it wasn't bad, and the Director's face thawed slightly as she saw some of the doctors nod in agreement.

All might have ended well, has Steve not chosen that moment to throw the half-eaten seed bar through the door of the book centre. He wasn't to know the doctors were in there, of course. Everyone stood and looked at the bar, still half in its wrapping. Jane wasn't sure what to do, so she picked it up and started to chew. There didn't seem to be any more to say. Even Sir Galahad was silent.

"Let's see what's happening in the crèche, next. Thank you, Jane: very enlightening," and Stephanie herded her little group out, leaving Jane munching and thinking. 'I'm not the only one going to be torn off a strip by Stephanie later. It was very unprofessional of Steve to throw the bar like that – not to mention showing a serious lack of style.' Jane was disappointed in Steve. An egg left on her chair would have been acceptable, or a piece of cuttlefish carefully hung up in the stockroom, but to just throw the bar through the doors indicated he was seriously pissed off. 'Like a child throwing a tantrum,' she decided. Jim then appeared at the door, very contrite.

"Sorry, Jane. When they said there was a bird in the book centre, I thought they surely meant you, so I ignored it. But then someone said there was a real pigeon – where is it, love?"

"All gone, Jim. A knight in shining armour rescued me." She looked again at what she was chewing. "Have you ever tried these? They really are foul – I don't know why I'm eating it." Jim smiled at Jane's choice of adjective.

"Haven't you had enough bird jokes today, Jane?" he asked wryly.

Jane didn't answer. In her head she was already back at home, constructing another outfit, as Sir Galahad had given her a brilliant idea for her next alter ego…

Chapter Five

Jon and Amy in the Real World

The pub was crowded, but Jonathan pushed his way through to the bar, holding Amy's hand tightly. The sensation of being looked after and protected was new and satisfying to Amy. She remembered a previous boyfriend entering a crowded pub with her, looking with dismay at all the people, and just standing there, hands in pockets, staring truculently at her and saying: "Well, what do you want to do, then?" as if it was her fault and her responsibility.

At the bar, a man slipped off a stool as he greeted his friend and moved away, and Jonathan grabbed it quickly for Amy.

"What would you like to drink, Amy?"

"White wine, please." She had time to take in the feel of the place while Jonathan waited to get the bar staff's attention. The pub's popularity was understandable: it had a good ambience. Someone had managed to create a new pub that wasn't entirely soulless. They had even got the lighting right: bright but warm in tone, with no dark corners. Amy admired the muted old gold and ivory walls, set off with kingfisher flashes of colour at the bar and round the doors. She decided her dress didn't actually clash with the kingfisher, and then she studied Jonathan's clothes. It was a warm evening, but his arms were covered with a long-sleeve shirt; she peered closer and saw that there was a microscopically thin red stripe on the off-white background. Looking round the pub, Amy had a pleasing sense of them fitting in with the rest of the crowd there, and she relaxed a little.

Jonathan was standing very close to her perch on the stool. She could feel his heat, and inhaled a sharp lemon fragrance. The sensations intensified as he leant towards her, which happened frequently over the next few minutes. A guy with an order of several dozen drinks kept leaning into the bar to grab the next couple of glasses, and as Jonathan moved out of the way each time, the front of his shoulder nudged her arm.

'If I moved my arm, he would be moving against my breast,' flashed through Amy's head, but she kept her arm where it was, enjoying the light contact and warmth of him. At one point he glanced at her, checking she was ok, but with no trace of apology or awkwardness. It was as if he felt entirely comfortable up close to her, and Amy similarly felt it was the most natural thing in the world that they should be here, squeezed together at the bar, as if they had known each other for months, not days.

Jonathan got served eventually, and they stayed at the bar, chatting about their surroundings.

"Have you been to the 'King and Crown', Amy?"

"No, is it any good?"

"Depends on whether you like being ignored, or

scowled at by the bar staff and then told there is only one ale on that night. I thought about nominating them for an anti-customer service award." His tone was dry, and Amy laughed, then added her story.

"I know the café where their relations must work. You go in, they ignore you, but if you go to sit down, the manager comes bustling over and says: 'We ask our customers to *wait* to be seated, madam.' He then spends ages trying to find you a table, which is crazy, because the place is usually half-empty."

"I wonder why?" grinned Jonathan. "Hey, look, that group are going. Let's grab their seats." He swept up their drinks, and Amy slid off the stool and joined him at the table. She watched him swing the chair round so that he could stretch out his long legs and then lean precariously on a fraction of the table: she envied him his easy way of moving and wondered if he danced well too. She found that loose-limbed way of moving very attractive: it was what had first drawn her to him.

On the other side of the table, some very different thoughts were going through Jonathan's head. He had been quite relaxed up to this point, but now felt pressure to make scintillating conversation. There they were, sitting facing each other, and Amy was looking expectantly at him.

'Here's your chance to shine, Jon, if only you could think of something to say,' he thought, and then: 'What are women interested in? Shopping? You could write what I know about that on a bar code strip. But I know…'

"Amy, tell me something. What is it about women

and shoes? I was looking in my sister's wardrobe on Saturday – don't panic – I don't dress up or anything – she'd asked me to fetch my nephew's present down from its hiding place, while she cooked supper. But I was astounded to see so many shoes! I asked her – does Peter know you've got all those shoes? And she looked at me as if I knew nothing about anything. 'Of course,' she says, all superior. 'Why do you have so many?' I asked her. 'There must be fifty pairs of shoes there.' Then she gave me that look again. Mark started squealing at me to play with him then, so I never did find out the answer. Do you know?"

Amy's eyes danced with laughter, and she was clearly amused. "Yes, I know: it's called the 'search for the holy grail.'" Jonathan thought he must have misheard. Then Amy explained:

"Every woman is looking for the holy grail. All those shoes are the attempt to find it. All women have many pairs of shoes – well, most of the ones I know do. You see, you go to try on a pair of shoes. You want them to look stylish, fit well, have just the right size heel, be the right colour, and the right price. You can sometimes get two or three of these things in one shoe if you're lucky. But you convince yourself, out of desperation, that this is 'the one' and buy them anyway. You've been trailing round the shops all day and you've got to get something."

"'The one?' Or even 'the pair' maybe?" put in Jonathan, his eyebrows raised. But Amy hadn't finished. She appreciated that he was trying to be funny, rather than correct her, but there was more to explain.

"You later find out that they are not so comfortable after all, or that the colour just misses going with your new dress – "

"I told you I don't dress up!" Jonathan interrupted again, but Amy carried on regardless:

" – so you go back to wearing your old ones, but your old shoes are wearing out, and you must get a replacement pair, so you go out looking again…we call it the search for the holy grail." Jonathan was astounded. Surely there were better ways of spending time?

"Why is it so difficult? I go into a shop, I find a pair I like, and they are usually comfortable. I've never tried on more than two pairs of shoes at one time in a shop in my life!" Amy laughed out loud at such an impossible scenario.

"Women's shoes are different – you must have noticed. And besides, we want to look good too. For example: heels make legs look longer and more shapely, but it is always a balance – literally! Good shoes balance well and you can get away with a higher heel and still be comfortable. But good shoes are expensive."

"Hence all the queues at sale time. Amy, this is beginning to make a sort of sense." He glanced down at Amy's feet under the table. "Those shoes have quite a high heel, don't they?"

"That's because I knew I wouldn't be walking far! There's no way I could wear them at work." Amy looked down apologetically at the poor neglected shoes, which only came out to play on rare occasions. Jonathan was hoping she was wearing them also because she wanted him to admire her rather lovely legs and feet – that she wanted to attract him, but he had noticed that girls seemed to wear nice things for each other as much as the men they were with. So where did that leave him? He opened his mouth to bring that topic into the conversation, hoping to move things on a bit, when Amy suddenly changed the subject.

"Tell me about your family – do you have anyone else, apart from your sister?" Jonathan took a drink of his beer, while Amy studied the long fingers wrapped around the glass. What would they feel like on her skin? Unaware of the direction her thoughts had taken, Jonathan wasn't sure if he'd missed an opening or just missed the chance of making a total fool of himself, so with mixed feelings responded:

"Yes, two brothers as well, and one of them, Patrick, still lives at home. You?"

"No, I'm an only child. You are lucky – I would love to have brothers and sisters."

"Not these ones you wouldn't," Jonathan grimaced, but then smiled and Amy correctly guessed that there were no great problems there.

"Do you have family get-togethers?" asked Amy wistfully, and Jonathan resigned himself to telling family stories to entertain her for a bit.

"It's probably just as well Mum and Dad never moved: the house is still big enough when everyone comes back into it – just about. As well as us four, there are other halves and kids too: Nessa and Peter have got Mark, and Stefan and Laura have Joel. He's walking now so we're into stair gates, kitchen cupboard clips and all kinds of anti-Joel devices."

"Is Mark a toddler too? You mentioned playing with him."

"No, he's about six now, I think; certainly old enough to lead Joel into all kinds of trouble. Last weekend we had a big family lunch for Dad's birthday, and at one point found Joel in the bathroom, wrapped head to toe in toilet roll. Mark had got the idea from some television programme. Poor Joel is just standing there and letting him do it – he worships his cousin, and I reckon they both thought it was a great game."

Amy smiled. "It sounds like you have fun. In my family there is me; then my mum lives in Suffolk so tends to stay for a few days when she visits. You remember I told you about that after our first Alexander lesson? I've got an uncle in Wales and he's got a son, but we only exchange Christmas cards. That's it, as far as I know."

Jonathan was thinking as he listened: 'She hasn't mentioned a Dad; I wonder what happened to him – a bit early to ask. She seems a bit sparse on the relations side. If tonight works out I could invite her to the Chinese meal we're going to in three weeks' time, and if that goes well, there's Mark's birthday party – she'd love getting involved with that.' Jonathan did not flinch, as some men do, at the idea of introducing Amy to his family at an early stage in their relationship. He had done this with girlfriends before, and found it took a bit of the pressure off both of them: there were more people around to make conversation, and he had always felt comfortable in his family environment. His mum and dad were great at making the girls feel welcome, without going over the top, and when the relationship had run its course, the girls filtered out of their lives quite naturally.

'They would love this one,' he thought, and Amy was taken aback by the sudden warmth of his regard, not realising she was only part of the story.

[1] "Ci sono molti ragazzi qui vicino, ma tu sei bella di pui, carina. Desiderate ancora un bicchiere di vino?" The warmth had somehow got into his voice. The effect on Amy was electric. She didn't know it was possible to both melt and have a live current sparking through her at the same time. She felt the flush move over her skin, and felt totally confused. The comfortable feeling had gone and in its place was an intense excitement. But what kind of girl was she, she wondered, that she could be affected so much, simply by Jonathan speaking Italian to her? The nice, ordinary young man had metamorphosed into an exciting lover, and all he'd had to do was speak to her in that oh, so different voice. She thought that she must be one of those women who are attracted by superficial things, but that was not how she had thought of herself before. Shamed, confused, excited, Amy excused herself abruptly and retreated to the Ladies Room as quickly as those high heels could carry her.

Jonathan watched her go and cursed himself. 'Why did I have to go and show off? Now look – she is embarrassed for me – I could see it in her face before she ran away. You stupid plonker. And you didn't even get the grammar right. Not that she knew that.' Desperate

---

1   "There are many girls here, but you are the most beautiful, darling. Would you like another glass of wine?"

for a cigarette, but unwilling to have Amy find him gone when she returned, Jon got more drinks from the bar and played with the beer mats as he waited. She wasn't gone long, but couldn't quite meet his eyes as she wriggled back into her space behind the table.

"Is your job interesting, Jon?"

Jon looked at her soberly and considered the new topic of conversation. 'She's a bit pink,' he thought, 'but I don't think she's unhappy with me. If she'd been embarrassed by me showing off, she would have made an excuse to leave, rather than start a new conversation. Perhaps I got it wrong.' He started to speak and suddenly Amy put her hand on his arm.

"Whatever you do, please don't tell me in Italian," she pleaded.

It took Jon a whole five seconds to size up the situation, and he then took a gulp of his drink and covered her hand with his.

"Do you really want to know about my job, cara, or shall we just get out of here?" For one long moment Amy stared at him, then nodded.

[2]"Andiamo," he replied, and wrapped his arm round her waist as they left the bar.

---

2   "Let's go."

Chapter Six

Sasha's Story

18 July

Today I became a prisoner. Mum and Dad brought me to the clinic this morning. A woman called Catherine is in charge. I hated the way Mum and Dad fawned over her, like she was doing them the biggest favour ever, by taking me in. I know they despair of me, but they are *paying* her, for God's sake; she's not doing it for free.

Catherine explained that this Unit is part of a bigger clinic called Yatross, and we share the grounds with the day patients there. I wonder what the other Unit patients will be like? I don't meet them until tomorrow. Most of the day was tests and measurements and doctors asking questions – oh, God, it's so boring. I've been through all this before. Why do they think that this time it's going to be any different? Just because they read something about this place in a newspaper, and then when they rang up there happened to be a space free for the summer, Mum thinks it must be fate or something.

She was crying when they left. I should be the one

crying – I'm going to be kept here all summer – but I don't feel anything. Except very, very bored.

19 July

My room is all right, and quite pretty. But I've never seen anything like the bathroom arrangements they have here. Nothing goes down the drain. Everything that comes out of your body gets passed into a holding tank so they can study and measure it. I could always be sick on the floor I suppose, but apparently (according to Laurie) one girl did that and they made her live with it for a day before allowing her to clear it up. It seems they play hardball.

22 July

There are all kinds of girls in my group, but no boys. Fat ones, thin ones, some with terrible wounds on their faces and bodies. The eating rules are the same for everyone, strangely. Every morning, we have to eat a bowl of cereal or porridge with milk for breakfast. If we don't want to, we don't have to eat anything for the rest of the day, but we have to eat all that breakfast.

The fat ones were relieved to know that they could also get dinner, tea and supper, though nothing in between. I couldn't believe how much food they managed to shovel away between them. It was disgusting. I watched them getting fatter as they ate.

Oh, and we also have to go for a walk every afternoon. Supervised, of course. It's like being in a prison camp.

24 July

We had more lessons today about the body: how it works and what it's made of. Loads of stuff about organs, blood, muscles, hormones. It's quite interesting, but difficult to relate to *me*. It's like I'm learning about some obscure African tribe or something.

25 July

Today we moved on to art and sculpture – they talked about artists who 'celebrated the female form.' What a lot of hateful old pervs they were. I've had more than enough of rounded breasts and buttocks today. We've seen videos of museum exhibits, books of prints, and a new lecturer talked to us about Art history.

It feels as if there is so much knowledge in the world, and I know nothing. I'm not sure what the purpose of all this is, but at the moment I'm feeling very insignificant.

27 July

I wonder why we have to do these walks in the afternoon? One of the girls said it is supposed to give us an appetite, but I'm not sure that works in my case. The best fun today was teasing the old man who potters about in the gardens. We hid his tools, and he wandered about looking for them.

Jeanne refused to join in and stomped off on her own – spoilsport. When we all got back, she looked strangely at me and said: "You're not who I thought you were," all sort of accusingly. Well that's ok – I have no idea who I am, either.

28 July

This morning we were set up with drawing materials and artists' crayons. I liked the feel of the paper and the colours. We were each given a toy doll to draw – small at first, then bigger, then the size it actually was – a bit bigger than my fist. Then they put the doll next to the drawing to see how alike they were. My drawing wasn't very good, but then we went round looking at everyone else's, and I could see that very few were. Angela's was good – she's got real talent – but even she hadn't drawn the doll as thin as she actually was. We had all drawn her fatter than real life.

So we then had to have another go and try and get it closer in size. I was beginning to think my eyes were all wrong, but Barti, the guy who takes the class, said that I was doing just fine, and I just needed to persevere. I must say the teachers here are very nice to you – much nicer than they were at school.

30 July

They brought a real person into the class today, and we were expected to draw her, or paint her, if we wanted. She wasn't naked, thank goodness, but wore fairly close-fitting leggings and a jumper, so you could see all the bulges around her stomach and thighs. You wouldn't catch me dead looking like that.

She was difficult to draw – much harder than the doll.

Tomorrow we are going to work with clay – I bet it's revolting.

31 July

Yes, it was – it was revolting and fascinating all at the same time. First, we had to try and copy the shape of the doll, and we didn't do too badly at that, as the doll was still there in front of us. Then we had to try and make a small model of the lady who sat for us yesterday, from memory.

Linda said it was good, but I had made her much fatter than she really was. She passed round photos, so I could see this was true.

I've decided I've had enough of messing around with clay.

2 August

They are quite clever, making you eat breakfast. I am getting used to it, and eating more cereal as the days go by. My stomach is getting bigger – I can see the bulge. At lunch the other day (where I normally eat nothing) someone passed me the bread and I took a piece and ate it without realising, because I was talking to Laurie. There is now room for all this extra food in my ever-expanding stomach.

Catherine smiled with approval but I felt as if I'd betrayed myself.

3 August

Today we had another test where we had to grade pictures of people and make notes on what we thought of their shape and size. Then they took us through the results of the test we did when we arrived, to show us how our perspective on people's shape has changed. It turned out that the woman I'd labelled 'gross' a few weeks ago, I now thought was only 'fat.' I said it must be a different woman and that she'd lost weight, but the photos were date marked from the camera that took them, and in the end I had to accept it was true.

I felt cheated and confused. So now I know I can't trust the evidence of my own eyes. I liked the little black and white dog the woman in the photo had with her, though. Before I came in here, Dad promised that whatever weight I gained while I was in here, if I could maintain that for six months, he would buy me a dog.

9 August

Mum visited today and brought me some new clothes. She brought a size 6 jeans and they nearly fitted – only a bit baggy. "You'll soon grow into them," she chirruped happily, but the thought of growing into anything fills me with horror. I had a vision, as she spoke, of being fattened up, like a greasy pig, until I fitted the next size up, and then the next, and no-one would be happy until I was a size 16 or something.

10 August

It's been obvious for some time what their game is. Learning about my body has made me feel guilty when I don't give it what it wants – I'd have to be made of stone not to respond to it, like walking past a collecting box after seeing pictures of starving children. I feel like I mustn't let my body go without what it needs, or it will cry out in despair. All those organs and blood, hungry for calories so they can keep working.

Who am I betraying if I eat/don't eat? I really hate them for doing this to me. They have cheated, lied and deceived me, but it has started to work, sort of. I know I'm eating more now. Somehow I've got to work out a way of getting even with them.

11 August

A thought came to me today: thank goodness I haven't started my periods again yet. I don't think I could cope with all that yet. I suppose it will happen one day, though. If I eat enough.

13 August

We sat on Laurie's bed last night, gossiping about the other girls. She told us about how she went out with a boy to the cinema, and in the dark, he put one hand on her breast and another on her bum. On finding nothing there, he cried out: "Oh God, it's a boy!" We laughed like drains, and Geri came in to shush us and send us back to bed.

14 August

We've done a cooking class every week, but now it has stepped up to a daily session in the kitchen. We're also doing things like finding herbs in the grounds, doing virtual food shopping, and learning where food comes from.

    I have to admit that if I didn't have to eat it, I'd quite enjoy messing around with food. Again, the colours attract me, and I've been taking real pleasure in creating a plate of food good to look at. Sometimes we eat each other's food, and the girls all fight to have what I cook, because they say it is so good. It is lovely to have people like your cooking, but I do wish I didn't have to eat it as well.

Catherine tells me I'm doing very nicely and will be ready to leave as planned, at the end of the month. Then what?

16 August

Today we cooked for a party we had tonight with all the parents. I did enjoy the stunned looks on some of their faces. Most of them had sent in girls who could just about tear off a corner of a roll, and called that preparing a meal. Everyone's made a lot of progress in cooking.

The table looked great, but it was a shame everyone messed it up by eating it. The plates looked horrible when everyone had taken bits of food from them, leaving smears of sauce, and pieces of lettuce scattered over the tablecloth.

I didn't eat anything, of course. I wandered about with a bit of quiche on a plate and picked it up a few times so that it looked like I was eating, but I saw Catherine's eyes on me. She hasn't said anything yet. I'm going to make the excuse that I was too excited to eat.

20 August

I'm doing a pretty good job of making out to everyone that I'm cured. If I don't, they won't let me out at the end of August. I can't wait to get out of here so I'm playing along for now, eating my cereal like a good girl, and picking at a few bits at dinner and supper, and pretending to enjoy it.

My weight has stabilised, and I can tell they are disappointed that I haven't gained more. But I must not get any fatter – I feel like a pig even now.

22 August

They are talking about how we can support each other after we've left, by forming little groups. We're supposed to get together at regular intervals during the autumn, cook for each other, and generally watch out for problems. A bit like a spy then. Laurie, Jeanne and I have said we'll make up a group. I'm not entirely sure I can trust them though. What will they do when they find out I'm losing weight – report me to Catherine? But it will be too late then: Catherine won't be able to do a thing about it.

27 August

I've worked out what I can do. I'm not going to eat so much during these last few days, so that my weight drops, and then I won't have such a high target to keep to when I get home, and I might still get my dog. Catherine won't like my weight drop, but there won't be a thing she can do about it at this late stage.

Also, they won't want to admit that their programme has failed, so they'll tell mum and dad that everything's ace, which is what they want to believe, anyway. So everyone's happy.

30 August

At last! I'm free! My last weigh-in wasn't too bad – not enough to ring any alarm bells. Mum and dad are really happy, as they think I'm cured. I feel a bit sorry for them, actually. They were a lot happier to see me than I was to see them.

It's heaven to be back home, in my own bedroom, with all my stuff around me. And no more cereal! I'm not sure what I'll eat for breakfast, but it is not going to be cereal.

I expect I could get through an orange.

Then if I eat a yoghurt at dinnertime, no-one can expect me to eat more than that in a day, surely?

Chapter Seven

Lizzie's Lucky Day

Lizzie drove into the car park just before 8.00 a.m. and reversed skilfully into her usual space. She turned off the radio, checked her hair in the driving mirror, gathered up her things and opened the car door. The scent of herbs wafted up from the sunny patch nearby, and she breathed in their fragrance on the short walk to the back door of the clinic.

'How lucky am I, that I get to smell that every morning,' she thought, as she opened the door. "Morning, Jim," she called to the round, sandy-haired man perched on a ladder in the corridor. No answer from Jim, as he continued to wrestle with the light fitting above his head. 'Deaf old codger,' she thought, and continued to her office. 'First things first. Tea.' Lizzy turned round, to find Mariella had heard her come in and was holding out a mug for her.

"You are an angel, Mariella; thank you, and good morning," and the tea was on its way to her lips before she had finished speaking. The sound of whistling, away down the corridor but getting louder, indicated that

Simon was also in, and Mariella indicated that she would go and make him a cup of tea also. Simon leant against Lizzie's doorframe.

"Well, and isn't it a wonderful morning, Lizzie O'Sullivan? Is that a new blouse you're wearing? It suits you – matches the blue of your eyes if I'm not mistaken." Lizzie wasn't entirely immune to Simon's flattery and smiled at him.

"It's Mariella you need to go and charm, so be off with you, you great lunk: you're taking up too much space in my doorway, with your enormous rucksack – what *have* you got in there?"

"There'll be a few new paint tubes, but mostly it'll be soda pop, and vittles to keep the hunger devils at bay. As you say, I'm a great lunk and this body needs a lot of fuel. Wait a minute – shouldn't that be hunk, not lunk?"

"Lunk is the word; now, leave me in peace. Look, there's Mariella with tea." Simon turned to take the cup and started the usual pleasantries with Mariella.

"What would I do without you, my flower? I swear this is like nectar to my parched throat – "

Lizzie pushed the door shut and brought her mind to focus on the day's tasks. Her tablet told her she had four appointments with patients this morning, a catch-up session with Stephanie this afternoon, and an appointment with a sales rep towards the end of the day. She smiled to herself when she thought of how hard the rep was going to work to try to persuade her to buy his café supplies, when in fact she had pretty much decided that his was the best deal available at the moment. 'No point in letting him win too easily, though. He might have persuaded his boss to agree to an even better deal by then.'

The catch-up with Stephanie was routine: she brought up on to the screen her list of items to cover with the Director, and decided there was nothing contentious there. Lizzie often thanked her lucky stars that she worked for someone who trusted her with the task of running Yatross on the non-clinical side, and rarely interfered with or demurred at Lizzie's plans.

Another few clicks, and she was looking at the profiles of the patients she was due to see, to negotiate terms of payment for their treatment. This had to be the most difficult aspect of her job, but part of her loved the challenge, and the battle of wills that could sometimes be enacted before an agreement was reached. At 9.00 a.m. she was due to meet Louise Smith, who was to have a course of treatment with the homoeopathic practitioner. Lizzie calculated the relevant rates, made a note on the profile, and then studied Louise's details to see what the alternatives might be, if she could not afford the fees.

'Could she be a Helper? She has a job as a care worker, looking after the elderly, and does shift work – that could be useful.' Lizzie typed in 'creche, res. unit, coffee shop,' next to Louise's name, and continued reading. 'Aged forty, no children, no husband. Better and better. I've lost count of the number of patients who tell me: "Oh, no, dear, I couldn't do that: my husband wouldn't stand for it/ my children have to be picked up from school at that time/ my mother needs me to be there," and every other excuse under the sun. Now this is interesting. She belongs to a Fuchsia society, and is a keen gardener. Tom has been lamenting a gap in his shrubs over the far side of the grounds and a hardy fuchsia of a reasonable size could be just right to fill the gap.' Lizzie made another note and glanced at her watch. There was time, she thought, to read one more.

At 9.45 a.m. a family called Decker was due. Mum, two adult sons and a young daughter. They were attending for family therapy at 10.30 a.m., which didn't give her long to sort out an appropriate package, should it get complicated. Lizzie read that Mrs. Decker owned a butcher's shop in town, and the sons worked with her there. Relations between the three of them were very poor. The young daughter was reacting badly to this and playing up at school. In the shop, the sons shouted abuse at each other and their mother. Knives had been thrown, on occasion. Checking her watch again, Lizzie rang down to reception.

"Anna, could you just check that I've got the corner interview room for my 9.45, please?"

"Hi, Lizzie, just a sec…yes, all booked for you. The 9.00 a.m. one is in the room next door, though – is that ok?"

"Yes, I think Louise Smith is going to be safe enough, but I did want to check about the other one."

"Dicing with death again?" queried Anna, with a laugh. "I'll look out for you, and put Daniel on standby, shall I?"

"No need for Daniel this time, but I'll be glad of the monitoring. Thanks, Anna," and Lizzie ended the call. She sat for a moment, thinking. 'Some of the rows in the shop have been about money, so that might be tight. And time wasn't going to be in great supply either: butchers were always up early. Might there be spare time at the end of the day? Worth exploring, anyway. What about meat? The residential unit always needs supplies. But what about hygiene? No point in negotiating a deal where they provide us with meat in return for therapy, if everyone promptly goes down with food poisoning. It might be fine, but if the family is in crisis, is hygiene going to be one of their priorities?' Lizzie made some notes on the family profile and decided to wait and assess the situation at interview.

'8.40' in the corner of her screen reminded her that it was time to go. She scooped up the tablet and set off for a quick tour round Yatross, her usual routine in the mornings. She scanned the rooms as she passed, checking for problems; greeted various staff; made a mental note of a ceiling tile that had been broken by cable installers; and popped her head into both the crèche and the book centre on her way round to reception.

"Lizzie, I'm worried about the sharp edges on these book boxes – did you come up with any solution?" Sue was always raising a 'safety issue' for the children in the crèche, and Lizzie sometimes thought it was just a way of drawing attention to herself that was entirely acceptable, on the basis that no-one would dare say that the children shouldn't be protected from every possible hazard.

"Not yet, Sue, but I'll keep working on it," she replied pleasantly, and whipped through to the book centre before Sue could say any more. Today it was 'Sergeant Jane' or maybe 'Major Jane' or just possibly 'Colonel

Jane'. Lizzie was not familiar enough with military outfits and stripes to be able to tell the difference. She saluted anyway, and earned a brief smile from the slight girl standing to attention behind the counter. 'I hope the Deckers don't have to come and borrow books today,' Lizzie mused. 'The combination of the knife-throwing sons and Jane's authoritative stance may not be a good one.'

Out in reception, Lizzie carried out an all-encompassing scan of the area. It all looked very good. Anna and the reception team did a great job of keeping everything in good order, and generally Lizzie only had to deal with major repairs here. Anna nodded discreetly in the direction of Louise Smith, sitting on one of the chairs by the entrance, and Lizzie went to greet her first customer of the day.

∽

It was lunchtime in Agora, and a heated argument had broken out between Simon and Steve.

"If Heracles was only a demi-god," Steve was saying with emphasis, "then why did he have so many powers – killing snakes and lions and stuff like that?"

"We know he is only a demi-god," explained Simon with exaggerated patience, "because his mother was Alcemene, a mortal, but his father was Zeus, who disguised himself as a mortal one night when Alcemene's husband was away. Then when the husband came back, he sired a twin brother, who was, of course, mortal." As Steve opened his mouth again, Lizzie stepped in with a question, hoping it might defuse some of the heat in the room.

"Can you do that, then? Have twins fathered by different men?"

"Non-identical ones you can," chipped in Kirsty, who had also been listening. "Anyway, we're talking Greek myths here – surely anything goes?"

"It was as far as Zeus was concerned." Simon was able to use Kirsty's throwaway comment to resume the thread of his argument. "He screwed anything that breathed. His wife Hera was very jealous of all the resulting out-of-wedlock bastards: when Heracles and his brother Iphicles were in their cradle, she sent two snakes to squeeze them to death – "

"I knew the snakes were in that story somewhere!" Steve exclaimed, and Simon continued:

" – and it was Heracles, at only eight months, would you look at the little lad! that took hold of one snake in each hand and killed them."

Lizzie smiled to herself. Only in Yatross would such a conversation be considered normal.

"So, Simon," said Kirsty slyly, "is this the topic of that painting you're doing up in the loft, then?"

Simon threw back his head and laughed. "Oh, no, you don't catch me out like that, young Kirsty, and it's no good turning those bewitching blue eyes on me because I'm not going to tell you. Our esteemed Director has agreed I can keep it a surprise, and so it shall be."

Steve then joined in with trying to trick it out of him. "Twelve Labours of Hercules is a great theme for a painting, Si, but are you sure that's what you're doing?"

"What I'm not doing, don't you mean?"

"Ok, Kirsty, that's one eliminated; he's not doing that one – how many myths have we got left?"

Lizzie continued to munch on a sandwich and left them to it, tuning out and away from their laughing banter. She was thinking about Alcemene's husband, and what he would have thought when he realised one of his sons had supernatural powers and could not possibly be his…there was something tugging at her brain, and she drifted over to the window to gaze out over the gardens and let the thought come if it would … something about the Deckers?

As it happened, she needn't have worried about how they were going to pay for their treatment: Mum agreed to the standard rates without demur. But the hatred between the brothers was palpable, and scary. Lizzie's thoughts ran on. 'Mum obviously dotes on Ian, the younger, but I thought she seemed quite distant to Robin, the elder son. So could that be it? Different fathers? Is that why the family relationships are so rocky? Maybe Mrs D had really loved Ian's father, whoever he was, but not Robin's, and so had always treated them differently. That would definitely lead to resentment on Robin's part…the brothers are as different as chalk and cheese, which doesn't prove anything by itself, but still, it could be an avenue worth exploring by the therapist?' Lizzie's tablet was never far away, and she immediately left a note on their file, feeling that it might save a lot of weeks of going down therapy blind alleys if her instinct was right.

"You never stop working, do you, Lizzie?" It was

Denece's voice from behind her. From some people it would sound like a compliment, but Denece managed to make it sound rather more like an insult. Lizzie gave her a brief smile and said nothing. Denece crashed down into a nearby chair and began on a list of complaints.

"I couldn't believe it when I came in and heard Steve and Si arguing yet again about Greek myths – why don't they talk about sport or something, like normal men? It's so boring! And then there's Kirsty hanging on their every word, which just makes them show off even more. Lizzie, have you thought any more about us having a TV in here? That'll shut them up. I'm going to ask Stephanie about replacing these chairs too: I'm sure I can feel a spring in this one."

Lizzie, bored and irritated, looked at her watch and threw what she hoped would look like an apologetic smile in Denece's direction as she collected her things and left the room, before Denece could start on the next item on her list.

∽

Stephanie's room was cool and pleasant, and Lizzie settled into an easy chair with her tablet in front of her, while Stephanie finished a telephone call. The lady riding in the forest with all those out-of-place trees teased her eyes, until she had to look away. 'It's not logical. Why can't she have a nice Monet, or something?'

"Sorry about that." Stephanie had put the phone down. "That was Malcolm Treader, the new herbalist. He now can't start until September, because of family issues. Is that going to cause us a problem?" Lizzie consulted her tablet.

"August tends to be fairly quiet, with lots of people on holiday, so I don't think so. I can see just two herbal appointments on the calendar, so I'll offer them new dates for September. I'll change the pay system too: at least we won't be paying him for August."

This led into their usual discussion of income and expenditure, and Lizzie covered the main headings for the Director, together with key items for the October to December quarter of the year.

"One area of concern,' said Lizzie at one point," is that the residential unit is still making a slight loss, so is effectively being subsidised by our day patients. It's because of the high number of staff needed, as you know, and there's not a great deal we can do about that. I have tried in this last quarter to get more Helpers but whereas patients are happy to assist in the café and crèche, and even the gardens sometimes, few want to do sessions with disturbed adolescents and adults with mental health problems."

"It's the fear of the unknown," said Stephanie in her usual brisk manner.

"Partly," agreed Lizzie carefully, "but I also think it feels a bit too close to home for some of them. I did, however, manage to recruit a new Helper this morning. It was a great stroke of luck, actually. Louise Smith comes from a care background, but she told me her job is at risk due to cutbacks, and she may have to look for an alternative. As a way of finding out if it would suit her, she was very happy to be a Helper in the unit for several sessions a week, to pay for her treatment here. I think she is going to be an asset, actually: a sensible, kind-hearted woman with lots of good skills."

"That is good luck – let's hope she likes it, then we might be able to persuade her to stay. How are we on the cash to service ratio for day services?" Yatross needed to have at least 70% of its income in direct cash payments, as opposed to other contributions from patients by way of goods or services.

"We're maintaining 75 – 80% through the year as a whole," Lizzie reassured her. "This means we can afford to have the Bonfire Night party for patients and staff, as we did last year, and also a Christmas party for the staff at the hotel where we went before, or somewhere else if you'd rather? Anyway, we don't have to chip into any of the long-term accounts for these. I'm also planning a roof check this autumn: I want a contractor to check tiles and the roof windows, and do any repairs necessary."

Stephanie was thinking about the Bonfire night party, the roof not holding as much fascination for her as it did for Lizzie. 'Everyone had a good time last year,' she mused, 'and although Tom got a bit upset at the damage to his precious gardens, it has all recovered pretty well. Which reminds me – '

"How old is Tom, Lizzie?" Lizzie blinked at the sudden change of topic, but checked the staff and Helper database.

"Seventy-five. Why? What are you thinking?"

"We need to plan for the future: Tom is not going to want to be responsible for the grounds when he is eighty, for example. He does very well, but he is not immortal. Who have we got who could take his place?"

Lizzie sat for a moment, thinking. 'I'd like to see the person who could shift Tom from the Yatross gardens – it's not going to be as soon as Stephanie thinks.' She said out loud:

"Both Sheridan and Gavin are showing a lot of promise, but they can't devote themselves to it as a fulltime job. Shall we just wait and see how things develop, Stephanie? Tom is in good health at the moment, and is very happy in his work."

'In other words, back off,' thought Stephanie wryly. 'You win for the moment, Lizzie.'

"I know I can trust you to keep it all running efficiently, Lizzie," she smiled at her bursar, and they moved on to talk of other topics. Their meeting was almost finished, when Stephanie suddenly rose from the chair and went to her desk. Looking out of the window, she said quietly:

"Lizzie, I want you to know how glad I am that you are here, doing this job. It is such a weight off my mind, knowing you are so capable and reliable. Nothing escapes your attention, and Yatross runs smoothly because of you, not me. I'm very grateful." Lizzie was stunned into silence. Stephanie had never made such a speech before, although she knew the Director appreciated her. What had come over her?

"You're not going anywhere, are you?" Lizzie burst out, as the idea suddenly occurred to her. Stephanie laughed.

"No, I'm not going anywhere. Don't worry Lizzie,

I'm going to be here for a long while yet, just like Tom," and she smiled warmly as she turned back to face her bursar.

"Ok, so if you're being nice and appreciative and all that, is now a good time for me to ask again about removing that fish tank?" The fish tank, bizarrely, was one of the few things they disagreed on. The tank kept leaking, and needed expensive repairs; to replace the frequently dying fish cost yet more money. Furthermore, cleaning it was a major undertaking that Jim hated. Lizzie thought it could be removed altogether, but Stephanie maintained that it was calming for prospective patients.

"It's a really old-fashioned concept, now, you know," continued Lizzie craftily, "and you can get the same effect from a well-designed installation."

"I'm really not sure, Lizzie. Let's leave it for now, and see how it goes for the rest of this year. In January, bring me a summary of how much it has cost us to run for the past three years, and I'll make a decision then." Stephanie made a mental note to ask patients about the fish, so she could collect her own ammunition for the meeting in January. Lizzie was happy, as she felt sure her financial summary would prove the final plughole for those wretched fish.

So they parted in good spirits, and Lizzie hummed to herself as she went back down the corridor to get herself some tea to take out to the courtyard. "What a lovely day!" she exclaimed as she pulled a chair up towards the edge of the fountain, which was sparkling in the bright sunshine. She nodded briefly to the statue of Asclepius, the god of medicine, with his staff and serpent, (well, you never know when he might come in handy, and it cost nothing to be polite), sank on to the chair and swung her legs up on to the fountain parapet. She could just feel the faintest spray on her bare legs, and it was delightful. She lay back and closed her eyes, very content.

Lizzie had a few minutes of peace and quiet before a wolf whistle made her open one eye. It was Daniel, pulling up another chair and sitting next to her in that smooth flowing movement that was so characteristic of him. Unlike the wolf whistle. She would have attributed that to Si or Steve, not Daniel. Too relaxed to analyse any further, she waved a hand languidly at him and settled back for another few minutes of tranquillity. She was just thinking that she probably needed to go and get ready for her café sales guy, when Daniel spoke.

"Lizzie, don't move." His voice was urgent, and Lizzie froze. What was it? Wasp? Bee? Asclepius' serpent come to life?

"Your hair is caught in the back of the chair and if you try to get up it will be painful. Let me try and untangle it." Lizzie had opened her eyes but Daniel had already moved to the back of her chair.

"It's going to take a few minutes; sorry, Lizzie," Daniel was apologetic, but Lizzie accepted that there was nothing she could do and gave herself up to the feeling of Daniel moving his fingers against her hair and scalp, as he tried to untangle the problem ponytail. The feeling was surprisingly sensual. There were a few gentle tugs as he enabled different sections of hair to gain their freedom, but this just added to the awareness of sensation…such firm but gentle hands he had. 'Actually, Daniel,' thought

Lizzie, 'you can take as long as you like if it is going to be as nice as this. The salesman will have to wait.' Lizzie gave a sigh and relaxed even more into the chair.

"The thing that most people don't realise about Athena," said Daniel quietly, "is that although she was born with a spear in her hand, and fought next to Zeus in the Battle of the Giants, she was actually the goddess of wisdom. She was concerned with prudence, moderation and balanced judgement."

Lizzie thought: 'Did I drop off somewhere and miss the beginning of this story? How did we get on to the subject of Athena? I wonder if the lunchtime conversation in Agora had a Part Two, which I missed. Never mind, I'm sure all will become clear…'

"Did you know that the city of Athens could have been called Poseidon? Both gods wanted to be patron of the city, so they decided to each give the city a gift, and whichever one was judged to be most valuable, would win. Poseidon promptly produced water from a rock, but Athena stamped on the ground and an olive tree grew. Well, you can guess what the decision was."

Lizzie had not the slightest idea why Daniel was telling her this story. 'I'm used to Greek mythology permeating every aspect of life at Yatross,' she thought, 'but this is a new angle, pinning down and indoctrinating people while they're sitting peacefully in the courtyard, drinking their tea.' She was having trouble following the thread of what he was saying, as his soft voice, together with those firm hands gently massaging her head, were making it difficult to concentrate on the goddess Athena.

"Have you ever seen Athens, Lizzie? I'm going to

have to undo your hairclip to get this last bit free, is that ok? It's magnificent."

Lizzie was fairly sure that the adjective related to the city, not her hair, but by the time she had thought of anything coherent to reply, Daniel had somehow tapped a whole new source of sensation on different parts of her head, and she became aware of goose bumps rising on her neck and arms, despite the warm afternoon.

She had mentally tried on each of the men she worked with as a potential lover: 'Si? No, too wrapped up in painting and Greek mythology – women would come a very poor third in his priorities,' and 'Steve? Good-looking, but too much of a ladies' man and has a different girl every month – I have no intention of being Miss July,' but for some reason Daniel hadn't appeared in her mental wardrobe. He had an other-worldly quality which translated into 'asexual' – or at least, had seemed so until now. She gave a brief thought to his age: 'What is he? Ten years older than me, maybe?' but then dismissed it of no consequence. With hands like his, who cared about age?

Daniel was now no longer even pretending there was any hair left to untangle, and was unashamedly running his fingers through her hair and over her head, over and over, while he finished his tale:

"So Athena gave her name to the city, and since then has protected mankind and helped in any peaceful activity, such as weaving, pottery-making and writing poetry. So, not war-like at all, really." Daniel gave one last stroke to the back of her neck and then stopped. "I think you're free."

All the while Daniel had been conducting his

seductive massage, Lizzie had been absorbed by the sensations he was creating, but now she became aware of her surroundings and felt a deep blush rise up her face. She moved so quickly to bring her legs down off the parapet that her cup went flying, and she dived to the ground to rescue it. By the time she raised her head, Daniel had gone. She clipped her hair back into its confining ponytail, while running back to her office and giving herself a stern lecture.

'What *were* you thinking of, Elizabeth O'Sullivan? Now you're late for Mr Stewart, and what excuse are you going to give? This is not like you! You'd better pull yourself together...I wonder what he meant by saying: "I think you're free"? Was he just talking about my hair? Or did he mean something else?'

While Lizzie washed her face and tidied herself in an attempt to present a business-like front, Mr Stewart's anxiety levels were at an all-time high. This contract was important, and he'd thought he had it in the bag. She was late, and it could only mean one thing. She was waiting to hear a price from another supplier, and was hoping it would come in before she agreed the deal with him. He paced up and down in the reception area, and finally went outside to call his boss.

"Mike? Yeah, it's John here. Look, things aren't looking good here at the clinic. I haven't got time to explain, but if I have to, can I cut another ¼ % off the contract? Yeah, I know. Yeah, I know that too. Well, I may not have a lot of leeway. Ok, I'll do what I can. Yeah. Yeah. Right."

So it was with some surprise that Lizzie found John

Stewart eager to suggest a slightly better deal than they had already discussed, and as they worked through the finer details, Lizzie found herself wondering whether she was supposed to offer up a sacrifice to Hermes, the god of commerce, or to Aphrodite, the goddess of love, for today's unexpected happenings. She just hoped they weren't expecting a live goat, or something equally difficult to obtain.

'Definitely Aphrodite,' she decided, when, on leaving her office that night, she found herself walking towards Daniel, on his way to the back door from the opposite direction. 'What are the chances of that?' she thought. 'It can only be divine intervention. My turn to take the initiative.'

"Daniel! You know you have ruined my reputation?" He half-smiled and raised his eyebrows, but said nothing. "For punctuality, you understand. Lizzie the bursar is known to never be late, but I was today. Not that I'm not grateful to you for helping me out of a jam, of course." She wasn't quite sure what to make of his lack of response. Had she dreamed it all? She took a breath and plunged in, hoping that Aphrodite was with her, despite the lack of suitable sacrifice.

"Daniel, tell me something." By now he had opened the back door and was holding it for her as she stepped out on to the path.

"Daniel, was my hair caught at all?" She stopped walking so that he turned to look at her.

"Of course. Your hair caught me the first time I saw it. There you were, Athena to the life, striding down the corridor with your tablet under your arm, going out to do battle with some plumber or carpenter, and that hair bounced along beside you. It was like it had a life of its own, but was still happy to join in with whatever you had planned. I very nearly joined in the party."

Lizzie's logical half registered that he hadn't answered her question, and had twisted it round to answer a different question entirely, but the other half of her was glad that he had finally made his feelings clear, and that she hadn't dreamed this afternoon after all.

"You've never said anything," she complained gently, and he moved closer to her on the narrow path. Daniel looked down into her lovely, open, honest face, and smiled.

"I was waiting for a sign from the gods," he said, and she was aware of the laughter in his voice just before he bent his head to kiss her.

Chapter Eight

Coffee Break Conversation

Andy filled the kettle at the sink and calculated that this must be the eighth time he had undertaken this chore. 'Still, mustn't complain: one of the girls always makes the tea.' The water overflowed the spout and he looked at it in mild surprise. He always filled the kettle until it got heavy and he could feel the pull in his back. But that prompt hadn't presented itself today. 'Interesting. That means my back was able to take a greater load on it before complaining. How come I've not noticed that at work?'

Andy emptied a gulp of water, plugged in the kettle and switched it on, then wandered outside to the smokers' garden, thinking about work. Jonathan wasn't far behind, and the men contentedly smoked their cigarettes in silence for a minute or two.

"So, do you think it's working then, this Alexander Technique?" asked Jonathan, attempting to give his body directions at the same time. *'Let my neck be free…'*

"I was just thinking about that. Funny how it seems to work here, and sometimes at home, but I don't think I've cracked it at work yet."

"I'm pretty much the same," agreed Jonathan, blowing out smoke. "Once I'm in the classroom giving lessons, all my concentration is taken up with the students. I imagine it's the same for you, with lots going on, on a building site." Andy nodded. They stubbed out their cigarettes and began to walk back to the building.

"How's the romance going?" asked Andy with a smile. They had had several conversations about Amy since that first evening.

"Really good. We're even planning to go away for a break before the Autumn term starts."

"Where will you go? Italy?" Andy's wink was not lost on Jonathan who grinned broadly.

"I don't think so: too much competition! No, we'll just find a last minute cheapo somewhere."

"Glad it's working out for you, mate." They had reached the Alexander studio, and found their tea waiting for them and a cheerful conversation going on about holidays. Sheila was telling Amy about a cottage in North Norfolk she had stayed at in May.

"It was neat and clean, had all the facilities you could wish for, and was only about ten miles from the coast. If you think you'd like it, I'll email you the details if you want."

Amy glanced up at Jonathan, trying to gauge his level of enthusiasm for the idea, but his face was neutral. She turned back to Sheila and smiled. "Well, yes, thank you, Sheila. We haven't really decided what to do yet, and it won't hurt to have another option." Amy was careful not to commit them to anything, while thinking: 'A cottage in the middle of nowhere *could* be romantic, or it could just be...boring. Maybe Jon feels the same? We can chat about it later.'

"I stayed in a cottage once," recounted Siobhan, "where the owner boasted that the bed mattress was genuine horsehair! How many centuries ago did they make those, for heaven's sake? I told him the next morning that they must have forgotten to take the horse's bridle out, as there were bits digging in me all night: I didn't get a wink of sleep!" They all laughed appreciatively, even Tosca, though she looked a bit puzzled. Her world was narrow, almost entirely focussed on hurdling, and sometimes the things other people spoke about went right over her head. She was Daniel's star pupil when it came to Alexander Technique, though.

Daniel now said: "Have you tried using your directions when you can't go to sleep?" Only Sheila nodded 'yes' so he continued: "Try it sometime, unless you have no trouble sleeping?" The discussion moved on to sleep problems and solutions, and Amy got up and took her mug to the sink to wash. Jonathan joined her, so she took the opportunity to ask him quietly:

"What do you think of the cottage idea?"

Jonathan grimaced as he pushed his mug under the tap. "Doesn't sound much, does it? I think we'd be better off in somewhere with a bit more life." Amy agreed and they returned to the rest of the group, some of whom were trying to use their Alexander directions to get out of their chairs.

Andy handed Daniel an envelope. "Could you get this to Lizzie for me? It's a quote for some fencing work she wants done. I happen to know a bloke who can give her a good deal. You breed some right little tearaways here, don't you? I saw the state of some of the fences on the way in."

"We certainly serve a mixed demographic," agreed Daniel wryly, taking the envelope. He turned to include the others. "We'd better make a start on our second half, if you're all ready."

At the end of the evening, the group dispersed to their cars (and bicycle in Tosca's case) as usual, and called out the usual "Goodbye," and "See you next week," to each other. Amy had come in Jonathan's car tonight, and halfway down the drive, Amy exclaimed:

"Oh Jon, I've left my scarf behind! I thought it might be chilly later. Can we go back?"

Jonathan good-naturedly turned the car round, while saying with a mild exasperation: "For goodness sake, Amy, it's August! When do you think it might be warm enough *not* to need a scarf?" Amy didn't reply, as, despite what she'd said earlier about it possibly being chilly, she believed scarves to be essential items of clothing, warm evening or not.

As she went back into the building, she noticed Sheila still hovering by her car. She realised that in the eight weeks since they had started, she had never seen Sheila leave the car park before them. To Amy's mind, that could only mean one thing. She met Daniel on his way out, and he gallantly accompanied her back to the studio to retrieve her scarf. As she slipped back in the passenger seat next to Jonathan, she burst out:

"I think Daniel and Sheila are going out together! She's always waiting for him; had you noticed?"

Jonathan checked his driving mirror and briefly considered this new item of gossip. "Are you sure? They don't say much to each other in the lesson."

"Of course they wouldn't. Daniel is so professional: he wouldn't act as if he fancies her in front of us. Wait till I tell Siobhan!"

Jonathan shook his head at women's propensity to make up fiery romances out of what amounted to minor bits of kindling, and drove on to their favourite pub for a well-earned and much needed drink.

❧

A few days later in Agora, Sue and Denece were also discussing holidays.

"That's one of the many problems of being a single parent, Denece: holidays are either non-existent or a nightmare." Sue prised off the lid from her plastic bowl of salad and began to fork leaves into her mouth.

Denece nodded in agreement. "I did once take Lucy and Dom on a plane on my own, though, Sue. I don't think I'd do it again. A friend had a timeshare in Spain, and the idea was that we'd fly with her and her son together. But we couldn't get on the same flight." Denece sat hunched in the chair, staring at a point beyond Sue's shoulder, as she remembered the experience. "I was trying to get Dom to eat something, and Lucy was chasing another child up and down the plane aisle, and the cabin crew were no help at all. 'Madam, you need to control your child,' one of them said when he brought her back. 'Help me entertain her, then,' I said, but he just walked off. There was an old man across the aisle who took the trouble to talk to her, told her stories for a bit, and eventually she fell asleep in his lap."

"Oh, my God! Weren't you worried? Suppose he was – you know." Sue's anxious mind had gone into overdrive.

Denece's bushy eyebrows drew together as she frowned in concentration. "I think you have to use your instinct – he'd been so kind, and what was he going to do, anyway, in a sardine can like that, where people watch your every move? That was the bit I hated most: feeling that people were judging me and thinking I was a bad mother."

Denece's face was troubled, and, as if suddenly embarrassed by revealing such thoughts, she dived into her large green handbag, found an emery board and began sawing at a rough-edged nail. Sue clicked her tongue in sympathy and leaned forward, balancing her salad precariously.

"I know what you mean. We were all on a beach once; it was before Jeff left but he might as well have not been there, anyway. He was doing his usual stuff where he buried his nose in games on his phone and ignored me and the children." Sue munched on salad for a minute while Denece waited patiently for her to continue.

"It was actually sunny, and not too windy. He could have played games with them, taken them in the sea. But when I suggested it, he just grunted something about the day being all my idea, so why didn't I play with them and leave him in peace. So I did, and the kids had a good time, but I watched other Dads wrestling with their boys and building fortresses with them, and I just felt like the boys were missing out."

Denece fished a sandwich out of the green bag and looked for an opening in the plastic carapace. "Does he ever see them?"

"During the school holidays, for a day, from time to time. But I get the feeling he does it as a duty. Anyway, the bad mother bit. The boys and I had started a game of throwing balls to each other, and George kept throwing it far too wide and high for Harry to reach, so he ran off, crying. I told George off, then looked round for where Harry had gone, but he'd disappeared. I was running up and down the beach calling 'Harry! Where are you?' and all the other families were looking at me."

"But everyone's lost sight of their child at some point," put in Denece sympathetically.

"You'd never guess it, from the way they looked down their noses at me." Sue produced a good impression of their snooty faces. "I was getting really frantic, but after about ten minutes I found him back with Jeff and George, raiding the picnic bag for food. I was then angry with Jeff more than anything, for sitting there so unconcerned while I was running around like a madwoman. 'And how, exactly, is this all my fault?' he said, all superior."

Denece bit back an instinctive "You're better off without him," because she knew it was never that simple, and that Sue, like herself, would have conflicting feelings on the subject. Instead, she looked down at the sandwich she had just finished unwrapping.

"I don't believe it!"

"He did say that, I tell you, no-one could be more – oh, you're talking about your sandwich. What don't you believe?"

"I asked Mariella not to put any spread on my bread, just cheese, but look! That's the second time she's done that. I don't think she likes me very much."

There was no answer to that, as privately Sue thought so too. So she said: "It would be a lot easier if she spoke. I'm always wondering if she's heard what I've said, and I can hear myself speaking louder, as if she's deaf. But she's not."

Denece bit into her sandwich unenthusiastically and chewed a mouthful. "I know. I do the same. But now I'm wondering if she understands what I say to her. Where does she come from? Did anyone ever say?"

Sue took a sip of her coffee while she considered what she knew. "Everyone seems a bit vague about that. Some war-torn country between Europe and the East, I suppose. I don't suppose she's had much of a life."

Denece was morose. "She's all right now, though, isn't she? Everyone thinks she's Christmas. I get fed up with people going on about how wonderful her cooking is, and how lucky we are to have her. She's lucky to be here, that's what I think. And this sandwich is rubbish, anyway."

Sue laughed. "You sound just like George, complaining about the sandwiches I make him. Would it cheer you up if I made you a coffee?"

"Thanks, Sue, that would be nice." Denece was more grateful than the simple offer warranted, because no-one made her coffee any more. She sometimes worried that she would always be on her own, that no-one would ever be around to care about whether she wanted a coffee. Such a small thing! But Sue could always be relied upon to make her feel better, and with this came another thought.

"Sue, why don't we go away together, with the kids? It'll be a lot easier to entertain them between us. I know yours are a bit older, but they get on all right, don't they?"

Sue was glad she was busy with Denece's coffee cup when the offer was made, as she felt her face might have shown her dismay. She looked after Lucy and Dominic in the crèche every day, and she wasn't sure she wanted a holiday with them too. A holiday was supposed to be different to your normal day-to day activity, wasn't it?

"It's certainly a thought, Denece. I'll put it to the boys and see what they say."

Denece was predictably put out. "You could sound a bit more enthusiastic!"

"Here's your coffee. Sorry, I'm just not sure what the boys want to do, really." She then thought of a sidetracking ploy. "We're going to the farm animal place on Sunday for the day. Do you want to come with your two? Bring a picnic."

"They'll like that. We'll come if it's not raining. I hate traipsing round those places in the wet: mud gets everywhere and I spend the next week cleaning clothes, boots, the car, and everything."

Sue was just wondering if she could put up with Denece's grumpiness for a whole holiday, when Denece thought of something else.

"I know what I meant to ask you: what do you make

of this?" and Denece lifted her skirt slightly to show Sue a wound on the side of her knee. "It won't clear up, and I've had it for months. What do you think?"

Sue studied the wound suspiciously. "Is it sore?"

"Not really. I can't remember doing it, that's what's strange."

Sue straightened up. "I've got some cream that the doctor gave me for George, when he had something similar. It's out of date now, so I won't use it on him again, but he's just a child. It should be fine for an adult. I'll bring it in tomorrow."

"Thanks, Sue, that'll be great. I've got a patient in ten minutes, so I'd better go. See you tomorrow." Denece gave Sue a brief hug in thanks, and flew out of Agora, leaving her lunch debris behind her.

Sue surveyed the mess and grimaced. It was like clearing up after the boys. But as she disposed of Denece's part-eaten sandwich, wrapper and half-drunk coffee, she couldn't help but feel some pity for Denece. She was patently grateful for small things: someone making her a coffee, taking the time to look at her knee, even grateful for the offer of out-of-date skin cream. And Sue knew what that was all about. She just wanted someone to care about her.

'We'd all like that,' she thought wryly, as she made her way back down the corridor, 'except for some lucky people, like Suki and Anna.' She then watched with half envy, half amusement, as Suki shot out of the crèche as soon as Sue returned, eager to meet her darling Anna for a lunch break together.

Sue turned round to meet the headlong rush of Lucy

and Dominic, both of whom had run up to give her a hug. "Auntie Sue!"

She responded with genuine affection. "Hello, you two. Guess where we're going on Sunday? With Mum, and George, and Harry?" She snorted loudly and they jumped up and down in excitement.

"Pigs!" they said in unison, and began snorting too. Soon, the whole crèche: staff, Helpers and children, were giving a good impression of a large pigsty at feeding time.

'Try getting out of Sunday's farm visit now, Denece,' thought Sue, with just the tiniest wisp of malice towards her friend.

"Come on, let's make some pictures of pigs for the display wall," and she took the children's hands in each of hers and led them off to join the others.

Chapter Nine

Tom's Troubles with the Young People

It was August, and Tom had all the troubles of the world on his shoulders. August meant school holidays, bored kids, vandalism and torment. He woke up every morning and hoped it was September, but it never was. Somehow he had to hang on until September and hope that Mrs Harman didn't find out how bad things were. Just another three weeks…

Today, as he arrived at Yatross, he wondered what he would find. Yesterday he had spent most of the afternoon clearing human waste from the rose beds – the patients from the residential unit had deposited it there on their afternoon walk round the grounds. They were bored, that was the trouble, and were continually thinking up new ways to bait him. Sheridan kept saying to him: "You must tell Mrs Harman," but he would not. He knew that if he did, Mrs Harman would think he was Too Old For the Job, and that he couldn't cope. She would start talking about him cutting his hours down, and handing over to someone younger. But the gardens at Yatross were his, carefully developed and tenderly cared for over many years, and when he thought about losing them, a panicky feeling came over him, just like he used to feel all the time.

'I've just got to hang on till September,' he thought, and squared his shoulders to face whatever the day was going to throw at him.

The first missile came in the shape of the large shed door swinging open to greet him – the padlock had been broken, and his heart sunk. He could work all day to repair damage, but loss of things such as equipment was harder to cover up. He had already replaced various tools out of his own pocket, when the young people had run off with them before he could stop them.

Tom went into the shed, and stopped. All that appeared to be missing were two bags of compost. He maintained several compost heaps around the gardens, but sometimes he needed an ericaceous mix or bulb fibre, and it was the specialist bags that had been stolen. A strange item for the young people to drag away, he thought, and he wondered what their plans were for it, and where it would eventually turn up. He sighed, and made a mental note to replace the padlock later this afternoon.

He glanced up at the sky, wondering how long he had before rain came. It was forecast for around lunchtime. With any luck, it would be heavy enough to keep the little devils indoors. Tom loaded up a barrow with tools and set off to prune some shrubs that had flowered late and now needed cutting back.

He spent a couple of pleasant hours working before it occurred to him that he could do with a cup of tea.

He hesitated, but then took the tools back to the shed before leaving the gardens. 'No point in making it too easy for them.' At the main building, he approached Agora from the terrace side. A couple of staff were chatting at one of the outside tables, and Tom thought about what a superb working environment these people had, compared to what he had had as a young man. He was about to step inside when Lizzie appeared at the terrace door.

"Morning, Tom, how are you?" she greeted him, smiling.

"I'm well enough," he replied gruffly, wishing he were forty years younger, and single. He always thought she was like the girls of his youth: pretty, hair tied back, not too much make-up; unlike some of the women you saw these days, where it seemed to be plastered on, and their hair often looked like they had been dragged through a hedge.

"I'll get you your tea, and that'll save you having to take your boots off, Tom," Lizzie offered nicely, and Tom resigned himself to sitting on the terrace and submitting to a chat while he drank his tea. 'I wasn't actually going to bother to take my boots off,' he thought, 'but probably best not to tell her that. No point in upsetting the apple cart.'

Lizzie brought a couple of mugs to the table, and, as he'd expected, sat down with him. After a couple of exchanges about the weather and the likely accuracy of the forecast, Lizzie asked:

"So how's everything going, then, Tom?" Tom buried his face in the mug of tea, which Lizzie remembered was exactly what he'd done last time she asked him this question.

"Well enough, well enough,' he muttered, and cast around for something to distract her. 'Got to be careful around Mrs. Harman's spy,' he thought. Then he remembered the padlock.

"You don't happen to have a spare padlock, do you? I couldn't get my key in it this morning, and as I tried to force it, it broke. Flimsy bit of kit. They don't make things like they used to, to my mind."

"I'll find one for you, Tom. How big does it need to be?" Tom indicated with his hands and Lizzie made a mental note.

"And what about Gavin and Sheridan? Are they proving to be a good help to you?" Tom took another mouthful of tea while he tried to calculate what would be the best response to this. Was the bursar trying to work out whether he could be replaced?

"They don't do too badly,' he admitted grudgingly, but added: "Of course, they've got a lot to learn. And it's not like they're here all the time. Gavin can only do weekends, and while Sheridan is here quite a lot during term time, she is off somewhere with her children this week and next, so you can't really compare either of them to a full-time worker."

"Of course not, Tom, we really couldn't do without you," reassured Lizzie, seeing which way the old man's mind was working. "I have managed to get you some sessional help for next week, though. Can you find something for him to do?"

Tom sighed. These Helpers were all very well, but

most of them knew nothing about plants or gardening, and he spent so much time showing them what to do, he often thought he'd be better off on his own.

"I suppose so. What does he know?" he asked, knowing the answer before it came.

"He might just about know a rose from a peony, but don't count on it," Lizzie said, laughing, while thinking: 'Oh dear, Tom is very grumpy lately.' She continued:

"Paul Watson is his name. He is a young man who is contributing towards the cost of his treatment by working for us from Monday next for two weeks. He seems sensible, and looks like he might be able to carry a few bags of compost for you. Tom? What is it? Do you know him?"

Tom had hurriedly got up from the table and was turning to go. He couldn't stay any longer. It was the mention of compost: he felt just as guilty as if he had stolen it himself.

"No, never heard of him. Look, I can't sit here chatting all day. You send him to me next Monday – that'll be fine." With that, he was gone. Lizzie sat for a few minutes longer, watching Tom stomp off back towards the gardens. Something was wrong, she knew. 'Is it just that he is fighting against getting older, and the mention of the young man being easily able to lift things rankled with him? Maybe. I could wander round the gardens a bit next week, and use the excuse of having a new Helper to monitor. The problem is, Tom resents my hovering even more than having Paul thrust upon him. I don't want to use Paul to collect information, but perhaps if I worded it diplomatically? *"Paul, I hope you will come and tell me if you run into any problems at all, or if anything concerns you."* Something like that.'

Having gone as far as she could with resolving the problem for the moment, Lizzie picked up the mugs and went back into Agora.

∽

As he approached his shed, Tom noticed a woman standing nearby. She looked up as he came towards her, and smiled shyly. It was obviously his day, Tom thought, for being waylaid by women, and he scowled at her, wondering if she was yet another Helper.

"Hello, I'm Louise. The bursar said I'd find you here at some point. Isn't it a lovely day?" Her voice was light, musical and quite charming, but Tom was not charmed. He grunted and walked on into the shed to get his tools. Why couldn't they just let him get on with his work?

"Miss O'Sullivan did mention the fuchsias?" Louise was slightly disconcerted by the gardener practically ignoring her, but had worked with older people for too long to be surprised by anything they did. Not that he was as old as her patients, she calculated. Tom wheeled his barrow out of the shed and pushed the door shut behind him.

"What fuchsias? What's happened to them?" Tom had an image of the tearaways trampling his precious plants, and started to pay her more attention. Somehow, Louise thought, they had blundered into a blind alley. Not sure whether it was her fault or his, she tried again.

"Perhaps it would be better if I started at the

beginning. I'm working at the residential unit for a while –"

"I knew it!" Tom exploded. "Those wretched kids!"

"Why, what have they done?" Louise asked quickly, the fuchsia offer forgotten. While she was not the only one responsible for them, she definitely wanted to know what the young people were up to. Now it was Tom's turn to look confused.

"You were going to tell me – what have they done to my fuchsias?"

"Oh, no, this is about new fuchsias – I've offered some to Yatross, from the fuchsia society I belong to. If you'd like some, that is." Louise was wondering if Tom was older and more confused than she had estimated, but suddenly his face cleared.

"You want to give me some fuchsias – well, why didn't you say so? What are they? Hardy? Half-hardy?" The gardener was immediately all business, and a relieved Louise explained what she could provide.

"I've got a 'Phyllis', which I thought would be good, as it grows up to above your height, and will fill in a fair-sized gap for you. And it's frost hardy. If you want some bedding fuchsias, and the bed is in a fairly sheltered spot, I've got a 'Margaret Roe' and a 'Nancy Lou', both of which are half-hardy. Oh, yes, and there's a 'Mrs Popple' if you want another hardy one, but not everyone likes those as they can take over a bit."

Tom started to think about where he could put these plants, and spent a pleasant half-hour showing Louise the garden locations he had in mind. Louise then had to go off to her shift at the residential unit, and Tom went back to find his tools and start on some weeding. But back at the shed, two young boys in their mid-teens were battling with spade and fork, and a third was cheering them on, waving a hoe dangerously near their heads. Tom was more than dismayed. These boys were not from the residential unit, but he recognised them as local boys from when they had cycled over his plants, earlier in the holidays.

"Hey, put that down!" he shouted, and started running towards them. He wasn't surprised when they started running off with his tools, across the lawns, but then he suddenly had an inspiration.

"It's all right, son, I guess I've got the better of the deal," and he picked up their bikes and started stacking them side by side, as if to wheel them into the shed. Nothing could have brought them back faster. They didn't know the shed padlock was broken, and they dropped the tools on the grass and started running back.

"You leave my bike alone, you old git!" shouted one, as he approached.

"Just grab it off him, Ben," called the boy behind him, not quite so speedy.

"So, Ben, which one of these smart machines is yours?" Tom's mild tone brought Ben up short.

"The blue one," he replied automatically, and found himself waiting for the old man to disentangle his bike from the rest. Somehow Tom had turned the tables on them and it was like he was doing them the favour by handing out bikes. The boys weren't quite sure how this had happened. The reversal didn't last, though. As soon as they were on their bikes again, Tom felt he had to assert himself, and show these boys they couldn't just turn up and cause havoc.

"Now then, be on your way, all of you, and if I catch you messing about with my tools again, I'll call the police."

"Yeah, right," the skinniest one of the three sneered. "And if you do, we'll just smash your greenhouse again!"

"So that was you! You little monkey! What's your name? Come here!" Tom was furiously angry, but the boys rode off, making rude gestures as they left the site.

Tom, almost snarling with rage, strode over to where the tools had been dropped. At least he wouldn't have to replace them again. But he was fuming about the greenhouse: how dare they admit to breaking the panes? 'Today's kids have no respect for property, or their elders. If I'd even accidentally broken a greenhouse pane when I was their age, my Pa would have made me apologise to the owner, and then do extra jobs on the farm to earn money to pay for the replacement pane. But this lot of good-for-nothings are not only bragging about doing it, but threatening to do it again!'

Luckily, Tom was able to take out his frustration on the weeds of Yatross, and the flower beds looked pretty good by the end of that week. Tom found it therapeutic to push down hard on the fork with his boot, and imagine the skinny one's head in its place. A peace-loving man, not given to temper or violence, Tom metamorphosed into a Fury when his beloved gardens were threatened.

The following Monday, Paul Watson reported for garden duty at 8.00 a.m. sharp. On seeing Tom approach the shed, with his brisk walk and military bearing, Paul felt compelled to salute and stand to attention.

"Stand by your beds!" he ordered no-one in particular. "Flower beds, that is. Morning, Major," and he grinned at Tom. Tom stared at him, nonplussed, then shook his head. First, they send him a woman who couldn't get to the point, and now there's this comedian. Well, he'd soon wipe that grin off his face.

"They told me you were a hard worker. That true?" Tom demanded.

Paul's grin faltered a little. "Well, fairly hard, I suppose. What do you want me to do?"

"Today," said Tom with satisfaction, "we're going to dig up a bloody great rubrifolia. Get yourself a fork and spade, and follow me."

In the shed, Paul found a hand fork, about the length of his foot, but realised immediately that Tom had bigger game in mind, or even roobeewhatsits, whatever they were. He then found a substantial garden fork and spade, and hurried to catch up with Tom, already striding off towards a group of shrubs. Tom had made a start, having arrived even earlier than Paul.

"I want you to hold these branches while I saw some of the height off; then we'll dig around the roots until she loosens up, then we'll use the bits of branch left, to lever her out. Got it?"

Paul got it, and leapt into position to hold the thick stems, at which point he yelped with pain. Thorns!

"You didn't bring any gloves, I suppose," said Tom

sourly. "Get back to the shed and find a pair of leather ones."

Paul trotted back to the shed, some of his earlier enthusiasm waning. Insults and injury seemed to be his reward for being cheerful, but he found the gloves and went back to help Tom, thinking: 'At least it's only for a couple of weeks.'

They worked for a couple of hours, by which time Paul had developed considerable respect for Tom's strength and skills. Paul felt hot and sticky, but decided not to remove his sweatshirt out of an equally strong respect for the thorns. He really wanted a rest and a coffee, and wondered how long he would have to wait for either. Eventually Tom muttered something about not needing him for the next half hour, which Paul took to mean he was free to have a break.

Paul stretched as he walked, and pulled off the sweatshirt, letting his t-shirt dry in the warm sun. He noticed that many of the patients were sitting outside on the terrace by the café, and he anticipated a very pleasant break. Five minutes later, he had a sandwich and a coffee from the café, and was dropping into one of the chairs outside, hoisting his feet on to another chair. He consumed half his coffee at one gulp, and lay back in the chair, arms behind his head, and closed his eyes, feeling the sun warm on his eyelids. His mind slid back to Tom.

'Will I be like that when I'm an old man? I reckon I'm pretty easy-going, but then maybe Tom was a different man when he was younger. Is that what life does to you? I intend to have a good life, as hassle-free as I can make it.

Which reminds me – I'd better get a bottle of water from the café – Steve the Needle warned me the migraines would be worse if I got dehydrated.'

While munching his sandwich and drinking the water, Paul looked round at the people sitting at the tables. Quite a mixture, and you couldn't tell what was wrong with any of them. They could be at any coffee shop. There were mums with kids, a dad or two, old people, couples, singles...he wondered briefly what they were all here for. Would the acupuncture cure his migraines? There was no way to know just yet, but he had tried everything else, so had nothing to lose. Except perhaps an arm, he thought wryly, remembering Tom's energetic use of the pruning saw. He reluctantly picked up his sweatshirt and strolled back towards the garden action.

He heard them before he saw them: a whooping noise and loud laughter. Then as he rounded a clump of bushes, there they were – three teenage boys throwing – what? Rocks? Surely not. No, bulbs: he recognised them now. They had found some boxes of bulbs and were throwing them with great force at Tom, who was holding up his hands in front of his face and trying to get out of the tangle of rubrifolia stems that he had stepped into while trying to evade the onslaught.

Paul whipped out his phone and took a few photos of the boys, edging nearer to make sure he got their faces. Luckily they were enjoying tormenting the old man too much to notice Paul. Phone safely back in his pocket, Paul then shouted and ran towards them, hoping they didn't turn on him instead. But the boys ran off, and within seconds had mounted their bikes and disappeared.

Paul turned to Tom. "You all right, Tom?" Tom made no answer, but he was shaking as he disentangled himself from the last of the thorny stems. "Why don't you go and take a break?" Paul said casually, "while I clear up for a bit?" He knew Tom would feel humiliated by what had happened, so deliberately didn't look at him, but started picking up bulbs and putting them into the wheelbarrow, as the boxes had been trodden on and were useless.

Tom did actually go and get some tea, and Paul was pleased to see his face had a bit more natural colour when he came back. Paul knew better than to talk about the incident to this proud old man, but at the end of the day he went to find Lizzie.

Lizzie was shocked at the photos, and immediately took Paul in to see Stephanie Harman. The Director's face was impassive, but she took a lead from a drawer and immediately downloaded the photos to her computer. 'Thanks for asking,' thought Paul, and wondered if she operated in this high-handed way with everyone. She gave him back his phone, and spoke for the first time.

"How very fortunate we are that you were so quick-witted, Paul. Thank you. If the police want to use them as evidence, and if it becomes necessary, would you be prepared to provide a witness statement?"

Paul's brain raced to keep up. He hadn't thought that far ahead, but she obviously had. He remembered Tom's hands up in front of his face, trying to shield it from the bulbs raining down on him, and didn't hesitate.

"Yes, of course, I will. They should be put away, but I

bet they get off with just a caution. I hope it keeps them away from Tom for a while, though. He doesn't deserve this."

"Quite." Stephanie's voice was tight, and Paul wondered what it must be like, working for such an ice queen. Luckily, he didn't have to. Stephanie didn't look at him again, and he wondered if he was dismissed. Feeling awkward, he pocketed the phone and turned to go.

"Thank you again, Paul," came the Director's crisp voice, and he went home, feeling very sorry for Tom, but glad to be away from Yatross for a few hours. It was several days before he realised that the photos had been wiped clean from his mobile phone.

∽

Stephanie was still looking out of the window, and Lizzie thought that no more was going to be done about the incident today, and turned to go.

"You know I can't send those photos to the police, don't you, Lizzie?"

"You mean because of the bad publicity for Yatross?" Lizzie's tone was hard, and she came back to stand in front of Stephanie, so that she turned to meet her look. Stephanie impatiently pushed Lizzie into the chair and brought up the pictures on her computer.

"Look Lizzie, really look. What do you see?" Lizzie thought that identification of the boys was possible. 'You can see the face of one quite well in this picture,' she thought, 'and the other two, not quite so well, in that one. Surely the police could do something with this? Oh, poor old Tom. Such senseless violence. And he looked so cowed, so broken, so old. Oh dear.'

"It's Tom, isn't it?" she said in a low voice. "That's why we can't use them."

Stephanie was pacing up and down behind Lizzie, and stopped as Lizzie spoke. "Tom would rather be assaulted by a dozen youths than have his humiliation publicly displayed; which it will, if these photos go to the police. The police will involve the press: 'Have you seen these boys?' and Tom's picture will be in the papers. People looking at him, calling him a poor old man: he couldn't stand that."

"But what are we going to do? We've got to do something, before something worse happens." Lizzie sat for a moment, thinking hard. "We had a patient a few months ago who was a private detective. He was very grateful when he left – could we make use of him in some way?"

"Perhaps, Lizzie. Let me sleep on it and we'll talk again tomorrow. Can you ask Paul to try and stay close to Tom while he's here? Then we'll have a few days to try and sort something out. Lizzie, I can see you're upset. What are you thinking?"

"I can't help thinking that those monsters threw bulbs because they were the only things they could lay their hands on quickly. They probably wouldn't have cared if it had been stones, had they been closer. Mindless, vicious thugs. And next time they could throw something that really injures him. I just feel so helpless, Stephanie."

'Such a kind heart,' thought Stephanie. "Well, at least

we know now," she said dryly. "Has it occurred to you that this may not be the first time? We're well into the summer holidays – I wouldn't be surprised if they've caused trouble before."

Lizzie really didn't want to think about that. The idea of Tom being terrorised by those horrible boys, all through the summer, and him not saying a word to anyone…

"Why? Why did he not say anything?" said Lizzie. Stephanie had guessed why, but said:

"Let's not speculate on that now, Lizzie. We'll come back to it tomorrow, when we've had time to think." Lizzie knew it really was time to go now, and said "Goodnight," as she left the office, leaving Stephanie staring out of the window.

Certainly Stephanie might not have been so willing to wait a few days, had she been a fly on the wall in Tom's loft that evening. He had to move half a dozen boxes before he could find what he wanted: his old service revolver. He had no intention of using it – he didn't even have any ammunition for it – but perhaps the boys might think twice if they realised he wasn't as helpless as they thought. He would only threaten them with it as a last resort, of course, but meanwhile it could sit on the top shelf of the shed, ready for emergencies…

Chapter Ten

Sir Galahad and His Lady of the Overalls

Jane whistled loudly as she entered the book centre at 8.00 a.m., as whistling, she felt, befitted the person who wore overalls and working boots. Her thick chestnut hair was pinned up under a cap, and for added authenticity she had splattered paint about the cap's peak.

'It's odd,' she thought as she walked towards the counter, 'but I couldn't bring myself to put paint under my nails and on my face and hair. I think once I would have done. I wonder what that means, that slip in the level of commitment? Am I getting bored with this, finally?' Before she could answer this question to herself, a pleasant, well-modulated voice called out:

"Good morning! Is that Jane?" A tall man in a suit rose from a chair on the far side of the book centre. She recognised him instantly. It was Sir Galahad, her knight in shining armour, who was the only person in that group of visiting doctors who'd had any common sense. Or, more precisely, the sense to know how to use his jacket to dispose of a pigeon in the book centre. She'd liked his easy smile, his quiet confidence, and the way he'd looked at her as if she was his peer. It was just the same now, and he came towards her and held out his hand.

"I don't know if you remember me, but I visited Yatross in early July, with a group of other doctors. My name is David Yately."

'Nicely done,' thought Jane as she shook his hand firmly. 'No-one listening to him would guess that the last time we met, I was in a bird costume and had to be rescued from the inside of a stepladder.'

"Of course I remember you. Stephanie told me one of the doctors was coming to see me, but I didn't know which one. Can I get you a coffee or something?"

"No, I'm fine, thanks. Are you free to talk now? Mrs Harman said something about arranging cover for you." There was a mild impatience about his demeanour, which Jane did not take exception to but instead interpreted correctly as passion for his subject.

"I have Beatrice, one of our administration staff, coming in from nine to twelve, but she doesn't work in the book centre very often, so I may need to pop back occasionally. But we can have a general chat now – it's unusual to get patients in here before 8.30 a.m.. So come and sit down and tell me about your project." They took places at a nearby table, and Jane liked the way that he waited for her to be seated before sitting himself, despite her workman attire.

"I've been tasked with creating a teaching module for doctors, on mental health," he began, speaking so quickly that Jane found herself consciously changing up a gear in her brain, in order to keep pace. "It has not been well-covered in general doctors' training up to now, and the idea of this module is to provide an overview of the complete spectrum, from someone who is suffering a little, to someone who is suffering a lot, and everything in between."

As he paused, Jane thought how very delicately he expressed himself: avoiding the word 'normal', which most people would hardly be able to stop themselves using. 'As if anyone was truly normal anyway.' Unaware of the tangent Jane's mind had taken, David continued:

"I can fill the module with technical detail, statistics and mental health theory, but that's not all I want for our medical students. I want them to see real people behind the data. Mrs Harman has been very helpful in providing an outline of what Yatross does, but she is limited by confidential considerations."

"I can see why she thought I might be able to help instead."

David's face brightened in response to her understanding. "Yes, exactly. You speak to the patients, you know what books they borrow, and why. What they read is something that would provide added value: it would make the technical information come alive for the students. I can pull together composites in the module, so that patients can't identify themselves, and add in the relevant medical aspects of the issues raised. So, can you help me?"

Jane nodded. She would like to help this very nice man, one of the nicest she had ever met. "We never make the mistake of separating our patients with mental health issues from patients with a physical illness. We have to deal with the psychological roots and impact from both. Everyone at Yatross believes that the health of mind and body are completely interconnected, so that when we treat one, we are always mindful of the other."

David was nodding in emphasis. "Every doctor knows that in theory, but many have trouble bringing that principle into their practice. If we can bring it to life for the new doctors, then we can change things for the better." Jane heard the personal pronoun with a tingle of pleasure at the implied partnership. She was already thought of as a collaborator, and she anticipated the next couple of hours' work with real pleasure. She resolved to get a drink from Agora, to ensure her brain was fully hydrated and in good working order, before they started.

It was typical of Jane that she gave no thought at this stage to her workman's clothes, or to what David might think of her as a woman. It was her best brain that must be made available for this man, not her best outfit, or most elaborate make-up.

"I feel like I want to start now," she admitted, her voice revealing her eagerness, "but we can't, not in here. I've got one of the interview rooms booked, though. Until Beatrice comes, let me show you the book centre." They then spent an enjoyable quarter of an hour following the shelves, through self-help classics to novels and on to medical books, pamphlets and journals. David's eye alighted on the book of Greek myths that the boy Ben had borrowed and discarded.

"Hello, what's this?" and he took it down and began to leaf through with interest.

"Do you know much about Greek mythology?"

"I was very interested as a child, but I haven't read much on the subject for years."

"Would you like to borrow it?" Jane watched him wrestle with the temptation.

"I probably shouldn't get distracted at this time – "

"Would it help if I told you that the whole clinic lives and breathes Greek mythology? Not to mention eating it for breakfast? Many of the staff, and even some of the Helpers, hardly talk about anything else. Think of it as background to your project." David grinned and looked very young for a moment, and she liked him even more. "Go on, take it; you don't have to book it out. Just bring it back in a few weeks."

Beatrice came in at that point and took in the scene: the doctor standing close to Jane, and the pair smiling at each other, oblivious of Beatrice.

'At last!' thought Beatrice with glee. 'We've got someone for Jane! And he's normal! Well, he seems normal, anyway.'

Beatrice had been on reception duty that morning and had immediately taken to the well-spoken doctor with a precise, slightly dry manner, which nevertheless managed to convey warmth and interest. 'I can't wait to tell Anna,' was her next thought, but then Jane noticed her, and started briefing her on book centre procedures. Beatrice, never subtle, raised her eyebrows and tilted her head in the direction of David Yately, now seated again and absorbed in his book. Jane ignored her, and continued to list the ten things that Beatrice simply mustn't do, to which Beatrice only half-listened.

'What a shame she's in workman mode,' thought Beatrice as she studied Jane's clothes. 'She can look really nice when she takes the trouble – '

"Beatrice, are you sure you've got all that? I'll be in the first interview room down this corridor if you need me." Jane felt some misgivings as she led David out of the book centre, and worried that she was leaving her precious domain in the care of someone who was too flighty to look after it properly. She turned round and caught Beatrice's eye, but Beatrice promptly demonstrated an explicit bottom and bust wiggling pose, and Jane hastened David out through the doors into the safety of reception.

"I thought we'd get a drink from Agora first," and Jane led the way down the corridor.

"Agora, yes: that's your staffroom, isn't it? 'Meeting place' in Greek, and how much more interesting! Stephanie's idea, I presume?"

"Most things are," said Jane dryly. "Here we are: help yourself from over there."

"What will you have?"

"Oh, a blackcurrant tea, I think." They made their drinks and Jane generously introduced her new friend to the few staff present. Michael, the CBT therapist, was alert to the possibilities in the project David briefly outlined, and munched on a biscuit thoughtfully while listening. When he responded, the crumbs that didn't get caught in his beard were sprayed widely around. Luckily, they missed most of David's smart suit.

"I'd like to contribute, if that would be helpful. I've a range of patients that I can combine characteristics of, so that they will be completely anonymous, as case studies for you."

"I would appreciate that very much. Would you provide them to Jane when you're ready, as she is my main contact here?" Again, Jane marvelled at his sensitivity. He knew that she would have felt offended or at least excluded if they had swapped business cards and dealt with the case studies between them.

"What is your specialism?" Michael asked with interest.

"Dermatology. I developed an interest in holistic medicine when I became aware that many of my patients' problems resulted from imbalances in their gut or their mind. The problem lay in trying to convince them of this. But I've been designing teaching modules on behalf of the profession for some years now."

Michael put his cup down and shook David's hand. "Good to meet you. I have a patient due, so excuse me, Doctor Yately."

As Michael left, David turned to Jane. "Did you guess that might happen? That we'd meet a therapist who could be useful to me, despite what Mrs Harman said?" His eyes twinkled at her in appreciation, but Jane was always truthful.

"No, I hadn't planned that, I must admit. I just wanted tea!" They both laughed, and left Agora for the interview room, to begin the serious business of the day.

"First of all," began David, when they had settled on either side of the table, "I want to reassure you that your role in this will be recognised, and your name and contribution acknowledged on the teaching module documentation."

"Oh, no; that is, I'd rather not, if you don't mind. I don't really want my name on anything."

"Are you sure? Well, you can always change your mind later. Secondly, I'd be grateful if you would allow me to record our chat. I'll make notes as we go along, but I can't hope to collect it all, and I don't want to lose anything." He smiled at her and she was happy to nod her agreement to that. It made sense, and she was glad that he considered that what she had to say would be so worthwhile.

"So perhaps I could start the ball rolling by saying that what has always fascinated me about mental health is the tightrope we all walk between functioning and not functioning in the world. Everyone is on that spectrum between well and not well, and can move with frightening ease between the two."

Jane heard this with a throb of recognition. She couldn't decide if he was saying this because he recognised that she was quite near the dodgy end of the tightrope, or whether it was just a professional observation.

"Leading on from that," David continued, "is the effect on others. I remember having a conversation with a man on a railway station platform, a couple of years ago. He was shabbily dressed, thin, dirty and unshaven, and he told me his story when I bought him a coffee in the station café.

"He'd been an interior designer, married to a lady in the same profession, and they made the decision to sell their house and drive with as many of their possessions as they could to France. The plan was to live and work there, and they had a number of promising contacts. Unfortunately she collapsed with a cerebral haemorrhage and died instantly, when they were only 150 miles into their journey. He was completely distraught. While trying to deal with both his grief and the authorities, he forgot to lock his car. It was stolen, with all his papers and a lot of his money. The Insurance officials were difficult, and he couldn't concentrate on what they were telling him to do. The outcome was that he spent his last cash on getting his wife's body home to England and then cremated.

"He had nothing left: no wife, no home, no career, and in his distressed state, couldn't deal with any of it. So a man that a few months ago led a life just like yours or mine, was suddenly on the streets. It occurred to me that it could have been a tall story, designed to worm cash out of me, but he disappeared from the café without asking for anything, and I think it was probably all true, sadly."

Jane swallowed hard. She felt a distant sympathy for the man, whoever he was, but her focus was on two particular aspects of the story. One was the reference to 'a life just like yours or mine,' which she heard with profound gratitude, having been labelled as mentally unstable by most of the medical profession she had encountered so far in her life. The other aspect was an awareness of how she could have ended up like the stranger, had she not found Yatross and been treated by the skilful practitioners here. She didn't want to think about that any more and sought to change the subject.

"His grief drove him mad, in a way," she said quietly. "We don't have many patients in that position, as people like that are not usually motivated to recover. When I consider what problems our patients do have, some of the biggest have to be related to communication. I wanted to start with that topic, as our books can help, if patients are willing to read them and learn the lessons they teach."

"Do partners come here for couples therapy?" asked David, realising that this was one topic that Stephanie Harman had not mentioned on his first visit.

"Yes, and therapists recommend a number of different books for them. 'Couples: how we make love last,' is a popular one, and has hundreds of mini case studies that individuals can relate to. Partners will often need different books, and I remember that one of our therapists recommended 'Women who think too much' for one of his patients, because he recognised that her negative thinking was becoming destructive to her relationship with her partner, and he wanted her to develop strategies to stop the overthinking early on in their conflicts, instead of letting it get out of control."

Jane stopped speaking for a moment as David made notes on his tablet. She realised she was becoming warm in the enclosed room, and removed her cap. David's eyes flickered to her pinned up hair for a moment and then focussed again on the screen.

"One of the issues," continued Jane, only slightly self-consciously, "that can be a surprise to our women patients, is the discovery that men can be just as indirect as women, when asking for what they want."

David's eyebrows lifted in surprise. "That doesn't sound like any man I know. Do go on: this is riveting." He did look riveted, sitting upright at the table, leaning forward towards her, eyes on her mouth, completely focussed on what she was saying.

"A patient who was a frequent visitor to the book centre told me that she and her husband were always fighting, and she became very stressed because she never knew what he wanted from her, and he didn't understand why she didn't know. One of the books the therapist gave them both to read provided the answer. The husband had been in the Army, and his superiors taught him that if they said: "I've left my clipboard behind in the office," they expected one of the men to run and fetch it pronto, not stand there thinking: 'Oh, what a pity.' He was using the same strategy at home, but she just wasn't tuned into it. I think they still fight, actually, but at least she understands why! And this makes all the difference to her mental health – it was the not understanding that was making her ill."

David threw his head back and laughed heartily: a very good sound. "What about sex? I assume," he continued, as if Jane hadn't changed colour completely at his first words, "that you have sex counsellors?"

The pink gradually subsiding from her cheeks, Jane replied: "Because sex problems are rarely just about sex, they are dealt with by all the counsellors, although Sarah has the most experience and would deal with the most difficult problems."

"And children? I'm very concerned that mental health problems in children are not being picked up by doctors, but are put down to behavioural problems, or faulty parenting."

"Yes. We have Denece, a specialist children's counsellor, who is highly regarded in the field. I'll ask her if she can provide some helpful pointers for doctors, shall I?"

"That would be good. Now, give me an example of a book that brought about a change that the clinic wasn't expecting. The students will have preconceptions of their own, and I want to surprise them out of their comfort zone."

Jane thought for a minute. "One of our patients was a doctor himself, and repudiated everything that therapists tried to help him understand about his own state of mental health. Conflict seemed to be a normal state for him, and he contradicted everyone. He did not believe in the mind/body connection, and thought that if only we would supply him with the drugs his doctor had refused him, all would be well. Our therapist was concerned about the side effects of the drugs, and wanted him to try other methods. In desperation, she persuaded him to read Candace Pert's 'Molecules of Emotion,' and this provided him with the scientific basis for the whole package: how negative feelings are retained in the cells of the body and the role of our brain receptors to both internal and external chemicals. He finally got it, accepted the therapist's advice, and began to get better."

"I like that story."

Jane smiled back at him, feeling completely in accord. "So do I."

"Let's do one more, and then I want to review what we have, and where to go next. What do you have for me?"

Jane loved this sort of challenge, and scanned the computer of her brain for a good story. "I remember a patient who wanted to become a counsellor himself. He thought that all his terrible self-destructive thoughts would go away if he could get involved in other people's problems. No amount of explaining that he needed to get himself sorted out first, made any difference. Eventually the Yatross counsellor pretended to go along with it, and said that first, he needed to read 'On becoming a counsellor,' by Kennedy and Charles. I saw his bookmark place when it came back into stock, so I'm fairly sure he only got about a quarter of the way through the book, but I know for certain he completely gave up the idea of becoming a counsellor. He realised how technical a profession it was, and realised too that he didn't have a hope of undertaking the training, as ill as he was."

"Did he start to address his own problems?"

"No, I'm sorry to say. He gave up all treatment and we never saw him again. This is something the staff here have to get used to – it does happen from time to time."

David made some more notes and switched off the voice recorder. "Jane, there is some brilliant material here already. And we've got the potential of more from Michael and Denece. You know, this is going to be one hell of a teaching module." A pause. "Why don't you want your name on it?"

Nothing indirect about that question: he'd obviously never been in the Army, thought Jane. She voiced the observation, much to his amusement, but he still sat there, waiting for an answer. Jane played with her empty cup for a moment, thinking hard.

"I expect you think I love drawing attention to myself, with the different costumes I wear," she began, and stopped. His face stayed the same, open and interested, and Jane noticed for the first time that his hazel eyes had flecks of gold in them. Mesmerised for a moment, she stared, not speaking, but then he blinked, as if releasing her.

"Actually, it's the opposite. I can submerge myself in another identity: I don't have to be me. Having my name on something like your module – well, that would definitely be me. I'm not sure I could deal with that."

"I understand all that, Jane. You don't have to worry. I'm not going to insist on you being you if you don't want to be. Though I would like to meet Jane one day, if she's available."

Jane stopped herself just in time from saying: *'But you've had me! I am more me when I'm with you than I've been with anyone! This is me, this is the real Jane!'* because that would be too much, too honest; and besides, suppose he was disappointed? Suppose he'd thought there was more? She couldn't face that.

"Let's go and get some fresh air," David suggested, rising from the chair and folding up his tablet.

"I'd better go and check on Beatrice. I'll catch you

up," Jane threw back over her shoulder as she hurried out of the door. She needed some space to get her equilibrium back. Jane had begun today by thinking of Doctor Yately as an interesting companion, but little by little he had got under her skin, and now she saw him for what he undoubtedly was: a very attractive man. Somehow she had to get her professional detachment back, otherwise she wouldn't be of any use to him. 'A first step, Jane,' she told herself firmly, would be to get that cap back on. Get back into workman mode, so that he doesn't see you as a woman. Then everything will be fine.' She crammed the cap back over her hair as she walked back to the book centre, hoping that Beatrice hadn't caused too much chaos in there this morning.

"So, is it going well?" asked Beatrice archly, as Jane took her place at the counter.

"Yes, very well, thank you, Beatrice," replied Jane evenly. "Would you like to take a break for twenty minutes?" Beatrice realised that she wasn't going to get anything else out of Jane, and sashayed her way out of the book centre, winking at Jane as she went through the door. She came back in instantly. Throwing a quick glance in the direction of old Mrs. Nicholls, sitting nearby, she hurried over to Jane, her eyes wide and scared.

"Jane! There's a man in reception and he's got a knife!" Jane stared at her for several seconds before collecting herself.

"Did he see you?"

"I don't think so. Jane, what shall we do?"

"Be quiet a minute and let me think. Ok, now you can get through to the offices via the crèche. As soon as you are somewhere where he won't hear you, phone the police. Tell Suki on your way through to keep all the children in, and not let them go anywhere. Make sure she locks the door to reception and the outer door to the play area. Alert everyone you can find, but don't let them come into reception. Wait a minute, who's in today…?" Jane recollected that Lizzie and Daniel were on holiday together in Athens, celebrating their new relationship, and that Stephanie had gone up to the residential unit for a meeting with Catherine. Stephanie needed to come and take charge of this situation.

"After the police, phone up to the unit and tell Stephanie what's going on. Now go."

Beatrice needed no prompting. The man with the knife was scary.

Jane wondered whether Beatrice would remember this set of instructions any better than the ones she'd left her with earlier today, and thought, rather belatedly, that perhaps she should have just rung the police on her mobile. Her instinct, though, had been that the man might come in at any minute, and they would all be trapped. She walked quickly over to the old lady, still placidly reading and oblivious to the women's conversation.

"Mrs. Nicholls?"

"Yes, young man?"

"I'm afraid someone's been very sick in reception

and there's quite a mess to clear up, right outside the door. Do you mind staying here for a bit, while we clean up? I'll come and get you when you can safely leave."

"That's fine. I'm quite happy sitting here, reading. This is a very interesting book. Did you know – ?"

"Got to go and clear up the mess now, Mrs. Nicholls. Now stay put, won't you?" Jane then cast her mind around for anything that might be useful in this bizarre situation. Yatross had had difficult and violent patients before, but this was the first time that a knife had been involved. What did the book centre have? Sticky tape? Pens? Hardly useful now. In the end she settled for her trusty stepladder, thinking that at the very least she could create a distraction as she entered, and it might also provide a barrier to a thrown knife.

Mrs. Nicholls watched her leave with the stepladder, and shook her head in disgust. Fancy someone being so sick that it had to be cleaned from high up on the walls!

Reception was more peaceful than Jane had imagined: there were a couple of people waiting for appointments, and only Anna, and David Yately, who must have stopped to chat to Anna on his way out, behind the reception desk. Jane's attention then focussed on the boy, probably about twenty years old, with a shock of fair hair, and holding a carving knife in front of his chest. He stood by the desk, looking smug, as if he knew he was the one in charge here.

Jane's inevitable clatter with the ladder had him swinging round, knife raised to deal with the unknown threat. He lowered it again as he realised it was just the handyman.

"Hey you! Where's that bitch of a Director of yours? Where's she 'iding?" Jane's heart sank. He obviously had some kind of grudge against Stephanie. Stephanie, who was probably at this moment making her way down to reception from the residential unit, if Beatrice had done what she'd asked.

"Not seen her this morning," she said, in as gruff a voice as she could manage. Jane felt compelled to maintain the handyman disguise, thought she could not have said why.

The boy waved the knife around a bit more and sneered: "Well, we'll 'ave to all wait for 'er then, won't we? She's not gettin' away wiv what she did to my bruvver."

"What did she do?" asked David in a level voice, "if you don't mind my asking?"

"Oooh! Ain't we posh? You think you're talking to the Queen, or summink? Well, I do mind. It ain't none of your bleedin' business. So you just siddown and shut up. You too, girlie," and he waved the knife at both David and Anna, who subsided obediently on to reception stools.

Jane looked round at how the two people waiting on the other side of the room were coping, and only just stopped herself from laughing hysterically. Two middle-aged women sat together, watching the proceedings and munching on sweets from a bag, just as if they were at the cinema. Perhaps they thought they were. Certainly the scene had an unreal quality about it. What Jane was all too aware of was that the seconds and minutes were disappearing: time moving towards the point at which Stephanie would walk unsuspectingly through that door – straight into the throwing line of the boy with the knife. She started to move her ladder towards the door, hoping to be able to alert Stephanie before she got too close, but the boy stopped her.

"Oi you! Stop right there. What d'yer think you're doin'?" Jane didn't have to manufacture a reply, as in the distance they could all hear the police sirens. The smug expression on the boy's face turned to fear. Then he looked at Jane, and he thought of a way out.

"You wiv the ladder! Gimme your overalls and cap – get 'em off quick before I slice 'em off you!" Jane unzipped quickly, stepped out of the overalls and handed them to him. A flicker of surprise crossed his face as he took in Jane's camisole and French knickers, but he put the knife down for a moment as he struggled into the disguise. Jane handed him her cap, thinking: 'Please get out of here quickly, please, please, before Stephanie comes,' and watched as the boy retrieved his knife and hauled the ladder out of the front door and down the steps, dragging it in a very unworkmanlike way on to the pedestrian path in the direction of the main gate. He obviously knew that traffic would arrive at the front door from the opposite direction; soon the relieved occupants of Yatross reception heard the noise from the police car sirens increase in volume to a piercing level, then stop.

Everything then happened at once. Various men in uniform ran into reception, and David quickly described the handyman outfit they needed to look for; two men set off in pursuit, but not before Jane called after them:

"And he's wearing a stepladder!"

Stephanie came in through the door with her usual hauteur: her expression would have unnerved anyone daring to mess about in her clinic. She raised her eyebrows at Jane's attire, clearly signalling: ' And what persona do we have today, Jane? French Tart?' Jane felt this was seriously unfair, considering that it was to try and save Stephanie from the carving knife that she had slipped out of her clothes faster than she'd ever done for any man. Anna had, meanwhile, been furiously banging on the door to the crèche, which now opened, and Suki fell out of it into Anna's arms.

"I thought you were dead! I had to stay with the children, but all I wanted to do was come out and drag you in here to safety!"

"Oh, darling, you were so brave. I'm fine, really; he didn't hurt me, but Suki – I was so scared!" They embraced, cried noisily, while a police officer waited patiently to ask them questions. Jane had started to shiver slightly, and David put his ever-useful jacket round her shoulders and studied her face anxiously.

"Does it make tea, as well?" she joked weakly, while trying to smile and pretend this was just like any normal day at Yatross.

"No, but I do. Inspector!" and he called across to the police Inspector talking with Stephanie. "This woman is going into shock. We'll be in Agora, the staffroom at the back of the building, when you need to talk to us. Come on, Jane," and he swiftly moved them both through the back of the reception and down the corridor. Jane was happy, for the moment, to have him take charge. She felt very wobbly, and tea was actually a very good idea. She might even let him make it.

In Agora, she sank into the same chair that she had sat in with her moulting bird costume all those weeks ago. For the first time, it seemed to her a daft thing to have done: to dress up in a bird costume on the day she knew a group of doctors were going to visit Yatross. 'Why on earth did I do that? And yet, it doesn't seem to have put David Yately off at all.' She looked down at her bare legs, now drawn up on to the soft cushions for warmth. 'So much for me not wanting him to see me as a woman! But how was I to know that today was the day a fugitive was going to need my overalls as a disguise? Not foreseeable, as even Stephanie will have to agree…'

"Jane: here's your tea. You are so quiet. Are you all right?" Jane nodded, and took the tea with gratitude. It was very hot, but she drank it straight down and David looked at her in alarm. "I wish I had some brandy for you; but then again, perhaps it's just as well I haven't." A strange expression twisted his face, but before Jane could analyse it, he sat down in the chair closest to her.

"Did you notice the tattoo on the boy's shoulder, when he was getting into your overalls? His t-shirt sleeve rode up and I got a good look. It was unusual, but I can describe it to the police, and it may help identify him. That is, if he hasn't tripped over your stepladder by now." David looked down at Jane's unblemished skin. "You don't have any tattoos, I'm glad to see. It would be a great pity to damage your skin. It is quite, quite stunningly clear, you know. Quite beautiful."

Jane looked at him through eyes that had filled with tears. "I used to wash it a lot. Perhaps that's why. But not any more." It was a turning point. She had said something significant about her past: something that would send any normal man running for the hills. How would he react?

"No, that's not why. This skin," and he picked up her hand gently as he spoke, "shows the kind of clear beauty that comes from inside. That is, in my professional opinion." The jacket fell back a little with the movement of her hand, and his eyes travelled up her arm as if to check that the rest of her was just as beautiful. Just then a loud throat-clearing from the Inspector provided a signal that any further exploration of Jane's skin would have to wait for now.

"I'd like a few words, if you don't mind, and an officer will take a full statement in a bit. Ah, is that tea?"

∽

Much later, two of the police officers stood outside the clinic, looked at each other, then by common consent moved towards the car park, away out of earshot.

"What do you reckon, then? That couple – that doctor whatsit and her in the knickers – what do you think? Reckon they were having it off somewhere while all this was going on, and got interrupted, yeah?"

The Inspector shook his head. "That was my first thought, but all the witness statements indicate that what they've told us is the truth. The doctor got caught up in it all by accident, while he was chatting to the receptionist. Mark found the stepladder, I understand?"

"Yeah. It looks like he threw it into the bushes as he legged it over the gate. So it was a grudge crime, from what you was sayin'?"

"It looks like it. We cautioned this bloke's brother earlier this week. The Harman woman made a complaint that the brother, Ben, had been throwing missiles at the gardener. Kids' stuff, but Harman was concerned, as the man is quite elderly, and the photos show a sustained assault. So we cautioned him, as I said, and it looks like this is his elder brother."

"Funny old place, ain't it? Weird lot. Is it kosher, do you reckon?"

"We've not caught them doing anything illegal, yet, though there have been several allegations, over the years. Most of the complaints relate to alleged supernatural happenings, believe it or not. There was this woman, once: she rung us up and said she had come here as a patient. Her chronic eczema had cleared up, but she couldn't work out how they'd done it, so they must all be witches and I should come out and arrest them all." The Inspector shook his head in mock amazement. "Nothing the public do will ever surprise me, Gary. See you back at the station," and they got into their cars and drove away.

Chapter Eleven

Michelle finds her Voice

Erin shifted restlessly in her chair in reception at Yatross: she was bored and uncomfortable. Michelle had told her to go, that she would make her own way home, but Erin thought: 'No, I want to be here when she comes out from her appointment. I want to hear what happened, and help Michelle make sense of it. God only knows what state she'll be in. There might be a lot of supporting to do.'

Erin had glanced at a few books in the book centre, briefly toured the grounds, sent some texts and made some work-related phone calls. It was nearly time for Michelle's appointment to end. 'Perhaps I could get some tea in the café now; I can always get Michelle a drink later.' Relieved to be moving, she rose from the chair and walked briskly to the café.

"Do you have fennel tea?" she enquired of the assistant behind the counter, and started to plan her second choice, expecting to be disappointed.

"Yes, of course: mug or cup, madam?" Kate usually called her customers 'love' or 'dear' or even 'sweetheart', but she sensed that none of these would do for this dark, well-dressed, rather haughty lady, with something very tight about her mouth. Kate grinned to herself as she thought about what her husband Mike would have said instead, but straightened her face as she handed her the cup and saucer she'd asked for. Money was dropped on to the counter in exchange, and Erin settled down at a corner table with a good view of the door, as she waited for her sister to appear. It was quiet and peaceful in the café, and Erin looked round with appreciation.

'This is, at least, a significant improvement over some of the places I've had to wait for Michelle,' thought Erin. 'How long ago was it when I sat in that dreadful hospital waiting room, when her doctor thought she had bowel disease, and then it turned out to be IBS? Then there was that grimy village hall, where Michelle had insisted on supporting some lame duck cause or other. I wouldn't have stayed, but I remember we were going on to visit Aunt Madge, and that duty is so much easier when Michelle is with me. So odd that Aunt Madge's senility doesn't bother Michelle, when she is so full of fear about so many things… there she was, chatting to her, soothing her, and neither of them making any sense at all: it always makes me feel so uneasy, that Michelle seems to be able to relate to her so well. I hope it doesn't mean Michelle is going to have mental health problems…'

Erin realised her fennel tea was cooling rapidly, and took a sip. She brought her mind back to why Michelle was here at this wretched clinic, taking up valuable time. She checked her phone again for messages. As it happened, there was nothing there that couldn't wait. Erin pictured Michelle's face when they discussed this appointment; Michelle had become unusually stubborn about it.

"I've been for an assessment, and this kinesiology is what they recommend. So I'm going to go along for at least the first session, and then decide what to do next."

Erin knew Michelle had problems deciding what to wear in the morning, so felt that the chance of her making a rational decision in these circumstances was zero. No, it was up to her, Erin, to help her see this claptrap for what it was. She ran her mind through some of the recent anti-depressants and anti-anxiety medication that had come across her path as a sales representative for a pharmaceutical company. She was just weighing up the pros and cons of two different medications that had recently come on the market, when Michelle appeared at the door, looking for her. Erin watched her hurry over to the table, and noticed that Michelle was clearly agitated. But before Erin could say anything, Michelle demanded:

"Have you got a pen and paper? I've got to write something down before I forget!" Erin, slightly put out at Michelle's tone, so unlike her normal diffident one, found a notepad and pen and handed it to her.

"Can I get you a drink?" asked Erin, finding her purse. There was no answer. Michelle had sat and was scribbling away, obviously unaware of her surroundings. Or of her sister, standing there, waiting. Erin made a noise of impatience, and abruptly sat down again. Michelle heaved a sigh, flicked her honey-coloured hair back and put the notepad down on the table. Erin read the upside down notes with ease:

Not valuing myself / valuing myself
Denying my potential
Belief ??

Erin sniffed, folded her arms, sat back in her chair and waited for Michelle to realise that she was annoyed. Unfortunately for Erin, this never happened. Michelle stared into space for a bit, looked back at the pad, and frowned. Erin could bear it no longer.

"Well? What happened? I was hoping to get away soon," and this with a glance at her wristwatch, which was a ploy that usually worked with both Michelle and work colleagues. Michelle looked at her properly for the first time since she had entered the café. At least, the woman sitting opposite looked like her sister Michelle, but the expression on her face was one Erin had never seen before. She tried to analyse it: elation, surprise, wonder – oh, my God.

"Michelle: what did they give you? Tablets, drops, what was it? Michelle, tell me what you've taken!"

Michelle responded with peals of laughter. "Erin! I've taken nothing – stop worrying." She made a conscious effort to come back to the world so that she could reassure her sister.

"She gave me things to think about, that's all. Well, she had to balance me up first, and then of course she had to balance herself to me and then there were magnets at one point but I don't remember what they were for, but mostly it was me thinking – Erin, I've never been able to think like that before. At least, maybe I have, but the results have never been so...so...I don't know what to call it. Effective, that's the word. Things I hadn't realised were going on inside me, all this time; and what is even more amazing is that this is just the beginning! I know there's lots more in there somewhere. And Zoe is going to help me work it out. She's amazing."

Erin listened to this rambling account with scepticism. Also with some irritation that Michelle was having trouble finding another adjective other than 'amazing.' She decided that the most important thing to do first was to establish the facts.

"Zoe was the therapist, I take it."

"Yes, and she does homeopathy and reiki as well as kinesiology. She says they all link up with each other."

'I bet she does. More chicanery to sucker in victims like Michelle,' thought Erin sourly. But while her instinctive response was to pour scorn on the clinic and everything they did, her sharp brain warned her that this would not work this time. Michelle truly believed Zoe had done something special. 'What has she done?' Erin wondered briefly, and then focussed on bringing Michelle back to real life.

"Do you want to tell me about this?" Erin asked, gesturing at the notepad on the table between them. She was careful to keep her tone neutral, and Michelle responded gratefully to her apparent equanimity.

"She asked me to lay still for a few minutes while I thought about those two concepts: 'not valuing myself' and then separately, 'valuing myself.' She told me that my body was holding some stress in it around that idea, and I was to scan my mind for what that stress might relate to. So I thought for a while, about not valuing myself. What did it mean? I asked her: is it that I don't value myself or that other people don't? Zoe said to try not to pin it down too much, as it could be either of those, or it could be that I have some fear around not being valued; she said to keep an open mind to the possibilities."

'Get-out clause one,' thought Erin cynically, but said nothing.

"I thought really hard," continued Michelle earnestly, pushing her hair away from her face again, "about what that could be, Erin. What did my body know that I didn't? I started to think about work: do they value me? How would I know? I think they do, but – "

"I value you, Michelle," put in Erin, suddenly feeling the need to say this.

Michelle smiled warmly at her. "I know you do. I don't think this is about you. But not having got very far with the first half, I then had to think about 'valuing myself.' I struggled to imagine what this might look like. I think I'm ok; at least, I think I think I'm ok – "

"It sounds like they've got you into a fearful muddle, I'm afraid," said Erin sadly.

Michelle, much to Erin's surprise, blithely brushed this away. "Oh, no, it was only because I'm not used to thinking like this. It takes a bit of practice, Zoe said."

'Get-out clause two,' thought Erin, even more irritated than before. She wasn't used to her suggestions being ignored. Michelle, not usually so insensitive to her sister's displeasure, continued with enthusiasm.

"The next one was easier: the one about denying my potential. When Zoe said that this was what my body wanted my mind to explore, I laughed and said: "What potential?" But she just said: "Everyone's got potential – you just need to find out what it is. It may be about how you make your living, about relationships, or just about what you contribute to the world as a person. Many people fail to realise their potential, Michelle, for a variety of reasons, but what came up for you was '*denying* my potential'. Think about what that might mean for you."

Michelle was silent for a moment, obviously thinking back to the session, and Erin sat and absorbed the details of the account. Suddenly, her mind threw up a scene from her own past. This was an unusual occurrence, as Erin tended to live in the present or the future. Her English teacher, who advised on careers at school, was talking to her about possibilities for a career. "You have a good mind, Erin: you are quick and incisive. I think your brain would enjoy having some hard work to do! I can imagine you doing a degree in business and economics: you have the potential to do well in the city. Does working in London, in a business environment, appeal?" It did appeal, and Erin had had a vision of herself as a trader on the Stock Exchange, making fast decisions that involved millions of pounds, but somehow, life had not worked out quite like that.

Michelle was speaking again: oddly in both a similar and opposite vein.

"I remembered my careers teacher talking to me about what I might do after school, but all the things she was suggesting I just couldn't imagine myself doing. I didn't really feel I had the potential to do anything worthwhile – so was that me 'denying my potential'? I know Mum and Dad wouldn't have stood in my way, whatever I chose to do, but at the same time they didn't seem at all surprised when I went to work at the newsagent's shop. He had a vacancy when I left school, and I thought it would do 'for now'. Still, I can hardly complain that Mum and Dad 'denied my potential'."

"I suppose you're going to tell me," said Erin, voice dripping with sarcasm, "that I've denied your potential by finding you that job as a doctor's receptionist, that you've been doing happily for ten years or more?"

Michelle looked at her sister soberly. "I do enjoy my job, yes, but could I have done more? I sometimes feel I'm drifting along, as if life isn't really touching me. Other people seem to have much more interesting lives, somehow."

"Interesting! You want interesting? You mean as in husbands who gamble their wages away, three kids under seven, a broken washing machine and damp walls in the bedroom? Or interesting as in having cancer, or Motor Neurone Disease, or a broken leg? Your life is safe, Michelle. You should be grateful it's not 'interesting.'"

Erin was emphatic, and Michelle looked at her with interest. Where had all that intensity about such problems come from?

"Aren't there other forms of interesting, though?" she queried.

"Like what? What do you want, Michelle?"

"I don't know yet, but Zoe has given me something

to think about. I'm going to try and work out what potential I might have for doing – oh, I don't know; maybe it's not even about work. It might be that there's something different I could do in my spare time."

"In other words, Zoe has made you dissatisfied with your life, whereas before you were perfectly happy with it."

'Was I?' thought Michelle instantly. 'Was I happy? Or was I just drifting, waiting for…what?'

"I presume this is it, that now she has upset your equilibrium completely, this is the finish, and you don't need to come back?" Erin was at her most imperious, and it took a real effort for Michelle to venture a reply.

"Well, actually, yes; I mean no, it's not finished, and yes, I am coming back. I've got another session booked for Tuesday week."

"For goodness sake!" exploded Erin. "Hasn't she done enough damage? You can't really be thinking of coming back again? Apart from anything else, how are you going to pay for it?" Erin knew Michelle didn't have much spare cash, and had expected this to limit her involvement at the clinic. Michelle had a surprise for her.

"When I went for the assessment, they said I could provide a service rather than pay fees. I had a chat with the bursar – she's really nice – and because of my background, I'm going to help set up the stores and systems for a new practitioner they have starting in September. Actually, it will be something different to do: I'm quite looking forward to it."

Erin looked at her in amazement. Who was this

woman, Zoe, that she could turn Michelle into someone else entirely?

"You can't be serious! When are you going to have the time to do that?"

"I explained I only had weekends free, and Lizzie, that's the bursar, said that was fine, and would I like to come in next Saturday and meet Malcolm Treader, the new herbalist who's starting in September. Then he can discuss with me what he wants in place before he starts. So I'll be coming in for more Saturdays after that."

Erin saw that Michelle was going to have a new life, or at least part of a life, that she, Erin, had no place in. It was a strange feeling. These people at Yatross were going to influence Michelle – were in fact already influencing her – in ways which she hadn't expected. In the space of a few hours, both Erin's and Michelle's worlds had been shaken up. They did not realise it, but the lid was about to blow on this particular cocktail.

Michelle, meanwhile, had been thinking. 'It's not fair: why is she not happy for me? She might not understand it all, but then neither do I. She could at least be a bit happy that I'm happy.'

"Erin, this is not going to affect you and me. You know that, don't you?"

"Well, I don't see how it can fail to, actually. You sit there, Michelle, and spout all this nonsense Zoe has filled your head with. I'm sorry, I don't know what's happened to you, but you just don't seem like my sister any more."

It was intended to hurt, and it did. Michelle, stung into fighting back for the first time in their lives, retorted:

"Then that's hardly surprising, as I'm not!" and then covered her mouth with her hand as she realised what she'd said. It was too late; the words were out there, hanging in the air between them. Erin was shocked into silence for only a moment.

"What? What are you talking about?"

Michelle's immediate impulse was to run away: out of the door of Yatross and into the grounds. She wanted to find a hedge or something big to hide behind. She even looked around, as if she could find a suitable barrier here in the café. As the futility of that struck her, she covered her face with her hands.

Erin's voice was sharp: "Michelle!"

Michelle drew a deep shaky breath. "I promised Mum that I wouldn't tell you. Oh God, I'm sorry, Mum. I'm sorry, Erin, but this wasn't supposed to happen." She had no alternative. This was hardly the right place or time, but she would have to tell Erin the truth.

"You're adopted, Erin. Mum and Dad adopted you when they didn't think they could have any children, but then I came along. You were first," she added in a conciliatory tone, but Erin didn't notice. She was still trying to absorb the fact of Michelle's first words, trying to take in the shocking, unbelievable truth. Michelle watched the changing expressions across Erin's face, and felt her own gut twist in anguish. She had hurt her sister, something she always thought she would never do. And she had broken her promise to Mum. She wished desperately she could turn the clock back a few minutes, but waited in silence for the inevitable questions. The first one was not what she expected.

"Who else knows?" Erin's face had hardened again as she rebuilt her protective shell.

"No-one else, as far as I know. Mum told me just before she died because she thought someone ought to know, in case of medical complications."

"So why did she never tell me? She should have told me – they both should have told me!"

"I know, I know. I said the same thing to her, but it was too late then." Michelle thought to herself: 'She wasn't strong enough at the end to face your anger,' but Erin was raging again:

"Mum and Dad could have told me when I was a teenager, at least. I had a right to know, Michelle!" Michelle knew that she was bearing the force of Erin's anger and shock, and she tried to stay calm, to think about the best thing to say.

"Of course you did, and I never properly understood why they didn't tell you. Mum said something about us being close and not wanting to spoil our relationship, but really I think they just wanted to pretend you were their own flesh and blood, and if they pretended long enough, then it would be true. You know what they were like."

Erin thought about this. Yes, she knew. Dreamers, soft as duck down: that was their parents. Just like Michelle. No wonder she, Erin, was so different. She'd thought she must take after her Dad's brother John, who had been a corporate lawyer and nothing like so wishy-washy. But it turned out she didn't take after anyone. Or at least, no-one she knew. So where was her real family?

Erin felt an overwhelming need to get away. There

was no way she could take Michelle back to work as if everything was still the same. This woman was nothing to do with her.

"I've got to go." Erin was standing, looking down at Michelle, and the look was that of a stranger.

"Yes, of course. Drive carefully, won't you?" but Erin was already on her way to the door. Michelle sat back and waited for her pounding heart to slow a little. She felt a strong need for comfort, and went to the counter for a mug of hot chocolate. Sipping it, back at the table, she began to feel a little better, and more hopeful.

'Erin won't be cross forever,' she reassured herself. 'We'll be sisters again soon. She just needs time to get used to the idea of being adopted, that's all. It was a terrible shock: what she believed to be true wasn't, and it will take a little while to – ' Michelle's thoughts on Erin halted as the word that Zoe had asked her to think about filled her brain. Belief. Was that what it was about? Erin had believed Michelle to be her biological sister. Erin also believed that Michelle was submissive and had no ideas of her own. Before the session with Zoe, so had Michelle, so she could hardly blame Erin for that. Now both Erin and Michelle had a new belief. Erin also had a belief that it was her job to look after her younger sister: what belief would she have now?

Michelle sipped her hot chocolate and cupped her hands round the mug, grateful for the warmth even though it was comfortable in the café. Her sister, the only relation she had in the world apart from Aunt Madge, had just deserted her, had left her without even saying 'Goodbye'. She should be feeling scared, bereft and lonely. There was a bit of her that did feel like that, but strangely, the rest of her was a seething mass of ideas and thoughts that were nothing to do with Erin.

Belief. Belief in herself, in what she was capable of, in what the future held. Surely there had never been a more important word in the world? If she had belief, she could do anything. Tomorrow she probably wouldn't feel like this, she knew. Tomorrow she would in all probability be back to dithery, spineless Michelle, who couldn't say 'shoo' to a sheep, and who wouldn't dream of annoying her sister.

For today, though, she had a voice, and she knew a deep gladness that she had finally been able to make herself heard.

∽

Chapter Twelve

Malcolm's Harbes

It was a warm day in mid-September, and Malcolm hung his jacket up behind the door of the herbal storeroom. Pausing before going back into the consulting room, he studied Michelle's neat, clear writing on the herb containers with pleasure.

'At my last practice,' he reflected, 'you'd have thought my assistant was studying to be a doctor, her writing was that poor. I was often in danger of giving someone the wrong herb: not now though. And it's heart-warming to watch Michelle blossoming in this role, tendersome[3] though she stays.'

There came a tentative knock on the door. It was too early for his first appointment, so he guessed it would be a member of staff. It was Denece's head that peered round in search of him, and he smothered the thoughts of 'frappy zawk'[4] that rose in his head and gave her his usual smile.

"Good morning, Denece. What can I be doing for

---

3   Easy-going
4   Short-tempered, silly person

you?" She immediately scuttled out from the door opening and sat in the patient's chair. Malcolm held back a sigh and went to sit down also.

"I'm looking for a remedy for this," she began, and immediately pulled up her skirt a couple of inches to show him the wound on the side of her knee. "I've had it for months and it won't heal," she complained, and waited while Malcolm studied the gash, which was about the length of a match but twice as wide.

"What does your GP say?" he asked at last, as he sat back and looked at her.

Denece shrugged. "I've not been to see her. I'm never ill – it wouldn't have occurred to me."

"My advice would be to go and see her, and ask her what she makes of it. She has your medical history and may be able to diagnose the problem."

"Aren't you going to give me a herbal poultice or something?"

"No, Denece; you need to find out what it is and why it won't heal. I'm sure your GP will be able to help you."

That was it. It seemed her consultation was over. She looked at him, disbelievingly. Everyone said how nice Malcolm was, how kind, how helpful – and he had now dismissed her as if she was of no consequence.

"But you gave Anna a herbal remedy for her headaches!" It was a whine, and Malcolm suppressed a sharp retort with difficulty.

"How long have you worked at Yatross, Denece?" he asked, as kindly as he could.

"Three years," she said sulkily.

"And I've been here only three weeks, but I still know, as you must, that different problems call for different solutions. Try your GP, and I'm sure she'll be helpful."

Malcolm continued looking steadily at her, and Denece got up reluctantly and went to the door. Not yet willing to give it up, she asked suddenly:

"If she can't help, will you look at it then?"

Malcolm thought: 'Probably best not to make an enemy of this lablolly[5] too soon,' and said: "Iss-fay, doan make me comical now,"[6] and waved her away.

Half satisfied, ('did he mean 'Yes'?') Denece was just closing the door when she heard a muttered "pilgarlic"[7] from Malcolm, and smiled to herself. Garlic pills, that was obviously what was needed, and Malcolm was just being difficult. Well, she could get those herself: she had seen them in supermarkets. No need to visit the doctor at all.

It was a pity Denece had heard that muttered exclamation of Malcolm's. She wasn't to know that where he was born and brought up, 'pilgarlic' was a person only worthy of pity.

By now, quite a few people in Yatross would have benefited from knowing more Devonian dialect. Most of the time, Malcolm spoke just like everyone else, except for a warm West Country burr. But under stress, or when he was feeling mischievous, the Devon words and phrases would appear. Conversations in Agora alternated

---

5   a silly person

6   yes, now don't make me ill-tempered

7   a person worthy of pity

from being great fun to great mysteries, depending on whether or not staff and Helpers understood what he had just said. "I'll have a snicket[8] of that cake, then," was easy to translate, as was "poorlified"[9] when talking of someone unwell, but he had to help them with some of the others. Sue told him about the uproar in the book centre when Jane dressed in her bird costume, and he commented: "Sounds like a real randy-voo."[10] Further explanation was also required when Malcolm said to Steve: "You feel fairy, then,"[11] as it turned out that this meant in good health and buoyant mood.

The general consensus was that he was a nice man, who had brought some new life and interest into Yatross. For Michelle, he had brought so much more. She had felt an instant rapport with this kindly man, who seemed to appreciate her ('he *valued* her!') so that she developed increasing belief in herself. Being told "Ee be too muty-hearted,"[12] or "Ee becoming a giglet[13] like young Kirsty," was like being mentored by an uncle, and she felt that personal comments in Devonian were so much more acceptable than any in English.

---

8   a very small piece
9   unwell
10 a disturbance
11 in a jovial mood, or in fine health, buoyant
12 soft-hearted, sensitive
13 happy-go-lucky young maiden

Meanwhile, Malcolm had put Denece out of his head and was nearly ready to see his first patient. He studied the notes provided by both Lizzie the bursar and Sarah, a counsellor. It seemed that Linda Collins was suffering from chronic insomnia. She was fifty years of age, divorced, with two children grown up but still living with her. He skimmed more notes: a variety of family problems, said Linda, kept her awake at night. Sarah recorded that the counselling sessions were continuing, but that she felt Linda would benefit from a herbal remedy now; the sessions with Sarah being a solution for the long term. Malcolm looked for any mention of a job.

'Ah, there we are: she's a sales assistant in a department store.' His thoughts ran on. 'She would likely be a real towser,[14] with those chillern[15] at home still, and a full-time job. No point, then, in asking her to brew herbal teas – it'll be tablets for this one. Let's see what her has to say.'

Malcolm looked out of his window and studied the effects of sunlight on the garden. He felt lucky to be working in such a pleasant environment, with pleasant people for the most part, and when Linda arrived for her appointment a minute or two later, she found a smiling man, content with his life.

---

14 a hard-working lady
15 children

Almost a week later, and the weather had changed. The sun, when it appeared, was watery, and there was a distinct chill in the air.

On Friday morning, Malcolm was asked to go to the Director's office, in between his patient appointments. On entering, he found that Stephanie's face had been afflicted by the weather: she looked pinched and sharp. The chill outside was matched by the slight frost in the office air that Malcolm had detected, and he began to feel uneasy.

"Sit down, please, Malcolm. We have a situation that I need to discuss with you urgently. Yesterday I was telephoned by a Linda Collins. I understand she is attending the clinic and seeing two therapists: yourself and Sarah. You prescribed a herbal remedy for this patient?" Malcolm nodded and Stephanie continued:

"She says that from a few days after taking the tablets you gave her, she has felt ill: sick and dizzy, and unable to go to work. Tell me: is this a possible side effect?"

"No."

Stephanie blinked. Well, that was definite enough. "Tell me more."

"She has been suffering from insomnia. Sometimes I provide herbs that patients can brew into teas, as I find that the preparation is a soothing routine that contributes to useful sleep. But Mrs. Collins has such a busy life that I prescribed tablets instead: a combination remedy of passiflora, hops, lime tree flowers and lady's slipper. It is safe and effective."

Malcolm delivered this account in a deliberate, unemotional tone of voice. His face was serious.

Stephanie knew that he was not pleased to be questioned on the attributes of the remedies he prescribed. However, she had a duty to the patients, and this came before his pride; she needed to follow up every possibility.

"What about the manufacturer?"

Malcolm made a tutting noise. "I have used them for years and trust them completely. However, I will report these symptoms to them and see what they say." He paused. "I have a patient arriving in a few minutes. Do you know if Mrs. Collins is returning for her next appointment?"

"I did receive the impression that she had rather lost faith in us. I think we'll have to wait and see what the manufacturer comes back with."

Malcolm nodded, turned briskly and left the Director's office. On the way back to his consulting room, various salty Devonian phrases were uttered, but luckily no-one within earshot had any idea what they meant.

A little later that morning, Malcolm had an opportunity to check Linda Collins' file again. As he already knew, there were no contra-indications in the medical history she had provided for him, that would indicate a response such as that reported. However, he had his own idea about what was going on here. The problem was that he had no proof, and was unlikely to obtain any. If only, he thought, he had been a therapist here longer. In his previous job, the Head of Clinical Practice knew Malcolm and trusted him implicitly. Any patient making a false claim would have been given short shrift. But here at Yatross he had yet to earn that level of trust.

It was interesting that Linda Collins had not come back to him directly with the problem. That alone was suspicious, in his view. He resolved to ask Stephanie if she would suggest to Linda that she come back and attend her appointment next week so that he could talk to her and make an assessment.

∽

The news of Malcolm's fall from grace soon reached Agora. Stephanie was no tittle-tattle, and Lizzie made careful judgements about which staff needed to know what information; both of them were frequently astounded at how often confidential information seemed to leak out, as if the Greek gods inhabiting Yatross were whispering snippets of gossip in mortals' ears.

Today it was Sue who said to Denece: "I hear that our new herbalist has been poisoning the patients – did you hear about Linda Collins? Malcolm gave her some sleeping tablets that have made her ill, she says. He never gave you anything, did he?"

Denece shook her head. She had had the sense to look up garlic pills on the internet, and had found nothing about them being able to heal wounds, so had changed her mind about self-medicating.

She replied: "So what's going to happen to him, then?" Sue noticed that quite a few occupants of Agora had stopped drinking tea, stopped unwrapping snacks, or had halted their own conversations, the better to hear this new piece of gossip. Sue was confident in her source, so said, without bothering to lower her voice:

"The manufacturer is going to be consulted, apparently. But if you ask me, herbal medicine is just too dodgy for words. It's never going to suit everyone, is it?"

~

Michelle came into Yatross on Saturday morning, and went to see Malcolm as usual to see what tasks he had for her. She knew he was still building up his stock of herbs, and she expected to be unpacking supplies and labelling jars and boxes. But Malcolm greeted her with:

"Good morning, Michelle. How would you like to do some research for me?"

"Of course. What would you like me to do?"

"You've been given access to the computers in Agora, I believe. I want you to take this list of herbs and look for medical studies that name them. Go back up to twenty years. I'd like you to record any studies where negative effects were found. I've listed here some other criteria for you to take account of, which will narrow down the list. I have a new patient to see shortly, but I'll come along a little after ten and we'll see how far you've got. Depending on your findings, we may need to adjust the research parameters, but don't worry about that for now." Malcolm took in Michelle's slightly dazed face. "I expect you're wondering why I'm asking you to do this."

"Well, yes. I mean, I'm pleased if I can help, but I get the impression that this is important. So why me?"

Malcolm smiled for the first time that morning. "Because I think you'll be thorough, and meticulous, and because I have too many patients today to do it myself. Yes, it is important, but because I want you to be objective, can you bear with me if I tell you what it is all about later today?"

"Of course. I'll go and make a start now."

As the door closed behind her, Malcolm wondered how long it would be before another member of staff told Michelle the news. He knew her loyalty to him was such (even after their brief acquaintance) that she'd be indignant on his behalf. He didn't want her subconsciously ignoring any negative studies, because of that loyalty. She was not a scientist, and could not be expected to employ a scientist's objectivity, but from what he knew of her computer skills she would be able to make a fair stab at what he had asked her to do. He didn't have long: patients all day today, Sunday to look at what Michelle had found, plus some research of his own, and then Monday he would be back in the Director's office again.

∽

Linda Collins declined to meet with the herbalist again, and also gave up her counselling sessions with Sarah, which worried and annoyed that lady in equal measure. Malcolm asked Stephanie to request some specific information from Linda: details of when she fell ill, how long after taking the tablets did the sickness start, did the dizziness come before or after the sickness, how long did it last, how many tablets did she take before she gave up and were there any other symptoms.

Luckily, Stephanie's GP training meant that she felt these were reasonable questions, and she was just as frustrated as Malcolm when Linda refused to provide the details. Stephanie began to agree with Malcolm that there was something behind her complaint.

Their suspicions were confirmed on the arrival of a solicitor's letter. Linda was claiming (the solicitor said) that Yatross had been negligent in supplying her with the tablets, and that this was a breach of the common law duty of care that the clinic owed her as a patient. Malcolm was tight-lipped when Stephanie showed him the letter, but Stephanie was surprisingly relaxed.

"At least we now know where this is going," she said, sitting back down at her desk. "I can pass it on to our Insurer, and their legal team will get on to it immediately. I'll send them that excellent report of yours, and they will then decide whether or not to contest the claim. Either way, there is nothing else for you to worry about, Malcolm."

Malcolm still looked stern. "You mean there is a possibility they will pay her claim, just to be rid of her? Is that what you mean?" He was incredulous, but Stephanie had been down this road before, and spoke calmly.

"It's possible, but it's out of our hands, I'm afraid. It will be the Insurance company's decision."

"And do we get any chance to have a say? What about my reputation? If she wins compensation, it may get reported in the press, and then patients will lose faith in both myself and the clinic." The kindly, good-tempered herbalist had disappeared, and been replaced by an angry, forceful man that Stephanie did not recognise. She realised that if this did not go the right way, she might be looking for a replacement practitioner quite soon.

"We're getting ahead of ourselves here. These cases take months to resolve, and I've plenty of time to put our case to the Insurer. Try not to worry: I'm sure it will all work out in the end."

Malcolm left her office, still unconvinced, still seething. It seemed completely against natural justice that a woman like Collins could lie to a solicitor, be believed, and because of that he might lose his reputation, and his job. This was the first time in his long career that he had been the subject of a spurious claim, and the sheer unfairness of it was a shock, like a dip in icy water. He went out to the courtyard, and paced it for several minutes, but it wasn't really big enough for his feelings to find sufficient expression, and he changed course abruptly and marched to the nearest exit to the gardens.

Here, he strode down the grassy paths, not really seeing much of his surroundings. The gardens began to work their magic though, and after ten minutes or so he could feel his body losing tension, his breathing deepening and his steps slowing. He waved to Tom, with whom he had developed the beginnings of a friendship, but did not go over to talk. Malcolm recognised he still had some calming down to do. Tea would help, and in search of this restorative he turned back towards the main building.

In Agora, he was very surprised to find himself and the solicitor's letter the main topic of conversation.

"...it was like a punch in the gut when it happened to me. And the woman who claimed my needles infected her was such a quiet, gentle soul. I think her husband egged – oh, hello, Malcolm, we're just discussing insurance claims. I hear you've been targeted this time?" It was Steve, completely unabashed to be found talking about it, and his forthright manner made it easy for Malcolm to join the group and the discussion.

"What was the outcome, if you don't mind me asking?"

Steve grimaced. "Settled out of Court. Insurance thought it was too costly to defend the case." Malcolm made a growling noise in his throat, and Kirsty stepped back in alarm.

'The lion has woken up,' thought Steve, but stopped himself from showing amusement. This was serious stuff.

"If it's any consolation, Malcolm, the Insurance company did a good investigation. They looked at all the angles before coming to a decision. But if they do decide to fight it, it may not be the best outcome for you, however professional you think you've been. Court means publicity, and there's always some idiot reporter looking for an angle on a story."

" 'Scandal Clinic Herbalist Poisons Patient' – is that the sort of thing?" It was Anna, on a break from reception duties. She was half laughing, and Kirsty couldn't help but try and lighten the mood too:

" 'Scandal Clinic' – is that us? I thought we were 'Witches Coven', or was it 'Pagan Place'?" Anna laughed outright and even Malcolm attempted a smile, but Steve drew him to one side, and offered to help.

"You're welcome to come and see the paperwork I've got on the case; it will give you an idea of what questions they ask, what angles they're interested in. One thing that surprised me was their interest in my own health. They wanted to know if I'd ever suffered from a blood-borne disease such as HIV or hepatitis, which astounded me at first. I then found out that they were exploring the possibility that I might be deliberately infecting patients with a virus."

Malcolm was equally astounded, and realised that Steve's case file could be very useful to him. They made arrangements to meet up later that week, at which point they spent a couple of hours going through the details of the case. Malcolm went on to submit a second report to the Insurer, covering all the issues that they might consider relevant, and so the correspondence between the solicitor and the clinic's Insurer gradually mounted up.

One morning in late October, Malcolm was called to the Director's office once more.

"Good morning, Malcolm. I've just had a phone call from Dave Macintosh at the Insurance company. He is of the opinion that Linda Collins is likely to drop the case. This is based on the fact that she has been unable to supply any corroborating evidence, whereas you have been able to show that you acted professionally at all times. The tone of the last communication they had from Linda's solicitor was quite different. They can't be sure, of course, but when I pressed them on probability, they estimated that 90% of claimants back down in similar circumstances. We probably won't know for certain until next year, but you can't walk around with that frown on your face for that long. So I want you to relax, try to forget all about it, and concentrate on your real patients."

Malcolm stared out of the window for a moment and Stephanie waited patiently for him to process the information.

"She wasn't a real patient, was she?" he said quietly, as if only just realising this fact.

"No, I don't think she was. Is that what's been troubling you?"

"I thought at first she was suffering, and blaming it on me, but now I'm wondering if she had anything wrong with her at all. She's just a chun,[16] a sclum-cat – "[17]

"Yes, well, we'll never know, but I think we can be sure she'll never come back to Yatross, that's the main thing," Stephanie interrupted him quickly, before he could get fully launched into Devonian. She didn't understand any of it, and felt it beneath her to ask him to explain what he meant. His next question took her by surprise.

"Do you want me to stay?" Malcolm asked in a flat tone.

"Of course. I believe you to be an excellent herbalist and a real asset to the team. The other practitioners and Helpers like you, and that's just as important, from my point of view. I like to have a content team around me: it makes my job much easier."

Malcolm merely nodded and left the office. He

---

16 a bad woman

17 a nasty or spiteful person

would think carefully about whether or not he would stay. This claim had soured Yatross for him, to some extent. It needed considered thought.

Later that day, he went to Agora at the usual time for afternoon tea and found that his friends had already decided for him. There was a party going on, to celebrate his return to the fold. Herbs were plaited into streamers and decorations, someone had made a spice cake, and there was a great array of herbal teas in fancy glasses. Helpers and staff who were not busy with patients had all appeared, and cheered him as he entered.

'What? How did they know? Truly this placed is ginged[18],' he thought, not for the first time.

"Congratulations, Malcolm; I told you it would all be ok. Now, try one of these: I made it myself, and it's really rather good," and Si Bevan pushed a glass into his hand.

Malcolm smiled across at Michelle, looking pink and happy on the other side of the table, and raised his glass to them all.

"I'm thinking it's time that you all learned a proper Devon drinking song," he began, and everyone in Agora roared their approval.

---

18 bewitched

Chapter Thirteen

Man, Waiting

"I had another dream last night. The telephone rang, and I knew it was Mary-Lynn, asking me to pick her up at the station. In my dream I picked up the phone, and she said: "Is that you, darling?" but her voice was cracked and broken, as if she hadn't spoken in a long while. And then as I woke I remembered she was dead, and it was like falling into a deep pit: the pain was so much deeper than I had felt before, because for a moment, I had thought she was still alive, still with me. Do you understand? Do you? The pain...I feel like I want to cut off a limb; I want to do anything that might make the pain go away.

"Today I knew I couldn't go on like this. This waiting in limbo for the agony to be relieved, for some kind of life to begin again. I wait, I exist, I think of her. That is my life. Some other man inside this body remembers to wash and eat from time to time, but that is all. I have not been to work since she died. I do not know what they think, and I don't really care. At some point my money will run out, I suppose, but I don't really care about that either. It is impossible to plan for a future without her in it, so I don't. I don't plan, and I don't have a future. I never imagined I would say that: it sounds so bleak, but it is nothing besides the bleakness of no Mary-Lynn, so again, it means nothing.

"I live in the past now. Always thinking back to times we had together. We were happy, you know? Really happy. I met her on a train, would you believe that? I saw her and thought: 'I want to spend the rest of my life with that woman, but first I have to ask her out, not just freak her out by staring at her every day.' It turned out that she had noticed me too, and didn't take much persuading to come out on a date with me. We went out to dinner at Romero's, and every part of that evening was magical to me. She smiled, she laughed, she asked interested and interesting questions, and at one point grabbed my arm when she got carried away with explaining something. I loved her passion, her animation, when talking about her work, her friends, her family: it was as if she had twice as much life as anyone else I knew. She would toss her long dark hair off her face, those dark blue eyes would flash, and I wanted her more than anything in the world.

"The first time I asked her to marry me, she said it was far too soon to think of such a thing, but I could see the idea intrigued her and I bided my time. I played her like a fisherman would play a fish on his rod and I waited a long time before asking her again. By this time she was terrified I would never ask again and she said "Yes" straightaway.

"No-one has ever looked more beautiful than my Mary-Lynn on her wedding day. White lace clung to her body as if it loved her as much as I did, and her hair was dressed with stars. Most of all I remember the look in her eyes, which said she was so happy to be marrying me. Everyone said what a lovely couple we made, and it never occurred to me that we would have any other future than a wonderfully happy one.

"She carried on working in Harrods, even after we moved out of London to that little flat in Croydon. She loved running her department and the management were pretty understanding when the trains let her down: they didn't want to lose her. I used to pick her up from the station when I was on the right shift – I worked at the Croydon Post Office. Maybe technically I still do. There's probably something about it in one of the envelopes I put in the bin from time to time.

"I loved going to get Mary-Lynn: driving to the station I was happy, and anticipated her face when she saw me. No matter what kind of day she'd had, she always had a smile for me. I'm not saying we never fought; we did, but she always got over it quickly, and seemed to love making up with me almost as much as I did with her.

"We loved each other, you see. It was as simple as that.

"So when we found out she was pregnant, it seemed we wanted nothing more. A baby would make us a family; it was what we both wanted. From the beginning, though, it didn't go well. Poor Mary-Lynn was so sick, and they gave her tablets for it. She didn't want to take them, as she worried that they would hurt the baby, but eventually she had to, and they helped a bit.

"Then I started worrying: about her dark strained eyes, her sallow skin, and her exhaustion. At about six months, she seemed to get a little better, but she was still tired all the time, and to me she seemed distracted by something. I would find her crying, and she tried to reassure me: "Don't worry, my darling, just my silly old hormones." I did worry, but not enough, not enough. I should have realised something was seriously wrong. That was my job, right? And I didn't do my job well enough.

"One morning, she said she felt rough, and would call work to explain she was sick. I asked her if she wanted me to stay with her, but she said no, she would try to sleep, and then maybe she would feel better. No alarm bells rang in my head, and I didn't call her from work, as I didn't want to wake her from a healing sleep.

"I drove home, with no other thoughts than that I would cook us both some supper, and how lovely it would be when the baby arrived. All was quiet when I got home, and I went quietly up the stairs, wondering how soon I could decently wake her.

"She was not in the bedroom. I opened the bathroom door and the room reeled about my head. I was back in time, at the cinema, watching one of the horror movies we used to scare ourselves with. The bathwater was red. A body lay in the bath, red lines on its wrists. My brain came up with the only explanation it could accept, and told me: 'Thank goodness this is not Mary-Lynn, not my heart, my love, my life.' And then came the realisation that it was so. I shouted "No!" and clutched at her body, pulling it out of the water, but it was very cold. She was no longer there.

"They said it must have been the hormones. 'Suicide while the balance of her mind was disturbed' was the verdict. You cannot know, cannot imagine, how many times I've wondered why my beloved wife, seven months pregnant with our longed-for baby, would take her own life. And why I never knew her mind *was* so disturbed that she could carry out such a thing.

"People said to me: 'You must have noticed something wrong – she must have been unhappy.' But I thought we were both blissfully happy. And then that makes me question every part of the life we had: was it all a lie? When she laughed at something I said, was she thinking of something else? When she reached for my hand, was it to pretend to comfort me, not because she wanted to? I have revisited and rewritten every part of our lives that I can remember, and it is a very special kind of torture. It's like I was dreaming, and now I've woken up, and the daylight world is more hideous than I could ever imagine, and all I want to do is go back to that dream world.

"And so I do. I don't know if I'm asleep or awake or dreaming, most of the time. I walk streets for hours and hours, not knowing where I go, and whether it is day or night, sun or rain. But I think on the touch of her hand, the feel of her skin, that twitch of her mouth just before she said something she knew was outrageous. I remember her throwing our wedding photo across the room because she was cross with me, and then immediately crying because the glass had shattered and the photo was bent and ruined. She couldn't keep plants alive, I remember; she thought my green fingers with them were nothing short of miraculous. I will never forget the smile she gave me when I once brought a dying plant back to life, because it had belonged to her mum.

"I've wondered about that, of course. She was desperately upset when her mum died, and she was only three months' pregnant then. She knew how her mum would have loved to see her first grandchild. I know Mary-Lynn was grieving, but I believed she was coping, and coming to terms with the loss.

"I've always had a very analytical brain, and I put that to good use from time to time, dissecting every conversation I can remember, every expression on her face, her voice in telephone calls. What was going on in her head? Will I ever know? And so the torment goes on. Sometimes I lay on our bed, hoping for a little sleep, or at least for happy memories to send me to her for a while. Sometimes I do sleep, worn out and hopeless somehow. But then I wake up, and the fall into the pit is a terrible thing. I now don't want to go to sleep again, with that waiting for me. I wish I could believe in some sort of afterlife, but neither of us did. I know there is no happy-ever-after, no place where we will be together again, so there is no comfort.

"No comfort. No comfort."

Finally, it seemed that there were no more words, and Anna disentangled her hand from his. Her hand and arm were stiff and uncomfortable, but she stopped herself from flexing them, for his sake.

"Trevor, I am so sorry about your wife, but I am very glad that you felt able to come in and talk to us about it.

But it isn't me you should be talking to: it's Kirsty. Will you wait there for me while I go and get her? And I'll bring you back some water."

At the door, she paused. "Trevor, did you ever leave a note for Kirsty?"

Trevor looked blankly at her. "Kirsty? I'm not sure who – "

"Don't worry about it, I'll be back in a minute." Anna shut the door of the interview room, and then cursed her way down the corridor. 'Bugger Beatrice! It obviously wasn't him who left the message about 'Nice Tits'; she got it wrong. And all this time we've been treating him as a joke, when he's anything but. How could she have made such a mistake?' Anna felt drained and tired, and wondered how the counsellors did this every day, soaking up people's miseries. She found Kirsty in Agora.

"Kirsty! I'm so glad you're here. Trevor Browning is back, and he's talking at last! I was coming to get you as soon as I'd settled him in the interview room, but he grabbed my hand and started talking and then wouldn't stop. There was no break in it, Kirsty, and I didn't want to say 'stop, hold on,' in case he couldn't start again. I can see in your face that you're cross, but I didn't know what else to do. Kirsty, will you go and see him now? Oh, and there's something else you ought to know. I don't think it was Trevor who handed in that note to you back in the Spring. I'm so sorry."

Kirsty wasn't cross, exactly, but she did feel a curious mix of indignation, relief, and exasperation. All that time she invested in Trevor Browning, and finally it was Anna who reaped the benefit! It wasn't fair, she started to say to herself, but then her innate sense of justice subdued her annoyance.

"It's all right, Anna: you did the right thing. Show me where he is."

When Kirsty reached the interview room, she wondered if he would still be here, or if he had anything left to say. She opened the door and saw him immediately, slumped in an easy chair, fast asleep. She sat down quietly, and after a few minutes, when it seemed he wasn't going to wake up, she started writing him a note to read when he woke up, so that he would know he hadn't been abandoned.

As she wrote, Kirsty thought: 'Here we are again, Trevor and I sitting in a room, and him not speaking,' but knew that this time it was different. The floodgates had been opened and now he would be able to talk to her.

She walked quietly to the door, opened and shut it noiselessly, and slid across the sign that said: 'Do not Disturb.'

Chapter Fourteen

*'Teresa's tired, but wait a bit:
she just needs her coffee hit'*

'Oh, help me but I'm tired. And I've been tired for such a long time. Mm-mn, I can't remember when I wasn't tired: when was that, I wonder? I'm actually struggling to remember a time when I had energy, the sort of energy I see in other people. Look at that runner over there. Run? I've barely got the energy to walk. And yesterday in the supermarket, that man was whizzing round with his trolley as if they were both on speed. Even Dad's got more energy than me, despite all his other problems.'

With that thought came a familiar feeling: a sinking feeling of dread in her gut, coupled with a rising anxiety in her chest, so that the two tides were pulling away from each other in her body, neither winning the miserable tug-of-war that had been a part of her life since her mother died, and her father had become solely her responsibility.

Teresa blinked and looked around her. 'How did that happen? I'm here, at the clinic. I've heard of automatic pilot, but this is beyond that. I have no recollection of any of that journey. Scary. I bet I'm even – ' and she checked her watch ' – on time. I suppose I've now got to find the energy to open that door and get out of the car.'

Help to do exactly this came from an unexpected source.

"Teresa!" The door was opened with a volume of energy that Teresa could only imagine possessing. She was looking into the face of Alice, another student on the nutrition course.

"Lovely to see you! How are you? Did you make that cake she gave us the recipe for? It was scrumptious! I ate it all up in one day!"

Teresa looked up at Alice's face, and wondered: 'If I ate a whole cake in one day, would it give me that amount of energy and enthusiasm?' It was bursting out of Alice, like her body out of her clothes, like her black corkscrew curls out from her head, like words spilled out of her large, generous mouth.

"Give me a tug, Alice," and Teresa held out an arm to the big woman, who lifted her out of the car as easily as if she were a three-year-old. They went into the building together, with Teresa trying to keep up to Alice's faster pace. Alice was chatting all the while, and Teresa kept thinking about coffee, and how soon she could have one. But Geri was in the kitchen already, and making herbal tea.

"Good morning Alice, Teresa; I'm just making a hot drink. What flavour would you like?" Geri took in Teresa's downcast face, and added gently:

"How many coffees have you had already this morning, Teresa?"

"Two," was the muttered response. She did wonder though, if she should also count the one she had at 4.00 a.m. when she couldn't sleep.

"Then let's make this one something different. I'll make you a lemon and ginger tea. Both lemon and ginger give you zing, and the lemon will cleanse your digestive system."

"I'll have that cranberry and orange one," said Alice. "It's yummy." Alice thought that most things you could put in your mouth were yummy, but she had a preference for sweet things above all. While Geri was pouring hot water, Teresa noticed the fast move of Alice's hand from the pocket of her cardigan to her mouth.

'Very practiced,' thought Teresa. They had only started the course last week, and were already learning a great deal. Mostly about each other, and about how to defeat the restrictions that Geri put in place to try and control their addictions. Teresa herself had a few squares of chocolate in her pocket, as she found it a good caffeine substitute when coffee wasn't available. Geri had turned back towards them and Teresa abandoned the idea of trying to slide some chocolate out of her pocket. She took the tea with a half smile, which was all she had the energy for, and fell on to a stool at the kitchen table.

A voice rang out from the hallway, calling Geri. As she disappeared, Alice and Teresa both slipped chocolate into their mouths. Teresa then became aware that Robert's laptop was on the table. He wouldn't be far away, but she couldn't resist opening it up to take a look. Much to her surprise, the screen saver hadn't activated, and she was looking at the introduction to the book that Robert was writing on Yatross.

"Alice! Come and look!" Alice took an adjacent stool, and they read:

I am writing this in the large, cheerful, well-equipped kitchen in the residential unit at Yatross. Often this kitchen will be thronged with young people, learning about food and nutrition as part of a course to deal with eating disorders, for example. This kitchen will also produce all their meals while they are here.

Today, however, and for the next eight weeks, I am part of a small group of adults who are attending twice a week on a course that will address caffeine and sugar dependency.

Teresa and Alice looked at each other, both thinking the same thing: how much more real their problems seemed when written down baldly like that. The introduction continued:

Other issues are covered by the diet and nutrition team in different courses, such as addiction to junk food, helping with changes to diet such as high fat to low fat, or to reduce cholesterol. Many of the patients are referred by the main Yatross clinic, and some are undergoing counselling at the same time, where there are underlying psychological issues.

The team is led by the experienced nutritionist

Geri Peters. She has been a member of staff at Yatross since …?

The reason for Robert's absence became clear. He had gone to the office to find out. Teresa looked round, and was glad to see they were still alone. Not wanting to push their luck, she pulled down the lid and moved away.

"Geri told us that Robert was here to write a book for the clinic," Alice mused, chin propped up on her hand, "but I'm surprised if that's all he's managed to produce since last week. I could have knocked that out in twenty minutes."

"Shush, Alice, don't let them hear you. We shouldn't have looked, and anyway, it's none of our business. Maybe he's been doing research or something." Alice looked as if she would continue the argument, but then the sound of footsteps outside made Teresa add, loudly: "So that cake recipe worked well, then, Alice?"

If Robert noticed that Alice didn't reply, and looked at him instead, he gave no sign. Face impassive, he offered: "Good morning," and then sat at his laptop and studied the screen.

Teresa thought: 'He's the first person I've met who truly deserves the label 'enigmatic'. That blank face never reacts to anything we do or say, and he never volunteers a comment or a question. I suppose that technically he could be described as good-looking, and I do like the clothes he wears. It's just a shame he doesn't seem to have much of a personality, let alone a sense of humour. I don't think Alice and I will be fighting over him, somehow.'

Geri returned to the kitchen accompanied by a woman they had not seen before. The first thing they noticed was her shape: she was a classic upside–down pyramid, with broad shoulders and a large bust, a slightly smaller waist and narrower hips, thin legs, and ending in tiny feet.

"Sorry about that," Geri apologised for the time spent away. "We have a new member for our group. Robert, Alice and Teresa, I'd like you to meet Vivienne." As greetings were exchanged, the group assessed the newcomer. Vivienne looked to be younger than the other women, in her mid-thirties, perhaps, with honey-gold hair in curls, and a sweet expression on her round face. Teresa noticed that there was a slight twitch to Geri's mouth, as if she was amused by something about the new student. Teresa didn't have to wait long to find out why.

"I'm right-on pleased to meet you folks here,

But ah could surely sink some beer!"

Alice actually looked round to see which deep-voiced American guy had come in the room, but found no-one new.

Geri replied evenly: "I'm afraid it's only herbal tea at the moment. Do you have a preference, Vivienne?" Vivienne wrinkled her nose, but replied pleasantly:

"Mah name they made it far too long:

Vienne will do. Jest make it strong!"

Geri decided that liquorice tea would be a suitable choice, and swiftly prepared her a mug, leaving the bag in to brew.

"Let's get on, then," she said, and moved into a position where she could address them all easily. "I'm going to talk to you for a few minutes about the effects of caffeine and sugar in your bodies. I know we did something on this at the last session, but it will be useful revision for you two, as well as bringing Vienne up to date. Then we'll do some work on soups, which you will find very useful over the next few weeks. Soups are nutritious and filling, and now that autumn is here it is just the right time to have some interesting recipes to try. We'll also make soup for our lunch today. This afternoon we'll prepare dinner for you to take home, and then have a discussion about replacement options for those tricky times when the temptation to eat or drink the wrong thing is overwhelming. I want you to get into new habits quickly, and have some success at making dietary changes, and that means being able to deal with the inevitable cravings. So that I can be thinking during the day about the best way to help you, just briefly tell me now about when the hardest part of the day is. Alice?"

"That's easy. All day!" They all laughed, except Robert. "Well, if I had to choose, I think mid-morning is the worst time. All I can think of is cake. Or maybe chocolate. Sometimes biscuits. You'd think it would take away my appetite for lunch, but no matter how much I eat mid-morning, I'm still hungry at lunchtime." Alice turned to look at Teresa, who frowned as she tried to think through the fog of caffeine withdrawal.

"The first cup of coffee tastes the best, and the second one almost as good. The rest of the day I'm just trying to avoid withdrawal symptoms, until the evening, when I really enjoy a coffee after dinner." Geri made more notes, and turned to Vienne. They all knew what to expect now, and weren't disappointed.

"After sundown – that's mah special time;
Daytime eatin' would fit on a dime.
But after a meal at the end of the day,
Ah eat and drink the evenin' away."

Teresa noted that Robert had been typing away since Geri had started speaking, and she wanted to see what he'd written and whether he would include Vienne's unique way of speaking. They had all been assured that no-one would be identifiable in the book, but Teresa thought that Vienne's rhyming couplets would cheer up a boring book on healthcare considerably.

"Well, that's clear," said Geri as she finished making her notes. "Thank you all for that." She reached for some pages and distributed them as she spoke.

"I'd like you to have these diagrams of the body in front of you as I talk, so that you can see the body parts I refer to and understand better what is happening in your own body. Have a look and see if you can find your adrenal glands, and your pancreas.

"You may remember that last week I explained that caffeine stimulates the adrenal glands, and prolonged stimulation will exhaust them. This is why you are so tired, Teresa. When we have our individual sessions later, I'm going to prescribe some targeted supplements to help support your adrenals through to recovery."

Teresa looked down at her poor little adrenal glands on the body picture and sent a silent message: 'Hang on in there, adrenals: help is on its way.'

Geri continued: "Two other things caffeine does: it

is a diuretic, and flushes minerals and water out of the body. We'll also get you some mineral support in there, Teresa. And the third problem is that caffeine causes your pancreas to release insulin, which drops your blood sugar, also making you tired, and craving sweet things.

"Alice and Vienne: you need to be aware that chocolate contains a significant amount of caffeine. I noticed from your food diaries that chocolate forms a large part of your food intake, so all this applies to you too.

"Let's talk about sugar for a bit. You all know it is harmful in large amounts, but just what is a large amount, and how much can your body take before it starts to become ill? Do any of you know, in teaspoons of sugar, or by weight?" None of them did, and Geri distributed a sheet with a list of common foods, with the amount of sugar they contained in a standard portion. As they started to chat about some of the surprises on the list, the administrator Beatrice arrived.

"Sorry for the interruption, but I need Vivienne for a moment. Viv, it's about your daughter, she – " There was a clatter as a stool went over backwards. Vienne had moved fast, but Beatrice reassured her:

"Don't worry, she's fine. It's just that the crèche are asking about what to give her for lunch. What she's saying she'll eat doesn't match with what you told them, and they need clarification." As Vienne followed Beatrice out of the kitchen, she could be heard muttering something about "that girl" and Geri said:

"I'll come too, in case I can help, Vienne."

As soon as they were alone, Alice whispered loudly to Teresa: "Why does she talk in rhyme? Why would you do that?" Teresa shrugged, as much baffled as Alice. But Robert had the answer.

"It seems that when she was a teenager, living in London with her parents, they had young American students to stay with them on a regular basis; some kind of homestay programme at the college where her father worked. Over several, one would imagine, impressionable years, they taught her to think and speak in rhyme."

Teresa didn't know whether to be more amazed at the information, or at the fact of Robert sharing it. Alice was sceptical:

"How do you know all this?"

Robert looked smug. "I overheard her telling Geri when they were in the office earlier, signing some paperwork." Both women looked at him with dislike, while his expression didn't alter. They had independently decided he should not have told them private stuff he had overheard – he obviously had no conscience, in their view. While sitting on their moral high horse, they were nonetheless glad to have had their curiosity satisfied. Meanwhile, Robert was completely impervious to their cold stares.

As Vienne and Geri came back into the kitchen, they heard:

"That girl, I'm gonna whip her ass,

If she goes on giving me all that sass!"

Alice smiled at her as she sank down on to her stool again, and asked: "Vienne, do you ever *not* speak in rhyme?"

Vienne replied with a shift in her shoulders that was half a shrug:

"That sure doan make no sense to me,

When rhymes are there to be had for free."

Before Alice could come in with something else, Geri said: "We don't seem to be getting on very fast this morning. There's more I wanted to cover, but we need to get lunch preparation under way. We're going to make butternut squash and sweet potato soup, with chilli and lime. Don't worry if you don't like spicy food: the vegetables absorb the heat of the spices and we can make sure it's not too strong. Everyone has a job on this recipe sheet, so let's wash our hands and make a start."

The kitchen was soon busy with the sound of chopping vegetables and the clatter of tools, and then some wonderful smells started to emanate from the large pan on the hob. Even Robert was lured from his laptop to inhale the aromas. Geri, finding him not writing, sent him to find the bread that was sent up to the unit each morning by Mariella. He was back quickly, with a message for Teresa.

"Teresa, Beatrice has had a message from your father's neighbour. Could you call her, please?"

Teresa's lethargy disappeared instantly, to be replaced by twists of anxiety in her stomach. She checked her mobile but there were no missed calls. With an apologetic glance at Geri, she went out into the corridor and called her father's neighbour, Brenda. It was Brenda who had recommended Yatross to her, and they had been talking about Teresa's course only last night. As she waited for

Brenda to make her slow way to the telephone, a variety of scenarios played out in Teresa's head.

'What has he done now? Rung the Police because a starling has flown into his garden? Wandered out into the street in only his pyjama top? Shouted at the carer because she was wearing yellow? Or has he pinched a carer's bottom and she's complained to the agency?' It wouldn't be the first time for any of these, and Teresa wondered what she would do if the carers refused to work with him. She was used to the everyday trials of her father wrapping his false teeth and putting them in the rubbish bin, and eating out-of-date food, and setting off the smoke alarm with leaving something to burn on the stove. These were regular irritations, but manageable. Brenda finally answered the telephone and Teresa identified herself.

"I hope you don't mind me calling you at Yatross, dear. I couldn't get through to your mobile, and I knew from our discussion last night that you would be somewhere on the premises today."

"What's happened?"

"Stan knocked on my door this morning, and after we had resolved the issue of *clothes* – " Brenda's emphasis made Teresa wince; " – he told me that he could hear the Wilsons singing songs, through the wall. He insisted I went in to listen, and although I am a little deaf, I don't think the Wilsons were singing anything. They're not the type, are they, dear? So I'm afraid your poor father is hallucinating again. I managed to get him to drink a cup of tea with me, by joining in with the singing for a while, and then he seemed to calm down. But when I left, he had his ear to the wall, listening to the songs again. I think it is likely he will call on the Wilsons, and instruct them to reduce the volume. I thought I should let you know as soon as possible, in the event that they should telephone you. I hope I've done the right thing, dear?"

Teresa didn't reply immediately, as her head was a maelstrom of thoughts. The mix included relief that it wasn't a crisis she had to respond to instantly, worry about her father upsetting the Wilsons, gratitude to Brenda for being so sensible and caring, and the ever-present worry about her father's health. Such episodes as this were so much worse when he forgot to drink and became dehydrated. How could she make sure he drank enough? Teresa remembered that Brenda was waiting for her to speak.

"Thank you so much for helping, and for letting me know. Well done for the singing and tea-drinking bit. Did you know all the songs?"

"They were very old ones, dear, but Stan and I are both very old too. I remember singing one of them when – " At this point Vienne came up to Teresa, concern on her face, and Teresa knew it was time to bring Brenda gently to a halt. At the next gap, she promised to call in on them both tonight, and thanked Brenda again before ending the call.

"My father has dementia, and that was his neighbour, relating the latest incident," she explained briefly to Vienne. "Luckily I don't have to do anything right now. Is the soup ready?" Vienne studied her weary face for a moment, then said quietly:

"Old folks can put you in a spin,

When their mind's not what it bin;
But soup is here: Geri said to call
'Cos we gotta take care of you an all."

The simplicity of that struck Teresa with some force, but in translation. 'I need to look after myself so that I can look after him. I don't think I've heard it expressed so well before. 'Poetry distilling the essence of meaning' – who said that?' Something in her gut released as she followed Vienne back to the spicy-smelling kitchen. The coffee craving was still there, and the worry about her father, but for the moment she decided she would just enjoy the lunch they had made, and the company of these new, unexpected friends.

Geri had made a low sugar fruit drink, and was pouring it into glasses when Vienne and Teresa joined the others at the table. All raised their glasses to Geri's toast:

"Naste kala, may you be well," and they all replied: "Naste kala," and drank. It wasn't very sweet, and Teresa looked at Alice's face, expecting a grimace.

'That's interesting. There is no way that could be sweet enough for her, but there she is, smiling and chatting to Vienne. I wonder…' Then Teresa spotted a tiny paper triangle, caught on Alice's sleeve, and she hid a grin. Somehow, Alice had managed to add a sachet of sugar to her drink when Geri wasn't looking. As Teresa sipped her soup, which tasted very good, she felt her spirits rise a little.

'There's got to be a way to harness some of that creative energy – and from Vienne too. I'm sure their imaginations could come up with better ways of dealing with Dad than I've managed to come up with so far. I wonder what they would say if I asked them? We get another break later. I'll talk to them properly about him.'

Geri looked round the cheerful group and congratulated herself on the soup recipe. 'It's as I've always said: get the nutrition right, and everything else sorts itself out. And this soup is better than good.'

Chapter Fifteen

The Revenge of Typhon

'I am wishing not the fireworks. That will be a little later, I think, and I can perhaps leave before then. The food will be eaten, so my job will be done. Why so many bangs? The colours are very pretty, but the noise, it scare me. Noise like that mean war, guns, someone getting killed. They are like children, here at Yatross. If they had lived in my country they would have no fireworks, ever.'

While Mariella ruminated on her fears, a guest approached the table and asked for a hot dog with onions. Gavin had it ready almost before he had finished asking, and Mariella slid a few more sausages on to the grill barbeque, in preparation for the next customers.

"This is just like the barbeque I cooked for last August," said Gavin cheerfully, "only with a lot more people. Do you think the food will hold out?"

Mariella waggled her hand in the air in the universal sign for 'maybe' and smiled at her co-worker. Gavin was tall and muscular, with a plain face and a large mouth. He always said what he meant, and was very direct. As far as Mariella was concerned, his greatest attribute was that he treated her the same way he treated Sheridan, the other Helper in the gardens, or anyone else for that matter. 'Some people,' she thought now as she flipped sausages expertly, 'are very embarrassed because I do not speak. They don't know what they can say to me, so they say nothing. Or they treat me as imbecile, as if I have no brain. Gavin, he not do this. I like to work with him.'

Just then Paul returned with reinforcement burger buns and submarine rolls. "That's the last lot." He put his hands on his hips and surveyed the crowds milling around the grounds of Yatross. Solar powered lights provided intermittent glimpses of people, eating, drinking and chatting until the main event began.

"Surely they must stop eating soon? Did any of them eat today at all? Or yesterday, come to that?" Paul was only half-joking.

Gavin barked a short laugh. "It's this one's fault," and he gestured to Mariella. "She's put this incredible-tasting sauce on the sausages. I tried one just now for the first time and it's fantastic. Here," and Gavin swiftly assembled another hot dog for Paul to try. As his mouth closed round the roll, Paul thought back to last year's bonfire night celebration in his street, which he had been unable to go to because of yet another crushing migraine. Since the acupuncture treatment started, his migraines had reduced in intensity and frequency, so he kept the treatment going by continuing to work as a Helper. He felt his connection with Yatross had an added bonus in that he could work with Gavin and Sheridan, both of whom he genuinely liked.

"That really is good. What's in it, Mariella?" Mariella

just smiled shyly, pleased with their appreciation, but Gavin asserted:

"I'm going to kidnap her next summer for my family barbeque, and then she'll have to cough up the recipe!"

More customers appeared and kept them busy for a while, and finally they were down to a few burgers and rolls. Suddenly a firework went off close by, followed by the sound of young girls squealing. Paul had been standing close to Mariella, and he felt her jump, then start to shake. He instinctively put his hand on her arm reassuringly, and looked into her face. 'Why, she's scared of the noise,' he thought, mildly surprised to see such a degree of fear in her eyes.

"That's just the kids, pre-empting the proper display," he said quietly. Then, more loudly, to include Gavin: "Why don't we clear this away and all go over to the bonfire? I want to hear what Simon's got to say." They turned off the equipment and covered over the table, then took the last burgers over to the bonfire, Mariella walking between the two men.

"Snakes, snakes, pick your snake now!" shouted Steve as they approached, and they readily chose a toy rubber snake each from the large box he had at his feet. Mariella enjoyed the puzzled looks on the men's faces; neither had been here last year so were entirely unaware of what was in store. Just then Simon appeared on top of a mobile tower that had been erected to give him a platform, and he began to speak into a microphone to the waiting crowd.

"Ladies, Gentlemen, children, and any Greek gods

who may be listening!" Simon had the ponderous ringmaster delivery off pat and everyone stopped chatting and looked up at their circus leader.

"Welcome to Yatross! I hope you are enjoying our hospitality tonight?" A few cheers went up, and he continued: "I'm told the food is good – is that right?" and there came a chorus of 'yesses' 'hoorahs' and whistles. Having warmed up his audience, Simon continued:

"And so, good friends, to the main purpose of our evening. On this night, 5th November, Bonfire Night, we celebrate a particularly momentous event in the Greek mythological calendar." He paused for effect, but the audience were already with him completely. They didn't know, or care, that there was no such thing as a Greek mythological calendar, and they stared at the big man in his long overcoat and wild mane of hair, with his compelling voice, and some of them even forgot to finish the hot dogs held in their hands.

"Tonight we celebrate – The Death of Typhon! The largest monster that ever lived!"

"Oooh-ooh!" cried the crowd appreciatively, and there were a few giggles. Simon continued, in his finest dramatic form:

"His legs and arms were all serpents; his eyes flashed fire and his mouth spewed flaming rocks! He fought with the mighty Zeus on Mount Casius, and used all those serpent coils to hold him fast. Zeus used his power of the thunderbolt to fight back when Typhon threw whole mountains at him, and their fight finally ended when Zeus hurled Mount Etna at the monster, which subdued him forever. But if you go to Mount Etna today, you will know that Typhon only sleeps, as fire still belches from the mountain's core!"

There were several roars at this, but many of the crowd standing around had begun to talk to each other again; they had had enough of Greek mythology. Now they wanted a bit of action. Simon knew he had strung it out as long as he dared, and launched into his finale:

"So, in support of Zeus, the ruler of all the gods, I want you to get ready to throw your snake on the fire! Typhon's many serpent heads will crumble and burn, and the gods will no longer fear him. Are you ready? One, two, three – throw Typhon on the fire!"

Daniel and Lizzie, standing together near the foot of the tower, threw their snakes with gusto, and enjoyed the spectacle in front of them. Dozens and dozens of snakes flew through the air, illuminated by the bonfire's light. As they hit the flames, the snakes flashed blue and green as they were destroyed in the intense heat. The colours made many in the crowd gasp, but those in the know were aware that Simon had coated the snakes with chemicals that would react with the flames. Daniel and Lizzie had seen it before, but that didn't lessen their enjoyment, and they stood arm in arm, occasionally looking at each other and exchanging comments on the evening's entertainment.

Watching them watching the bonfire, were the Alexander Technique pupils. Their little family group had survived together so far, and were making slow and halting progress, in the case of Andy, Amy and Jonathan; and steady and useful progress, in the case of Sheila, Tosca and Siobhan. The snake event having finished,

Jonathan and Andy offered to get more drinks for the group before the fireworks started. As they disappeared towards one of the drinks tables, Andy's girlfriend Mira was chatting to Siobhan and Amy, Sheila had excused herself for a minute, and Tosca was holding Sheridan's daughter's hand while Sheridan took Luke to the main building to use the facilities. Nobody knew it yet, but the scene was set for Typhon's Revenge.

A few yards away, Mariella gazed into the flames, remembering how her own home was destroyed by fire, many years ago now. 'It is a terrible thing, fire. I watch people try to get back in, to save someone or something, but it is hopeless. Even the children try, but cry out as they get burned. The children…what is that boy doing? He looks like Luke, the young son of Sheridan, and he is trying with that stick to get snake out of the fire… … No!' Mariella rushed forward, and suddenly the 'No!' in her head became a screamed "No!" out loud and Luke looked up in surprise as he reached out to pick up his snake.

"Don't touch! Burn you!" He looked back at the snake but by then she was with him and swung him round out of danger. While Luke struggled to get out of her arms, crying: "I want my snake!" Sheridan was running back towards the bonfire, shouting "Luke, Luke, where are you?" Mariella was then surrounded by people saying: "Mariella! You spoke! That was you! And you saved Luke!"

It was a real randy-voo, as Malcolm would have said. Mariella, cried, laughed, then cried again; she muttered a few incoherent words, then cried once more. Luckily there was no shortage of professionals available, and the Yatross counsellor Sarah bustled over, and summed up what needed to be done.

"You need to go home, Mariella, but not alone." Jane was nearby, having been talking with Sarah, and now spoke.

"I'll go with her – I've got my car. Where's your stuff, Mariella? Let's go and get it." Sheridan by now had grabbed Luke from Mariella and was alternately remonstrating with him for running off, and hugging him to her, hard. Mariella gave him one last glance and walked with Jane towards the main building.

For those left behind, it was an anti-climax. Their heroine had disappeared. What now?

The answer came with the first rockets. Typhon was hurling flaming rocks from his mouth and they exploded in the sky. As the crowd began to exclaim over the firework display, Sarah looked thoughtfully after the disappearing Jane and Mariella. 'An odd friendship,' she thought, 'until you remember that Jane would appreciate someone who never judges her, and Mariella would admire someone who always speaks her mind and is afraid of nothing, except herself.' Sarah cast her mind back to when Mariella first arrived as a patient, just as the new clinic premises opened, about seven years ago.

'There she was, sitting in the patient chair and looking at me with such fear. She was thin, I remember: I don't think she'd eaten properly for years. She tried to speak, but couldn't. We tried writing, but her English was limited. In the end she drew pictures for me. Terrible pictures. She must have gone through hell in her homeland. But she had at one time been a cook, before she became too afraid to speak, and we needed a new one. I'm so glad I persuaded Stephanie to give her a trial. She sustains us, and now everyone loves her. It can't make up for what she's lost, but it's something. I wonder what will happen now? I will see her tomorrow morning and see if she can still speak, or whether that was a one-off, brought on by extreme stress. It's an interesting case.'

While Sarah mused over Mariella's condition, other members of Yatross were being kept busy. Tom had to go back and forth to the shed for sundries such as extra sticks for rockets, and he refused to allow anyone else to go in there. He fretted, in between his tasks, about what state his gardens would be in tomorrow. After Luke's near-miss, a patrol had been set up to keep the children away from the bonfire; luckily the fireworks helped divert their attention, and Steve had distributed the remaining unburnt snakes as fairly as he could. This, however, led to tussles between snake owners and the snake-deprived, so parents and Helpers had their hands full refereeing disputes, and cursed both Simon and Typhon mightily.

It was hardly surprising then, that the fire in the internal courtyard of Yatross was burning brightly before anyone became aware of it. Steve found his arm grabbed by a visitor he didn't know.

"Excuse me, but I've just come from the toilets in the main building, and there seems to be some kind of fire inside your courtyard? It looks real – " but Steve had gone. As he ran towards Yatross he could see smoke billowing out from the centre, and in reception he pressed the fire alarm to alert anyone who might be in the building. He could see the flames through the double sets of glass doors, and a kick of adrenalin vaulted him over the desk to reach for the telephone.

"Fire, and hurry, please. Is that the Fire and Rescue Service? It's Yatross, we're on fire in the central courtyard! Yes, the building is clear of people as far as I know, but I'll check as I leave. No, I won't. How long will you be?" As he put the telephone down, Daniel, Lizzie, Gavin and Paul appeared at the door.

"Can't we try and put it out?" asked Gavin, moving towards the back door of reception.

"No!" Lizzie shouted. "Don't open that door, Gavin! If one of the internal doors is open the fire will be drawn into the building. We can't take the risk. If all the doors from the courtyard are shut, the building is safe for up to an hour. How long will they be, Steve?"

"Fifteen minutes. They said to keep the vehicle route clear of people, and make sure cars are not trying to leave at the same time as the fire truck is trying to get in." Gavin was moving towards the door. If he couldn't fight the fire, he'd fight the public instead.

"I'll guard the entrance to the car park. It'll be easier if the gate is across, though. Lizzie, is there a padlock for it there?"

Lizzie dragged her eyes away from the blaze. "Yes, but Jim has the key. He's helping Si with the fireworks. Ask them to spin them out as long as they can, will you?" Gavin ran out of the door, almost falling over a young woman with a toddler at her feet.

"I'm sorry," said Steve firmly, "but you can't come in.

Take him up to the other building at the top end – there are toilets open in there."

"But we'll only be a minute. Look Mikey, see all the flames? It's just like the bonfire." Daniel knew that Steve was about to explode faster than any of Simon's rockets, and he stepped forward and took the child's hand.

"Come on, Mikey, let's go and see if we can find any more snakes. I bet I know where we can find one." Steve and Lizzie looked at each other with relief. Paul had been quickly checking the rooms off reception, and confirmed all was clear.

"Can we lock this area now, Lizzie?"

"Yes, I've got my keys – let's go." Lizzie turned at the door and took a last agonised look at the reception area. The fish in the corner tank swam unconcernedly around. 'As much as I hate you, I wouldn't have wished this on you, fish,' she thought, and then she glanced once more at the fire zone panel. None of the lights were activated. Which meant that the building was holding up so far.

The outer door slid shut and was firmly locked by Lizzie. Outside, life still seemed normal. People still watched the fireworks, children were waving sparklers around, and the bonfire was starting to die down. They all looked towards the main gate, despite the fact that they all knew it was too soon for the fire truck to appear.

Teresa, followed at a short distance by Alice and Vienne, appeared out of the semi-darkness. "We heard about the fire: is there anything we can do to help?" It was Teresa speaking, as Alice and Vienne were still puffing a little from their enforced brisk walk.

"That would be good, thank you. Teresa: would you

hover between here and the fireworks, and if you see people wander this way, try to head them off? If they want the facilities, direct them up to the residential unit. Alice, would you go up there," Lizzie continued, turning to the next in line, and failing to notice Alice's face falling as she realised more walking was required. Alice had boundless energy for some things, but walking was not one of them. "Please make sure they find what they need, and reassure them that no-one is in danger, if they ask about the fire. The Fire Service has asked for the route into Yatross to be kept clear, so people will be able to leave as soon as the fire truck arrives. Can you do that ok?"

As they moved off, Lizzie turned to Vienne. "Would you stay here, Vienne, and redirect people to the residential unit if they get this far? Make sure they don't go round the back, looking for another entrance." Vienne smiled, glad to be given an important job to do.

"You can be sure they won't get by,

"'Cos I am *known* for mah eagle eye!"

Lizzie, Steve and Paul walked away, Lizzie's brain working at top speed, thinking about what else needed to be done. But her comment about people going to the back of the building had triggered a thought in Steve's head.

"The visitor car park is a reasonable distance away, but our cars are right at the back of the building. Not good, when they are full of fuel! Shall we try and move them further away?"

"Good idea. Find as many staff as you can and get their keys off them, so that it is only you two moving the cars. I don't want a stampede of staff towards the main building: it's just the kind of thing that will panic everyone."

Steve and Paul ran off, relieved to have a concrete, useful task to do. Lizzie stood still for a moment and allowed herself to worry about what Stephanie's reaction would be when she found out, as at the moment she was in the USA at an alternative health conference. 'Let's hope we can save Yatross for you, my friend,' was Lizzie's last thought before the sound of the fire trucks coming sent relief through every part of her.

∽

The next morning, Lizzie surveyed the damage in the courtyard and decided that they had been very lucky. The fire, reflected in all the glass, had looked much worse than it actually was. Also, it had soon run out of material to burn. The courtyard was mostly plants and shrubs, and these had not burned quickly in the damp November air.

The biggest casualty was poor Asclepius. Being a concrete statue, he had not lost his shape, but he had been blackened by the fire, and his paint had peeled and blistered: he looked very sorry for himself.

A wave of emotion held Lizzie still for a moment. 'The courtyard was where Daniel and I... and now look at it! And poor Asclepius: I always greeted you and you always watched over us. We don't seem to have looked after you very well. But I promise you will have new paint just as soon as I can organise it.' Lizzie gave no thought to the fact that it was the god of healing that had been damaged, and what that might mean for Yatross. Her thoughts were occupied mostly by what the fire officer had told her earlier that morning.

"We thought at first that a rocket had fallen into the courtyard and set light to something there. But the seat of the fire was too intense for that. We now think that someone set light to half a dozen fireworks, together with some cardboard, in order to make a proper little fire. Who had access to the courtyard?"

Lizzie had been stupefied. Yatross had enemies? "No-one, other than the handyman and myself. We checked the doors first thing, and all the internal ones were locked."

"What about the ones we went through last night – we went straight through to deal with the fire. Had you unlocked it in advance?"

Lizzie had felt foolish. "You're right. Those must have been unlocked. I don't know how, but – "

"You need to review your security, madam." The fire officer had become brisk, professional. Miss O'Sullivan was just another careless duty-holder who couldn't remember whether the doors were locked, before holding a semi-public event with inadequate numbers of trained staff. He soon took his leave and said he would be sending a summary report.

Now, Lizzie was still wondering and worrying about those unlocked doors. Jim always locked up, and he would have been particularly careful yesterday, knowing that people would be in and out of reception all evening. She went to find him at his morning break time, and he brought his tea into her office.

"Something a bit odd, Miss Lizzie, last night. I was surely going to tell you later. A woman came up to me when I was helping with the fireworks and said she'd been told I would have the keys to get into the courtyard. She seemed in a bit of a state, I thought. She went on and on about how some young lad had grabbed her handbag and flung it over the roof. She reckoned it must have surely landed in the courtyard. Well, Miss Lizzie, we went in and looked everywhere for that bag, but it weren't there. We looked out the back, and then she went back in the courtyard again, but in the end we had to give up. I wanted to get back to help Simon. I did lock the doors again, I'm sure I did."

"What did the woman do?"

"I'm sure I don't know. I didn't see her again, so she must have found it somewhere."

"Thanks, Jim: that's been helpful. What did she look like?"

"I'm sure I couldn't tell you. Your build, I suppose, and dark like you, but I never looked at her face. Too busy looking for that flamin' handbag."

After he'd gone, Lizzie made some notes from what Jim had told her. It seemed clear they had found their firestarter, but who was it and why would she do such a thing? She sighed, checked her watch, and lifted the telephone to make the difficult call to Stephanie, who, in another time zone, would just be getting out of her hotel bed.

Chapter Sixteen

Friends, Enemies, and Lovers

A few days after Bonfire night, the following email appeared in Lizzie's in-box:

From: Andy Harrison
To: Elizabeth O'Sullivan
Subject: How's yer bushes, bursar baby?

Hiya Lizzie!
Hope you've recovered from the excitement of the other night? Must say, it was good of you to lay on so much entertainment! Seriously, I realise you must have your hands full at the moment. Let me know if you need any help with anything. I'm sure I could muster a few Alexander Group volunteers to help sort out the courtyard, if you need it.

To business: Ryan said he's looked at the potholes in the car park and will be dropping in a quote this week. I think you'll find it pretty competitive. Let me know if you need help with anything else.

    Regards, Andy

    PS Hope the subject line got past the censor?!?

Lizzie grinned to herself and sat thinking for a moment. She and Andy had developed a good relationship over the last few months, and he had proved a useful contact for building related work. She typed back the following reply:

From: Elizabeth O'Sullivan
To: Andy Harrison
Subject: Bushes in hand, thank you

Hello Andy
Very good of you to offer, but we've already started work on the courtyard, and all the burnt stuff is cleared away now. Tom is in his element, re-designing the layout.

    Thanks for the info re Ryan – I look forward to receiving his quote.

    As it happens, there might be something else you could help me with. I've asked three contractors for quotes for checking the condition of the roof and carrying out any minor repairs needed. The sums they have come back with have been ridiculous. Do you know anyone who could do it at a reasonable cost? I've got a detailed spec I can send you if so.

Hope to hear from you soon, regards from Lizzie

PS Hope my subject line also got past the censor?!?

She clicked on send, and sat back, feeling hopeful about the roof work for the first time. She began to look at the list of work resulting from the fire on Bonfire Night (or the 'Revenge of Typhon' as most of Yatross called it) and then there was a knock on the door. It was Daniel, and she greeted him warmly.

"Good morning, my love, and how are you?"

"Glad to see my goddess, but hoping she won't wreak vengeance on me after I tell her what I plan to." Daniel sat down, obviously ill at ease. Lizzie leaned forward, puzzled but not yet alarmed. Daniel began:

"You said that Jim told you the woman who'd lost her handbag was your build and dark, like you?" Lizzie nodded assent. "This morning I had an email from one of the Alexander group. She said that she would not be attending any more sessions, as she was moving up to Scotland to live with a cousin. It would be a permanent arrangement. Lizzie, I think the fire might have been started by her."

Lizzie's bewilderment was understandable. "Why on earth would she do such a thing? What does she have against Yatross?"

"Not us, Lizzie, me. Or possibly you and me. You see," and Daniel shifted about in his chair with some embarrassment, "I knew her from several years ago. She was a pupil, and what she did was not uncommon:

her back problems improved, and she fixated on me, her healer, as she saw it. She thought she had fallen in love with me. The problems started when she couldn't accept that I didn't love her, that I couldn't love her. She thought that if she persevered enough, loved enough, wrote, phoned and pestered enough, I would reciprocate eventually."

Lizzie stared at him. "So what happened next?"

"I took her off my list of pupils, gave her the details of another teacher, and explained that I couldn't see her again. Eventually all the contacts faded away and I thought she had given up. It was at least eighteen months later when she contacted Yatross, saying she would like to be part of the group Alexander teaching that she had heard was starting up. At first I refused, but she came to see me, and assured me that all that 'silliness,' as she called it, was finished with. I thought that as it was a group, she would be unlikely to make a nuisance of herself, and decided to give her another chance." Daniel grimaced at the recognition that this had been his first mistake, and that if he had followed his initial instinct, none of the rest of it would have happened.

Lizzie folded her arms, her expression unreadable. "When did you find out that she still loved you?"

"It wasn't love, Lizzie. I told you: it was obsession. She didn't know me, not really. She was waiting for me in the car park, after the first session, back in the Spring, and I could see from her face what she wanted. I refused to engage with her. She carried on coming to the group sessions, and behaved perfectly well during the session, so I had no reason to expel her. But she always waited for me in the car park after every lesson. It was as if she was saying: "I'm here, if you change your mind." But I never spoke to her at those times, never encouraged her. I thought she would give up eventually. Now, though, I'm thinking that she saw us together on Bonfire night, and this sparked a mad jealousy."

Lizzie was thinking hard. "But how could she have known that it was the courtyard where you and I first ... unless you told her?" Her tone became hard, and Daniel attempted to reassure her.

"As I said, I didn't speak to Sheila on personal matters, only about Alexander Technique in the lessons. She couldn't have known the courtyard was special to you – to us – it was just a co-incidence. She thought of a way to have her revenge, and the courtyard was a convenient place. I expect she hoped the fire would gain a foothold there, out of sight. That is, if it was her. I hope I'm not accusing an innocent woman, but the evidence seems strong."

To Lizzie, the evidence was overwhelming. She felt a multitude of emotions, some of which would have to be dealt with later, but for now, the next step was clear.

"I need to call the Police."

"Lizzie, do we have to?" Daniel heard the pleading note in his own voice, and hated it, but he could not help himself. This was all his fault, and he had to find a way of putting things right.

"You're sticking up for her? The woman who tried to burn down Yatross?" Lizzie was incredulous, and rose to her feet with the onrush of emotion. Daniel rose too, and held out his hands in a gesture of appeasement.

"She's going to Scotland, Lizzie. She's not coming back. She can't hurt us again. I think she's a damaged woman, but in a different environment, she may heal. What would be the point of criminalising her, imprisoning her perhaps, for a moment's crazy impulse?"

Lizzie stared at the man she thought she knew. "Daniel: you are the crazy one! Of course I have to tell the Police. She's dangerous – who knows whom she will fixate on next, and possibly try to injure? It doesn't make any difference whether she's in Scotland or Cape Town!"

Daniel turned away with an exclamation of exasperation. "I should never have accepted her into the group."

"I expect you thought you could control her," replied Lizzie, in a softer voice than she had used so far.

"No, I thought she could control herself. Lizzie, please don't do this." He looked straight into her eyes, but she hardened her heart.

"I'm sorry, Daniel, but I have to. For everyone's sake. Excuse me," and she picked up the telephone as Daniel threw up his hands, but then left the office.

As she waited to be put through to the officer dealing with the firestarter case, Lizzie looked up Sheila's details on the clinic database. The photograph showed an ordinary looking dark-haired woman of about forty: there was nothing on the profile that screamed 'arsonist.' At the same time, Lizzie's mind threw up images of herself and Daniel leaving Yatross together, as they did a couple of times a week, appointments and pupils permitting. She remembered other people being around sometimes, but could not really remember Sheila. Her thoughts ran on.

'She must have seen us together at some point, if she was waiting for Daniel on a regular basis. So Bonfire night was not the first time she would have been aware of us as a couple. So it wasn't a 'crazy impulse' as Daniel said. I think she planned it all along. She must be a seriously ill woman.'

"Is that PC Walters? Yes, that's right: Elizabeth O'Sullivan. I think I may have a new lead for you."

∽

Over the next week, Lizzie came to an agreement with Ryan about the roof work, as part of a package with the car park repairs. Ryan and his mobile tower scaffold became a familiar sight to the occupants of Yatross during the rest of November and into December. He'd explained to Lizzie that, if she wanted it done before Christmas, he would have to slot it in between his other jobs, so there would be a long lag between the start and finish dates. He told her that he would have to go into the loft area at some point, to check from the inside, but he would concentrate on the outside while the weather was fair.

Lizzie was happy to agree to all of this. At last it was finally going to get done: something was going right. On a personal front, things were very wrong: Daniel was avoiding her. Their relationship, which had seemed so promising, had taken a bad turn with their disagreement over Sheila, and she didn't know how to get it back on course. Their holiday in Athens seemed like a world away, as if they had been two other people.

'Thinking about it rationally,' Lizzie mused one day to herself, 'I guess the problem is that we approach things from two very different perspectives. Daniel is a healer: he thinks first and foremost about how someone can be healed, whoever they are. I am more practical: I think about how I can make things work, how to be effective. You'd have thought we'd make a good team, but maybe we are just too different. I want to talk to him soon and try and salvage something from this mess.'

Daniel and Lizzie may well have been able to resolve their differences, but a phone call from PC Walters threw them on to a different course. Sheila Candy, the police officer informed her, had left her flat in a tremendous hurry, and they were now trying to trace where she had gone. They could only deduce that she had received a tip-off. Did Miss O'Sullivan know anyone who may have alerted her?

Lizzie assured PC Walters that she knew of no-one who could have done that, and agreed with the officer that the most likely scenario was that Sheila had panicked with the realisation of what she had done, and fled.

When she put the telephone down, Lizzie put her head in her hands and wept softly. What future could she and Daniel have now, now that she knew what he'd done?

∽

The Greek gods that watched over the inhabitants of Yatross demonstrated their capricious nature this

Autumn. While Lizzie lamented the loss of Daniel, Jane was becoming closer to David Yately with every visit he made to Yatross, and everyone who cared about her pretended that absolutely nothing out of the ordinary was happening.

Although Jane usually did nothing by halves, her transformation into Jane 2 had elements of uncertainty about it, like a drunk trying to fit a key into a lock. She sometimes dressed up, she sometimes didn't; sometimes her hair and make-up looked planned, sometimes it looked like she had spent the night on a park bench, just like the aforementioned drunk. Jane did not want staff or Helpers speculating (although of course they did) on why she was changing, why she spent more time on clothes, hair and make-up, especially as she barely acknowledged those reasons to herself.

'I'm bored with all that costume stuff, and everyone's so used to it, that it no longer provokes a response. I'll go back to it sometimes, just to keep people on their toes.'

She articulated something of these thoughts to Sarah, after she had commented on how attractive Jane 2 was, but the offhand comments didn't fool the wise Sarah. She knew better than to refer to David as the trigger for the change, and left Jane to find her own way.

That journey was not without incident. For a meeting with David in the middle of November, Jane wore a sweater dress over leggings, with boots; and tendrils of her long chestnut hair pinned up, leaving some strands loose. It suited her: she looked gorgeous. Both of them were so overwhelmed with the significance of her altered appearance that they were desperately self-conscious, and the meeting was not a success. As they left the interview room, Jane found Robert hovering outside, and took out her frustration on him.

"Why are you always snooping around, Robert? I'm tired of falling over you every time I leave a private meeting. Can't you just leave me alone?" She knew she was behaving badly, and in front of David, a man she badly wanted to impress, but she couldn't help herself. Robert, thick-skinned as always, was completely unabashed.

"If you agreed to give me an interview, Jane, then I wouldn't have to snoop around," he retorted, and promptly introduced himself to David, whom he had not yet met. Jane was incensed at the idea of the two communicating with each other (possibly about her?) and practically dragged David down the corridor to Agora, despite Robert's protests.

If David had any doubts about Jane's feelings for him, these should have been dissolved by that day's happenings, but he was a modest man, with vulnerabilities of his own. So, from their enforced intimacy on the 'Day of the Knife', their relationship continued in a halting fashion, with Jane alternately advancing and retreating, and David so determined not to mess things up by going too fast, that he took them very slowly indeed.

Soon after this, Jane and Sarah happened to be on the same break one morning in Agora, and started discussing the mental health project, as Sarah had taken a keen interest in it.

"I've booked the lecture room for next Thursday, as David now has a draft version of the training module ready to deliver, and he wants me to tell him how it comes across in a real training venue," Jane explained with enthusiasm. Unnoticed by either Jane or Sarah, Robert had slipped into the room and was listening avidly. He suddenly spoke, making Jane jump.

"I would like to be present at that draft run-through, Jane," he announced with his usual arrogance. "I'm sure Yately wouldn't mind. He seemed a reasonable chap."

Jane was aware of Sarah watching her reaction and she managed to swallow the first, fairly obscene retort that rose in her throat. She replaced it with:

"That won't be possible, Robert. The module isn't ready yet for public viewing. When it is, we'll let you know."

"I know that Stephanie is keen for *every* aspect of Yatross to be included in my book, Jane, and I'm sure she would approve. Perhaps I'll ask her."

"Fine. You do that." After half a minute of waiting for her to back down, (he really didn't know Jane at all) Robert stalked out of Agora, and Jane allowed her face to reflect some of the anxiety she felt. Suppose Stephanie agreed with him?

"What are you afraid of, Jane?" asked Sarah softly, and Jane got up from the chair and went to the drinks table to distance herself from the question, which Jane felt had more multiplying serpent heads than Typhon ever had. Which one of herselves was afraid of David? Or of Robert? And why?

Finally, she turned and said: "It's not fair, Sarah. We're trying to develop this module, and it's at a really early stage. We may decide to revamp whole sections of it. Having him there is just going to… complicate matters."

"Would you like me to have a word with Stephanie? I'm sure I can arrange to see her before he can, even if he is the son of her best friend."

Jane's relief was evident in her voice. "Thank you, Sarah: that would be so helpful. You always know just the right way to handle Stephanie."

So it was that on a damp, murky morning at the end of November, Jane and David closeted themselves, and only themselves, in the large airy lecture room at Yatross.

"I'm so glad we've got all this space," said David with obvious pleasure. "I want to get your opinion on what this will feel and sound like when presented to a group of student doctors." David looked away from Jane in an effort to hide a grin. "In addition, it will give you plenty of room to practice your fencing moves, should you wish to."

Jane blushed a little. She had no idea what possessed her this morning when she got dressed. The upshot was that she was standing in front of him now in full fencing gear.

"I can probably do without the mask and foil, for the moment, anyway," she admitted, and started to remove her mask.

"That suit outlines your figure wonderfully, Jane. I'm certainly not complaining about the view." He was frankly admiring, and Jane thought that perhaps the costume wasn't going to be a complete disaster, after all.

There was a knock on the door and it opened. He wasn't supposed to be there, but like an unwanted and uninvited guest who has no idea how objectionable he is, Robert had turned up anyway. Barely had he got a foot across the threshold, when Jane sprung. Mask on, foil at the ready, she leapt into her most dramatic fencing position in front of him, and had the satisfaction of seeing his face show genuine astonishment.

"Oh, this is ridiculous!" he exclaimed. He spun round immediately and walked out, at which point Jane closed the door decidedly behind him. David let out a huge guffaw, and as she removed her mask, Jane felt the uncomplicated pleasure of making someone you care about laugh. David finally stopped, and looked down tenderly at her.

"Mask off, then, Jane?" he asked, his amusement still evident, and she nodded. It was time, she decided, for the mask to be removed and for her to stop groping around with that stupid key. Opening the door as Jane 2 was easy when you had help from the right sort of friend.

∽

Christmas preparations were escalating by the beginning of December, and some staff and Helpers were looking forward to the change in routine. Michelle was particularly excited, and asked if the Christmas tree decoration could be done on a Saturday so that she could help. Anna good-naturedly agreed, and arranged for Jim to erect the tree in reception on the first Friday in December. Michelle arrived on the Saturday morning to see boxes of decorations taking up a whole corner of the reception area.

"Where's Anna?" she asked a harassed Jim.

"I'm sure she's on her way, Giglet, so don't you fret. It's very early still. I've put water in the base, but it'll need topping up by the end of the day. I'll just go and get the stepladder for you."

Michelle fairly bounced up and down with anticipation, and thought that her new nickname, courtesy of Malcolm but adopted by others, suited her very well. She knew she shouldn't start the tree without Anna, so trotted off to Agora for tea, to remove herself from the temptation. When Anna arrived about ten minutes later, she wasn't at all surprised to find Michelle in so early, and readily took her tea into reception at Michelle's urging. They set about opening all the boxes and laying out the decorations, and when Beatrice arrived to cover the reception desk, they started to decorate the tree in earnest.

"How's your sister, Michelle?" asked Anna, as she reached down from the stepladder to take the next bauble from the younger woman. For once, the Greek god whisperers had nothing to do with Anna's knowledge of Michelle's personal life: the sensible but kind-hearted Anna was a confidant of many of the staff and Helpers at Yatross.

"Do you remember I told you she was applying for that really high-powered job? Well, she didn't get it, and she was so gutted. Ever since we had that row, when I came here for the first time, she's been terrifically ambitious, and she pushes herself so hard. There are hardly any hours in the day when she doesn't work. I guess she's trying to prove something, but I'm not sure what."

"Do you see her at all?"

"For a few hours on a Sunday. Much less than I used to."

"Has she changed since she found out she was adopted? I'll have those gold-coloured ones next, Michelle. I suppose what I mean is: in what ways has she changed, other than working herself so hard?"

Michelle handed up the next decorations. "She's harder, definitely. There's a wall there that I can't penetrate. But she gave me a nice birthday card and present, so I suppose she does think of me as her sister again. I'm not looking forward to Christmas, though." Michelle studied the tree, as if it held the answer to her future.

"Why's that? Hang on a minute: I'm going to move this ladder to the other side of the tree. You were saying?"

"We usually find some pub or restaurant that is doing Christmas lunch, and then go and visit Aunt Madge for a couple of hours. I just feel as if the whole day is going to be a strain for both of us, trying to pretend everything is just the same as before, when it isn't."

Anna was thoughtful as she too studied the tree. She and Suki worked full time, and the days they had at home on their own were precious. How would Suki feel if she invited Michelle to share their Christmas lunch? Anna decided, as she climbed down the ladder, to resist making such an offer to Michelle. Apart from the consideration of Suki's feelings, she also realised that it didn't solve Michelle's problem anyway: she would hardly leave her sister alone on Christmas day.

"There! I think that looks beautiful. Let's switch the lights on and see it in its total, over-the-top glory."

In Lizzie's office, an even more important activity was taking place. Tradition had it that Lizzie and Michael always worked out the seating arrangements for the Christmas lunch, due to be held in a week's time. The pair of them made such a good job of this, that no-one complained afterwards (as they had many years before) that they had been seated next to a drunk/a bore/someone who wouldn't stop talking about themselves/someone who barely spoke/the clumsiest clot in the universe who always knocked a drink into a plate of food (not their own). Lizzie's pragmatism allied to Michael's expertise in human behaviour was a useful combination, and staff maintained that no-one else could be entrusted with the job.

This year, though, was fraught with new difficulties. The first of these was Michael's insistence that Lizzie be allocated a place next to Daniel.

"You always get the duds, Lizzie, but this year you shall go to the ball!" Michael expected grateful thanks, and was surprised when Lizzie brushed his gift aside.

"Let's not worry about that for the moment, Michael." She did not want to broadcast the awkward situation that had developed between herself and Daniel.

"My main worry this year is Robert. What on earth do we do with him?"

"I suspect," Michael replied solemnly, "that people have been asking that question for a very long time. But for us it's simple. We put him next to Stephanie. It's all her fault he's here, after all."

"What about his other side? Sadly, he has two."

"Actually, I think he has about ten, but that's probably just me being nasty. I'm afraid I'm not volunteering."

"I know: we'll put Jim there. Jim's half-deaf, so he won't care. Robert won't be able to bore him, and I'll put Suki on Jim's other side, as a reward. Jim really loves Suki."

"And Suki really loves Anna, so we have the quintessential love triangle. Perhaps we could make a Christmas play about it?"

"Michael, I don't think you are taking this seriously enough." Lizzie tapped her pen on her screen. "Come on, who do we put on Stephanie's other side?"

They both sat thinking for a moment. They liked and respected their Director, but, while possessed of a certain dry humour, Stephanie was not a sparkling dinner companion. In addition, none of her employees could forget they were seated next to the boss, which added an element of restraint to both their conversation and alcohol intake. That thought led Lizzie to another.

"I wonder if we could put a Helper there?"

"We could do," agreed Michael, "but what about Catherine? They get on well, don't they?"

"Yes, very well, but the last time we seated Stephanie and Catherine together they spent the whole Christmas lunch talking about the latest research in self-harm. Everyone near them complained that listening to all the different ways there were of cutting yourself with a razor blade made them want to go out and do it themselves, by the time they got into the second hour of it. You know what they're like. No, we need someone who Stephanie has to talk about more general topics with. That's why I'm thinking about a Helper."

"In that case, what about Louise? It's her first Christmas. She won't complain."

"Good choice! Right, she's in. Well done, Michael. You are finally earning that second mince pie. Ok, your third."

"I seem to remember we've got another couple of problem patients. Where are you putting Sue and Denece?" Michael was mumbling through a large mouthful of mince pie but Lizzie caught the gist.

"I'll have to put them together as usual, and they'll chat away quite happily. But the people on their other sides will have to have someone nice to talk to as an alternative. I remember last year Sue and Denece barely turned their heads to their companions."

"Funny how good they both are with the kids, though," he said reflectively.

"Yes, but can we find any kids to sit beside them in time for next week? Michael, this is so stupid, that you and I have to spend so much time sorting out something so trivial." Lizzie was apologetic, but Michael shook his head, and a few crumbs flew out from his beard with the vehemence of it.

"But it's not trivial at all. Seating arrangements in

tribes have always been full of significance. Who gets to sit next to the chief, who is at the bottom of the table, who gets invited in the first instance. In our case, when people know that their desires and feelings have been taken into account, they feel valued, they feel loved. They sit down at the table knowing they are going to enjoy themselves, because the company is congenial to them. To take the trouble means that the party will be successful and everyone will have a good time. Do you still want to give up?"

"Not when you put it so persuasively. Pass me a mince pie, please, Michael, and in a minute I'll go and make some coffee. Let's do a few easy ones. Next on my list is Kirsty. I was going to put her next to Malcolm."

"Why don't we give her an early Christmas present instead?" Michael was being mischievous, and they both knew it.

"He must know how she feels about him, but I think it's a point in Steve's favour that he never follows it up," said Lizzie seriously. "He is too old for her and she'll only get hurt when he moves on. Let's not put temptation in his way; Christmas parties are notorious for people losing their inhibitions."

"Plus a few other things," Michael grinned wickedly. Just then, there was a knock on the door, and in came Mariella with a tray of coffee.

"I thought – you may like – yes?" she smiled, and Lizzie smiled back her pleasure in hearing Mariella speak. It was still just a few words, but she was saying more every week.

"How did you know? Well done, Mariella," and

Michael took the tray from her. As she closed the door, Lizzie asked Michael:

"Next to Jane?"

"Next to Jane," he agreed, and the next piece went into the tribal seating plan.

∽

Thanks to Lizzie and Michael's efforts, the Christmas lunch in the second week of December went very well, and everyone was still talking to each other afterwards. Lizzie had sensibly decided that to not sit next to Daniel would cause more speculation than to do so, and resigned herself to an awkward couple of hours.

In the event, it wasn't awkward at all. Daniel assumed she had placed herself there because she had forgiven him, and he held her hand under the table all the time they didn't need those hands to wield cutlery. By the time Daniel had whispered romance into her ear and generally treated her as if she was the embodiment of his favourite goddess, she was seduced all over again. She tried to remind herself about why she was cross with him, but it didn't seem as important as it had been. Later, when they were alone, she finally forgave him completely when he said:

"I'm so sorry, Lizzie. I tried to put right one mistake and ended up making a worse one. But I swear that I would have left her to fry had I known telling her was going to threaten our relationship. You mean the world to me, my goddess. I love you dearly. I promise I will never take our love for granted again."

A couple of days later, Ryan knocked on Lizzie's office door.

"Hello, Ryan, how's it going?"

"All finished. No major problems. I'll send a report in; probably be first week in New Year now. All right?"

"Yes, that's fine. You got up into the loft ok? I know Simon was very worried about his painting." Ryan twisted his hands and looked at them as if they held the answer to a very important question.

"You haven't damaged it, have you? Simon will kill you!"

"No, no, it was all covered up, like he said it would be. I was just – well look, I must be off: I've got another job on. Have a good Christmas and I'll be in touch."

Ryan disappeared as if he thought Lizzie would detain him if he wasn't quick enough, and Lizzie wondered if he had damaged something while he was up in the loft, even if the painting was still in one piece. 'He looked so shifty! I'm going to ask Simon to have a look around, just in case. I'm looking forward, though, to telling Stephanie there will be no large bills for the roof in the New Year.'

Late in the afternoon, Andy Harrison appeared in reception as Lizzie was just saying goodbye to a new patient.

"Hello Andy! Ryan was in earlier."

"Glad I've caught you. Can we go and have a chat somewhere private?"

Lizzie started to feel hot. She was scornful of those

people who insisted that they 'knew something was going to happen,' but right at this moment that was exactly how she felt. Ryan, acting so strangely; Andy, with something private to talk about – something was very wrong.

"The thing is, Lizzie, Ryan was a bit taken aback when he got up into your loft. Mind you, so was I when he told me." They had reached her office and Lizzie sat down heavily in her chair. Her heart was racing, her skin was clammy, and she could not think of a single thing to say.

"You must have known he would find out, so what I want to know is – why did you send him up there? It has put both me and him in a very tricky position."

Lizzie finally got her voice back. "Andy. I really don't know what you are talking about."

"Come on, you can't expect me to – "

"Andy, listen to me. I don't like telling people this, but I have a phobia about heights. I have to ask other people to do any task that involves ladders, and I've never been in the loft here. So please just tell me – what did Ryan find?"

"You really don't know?" Andy stood for a moment, working out the implications of that, and then sighed. "In that case, wait here."

He was gone a long time, during which Lizzie's thoughts ran riot. She was about to run out of the office to go and find him, when he reappeared in the doorway.

"Shut your eyes and hold out your hands, Lizzie," and although she could have screamed with frustration, she obeyed.

When she opened her eyes and looked down at what lay in her hands, she understood, for the first time, the real meaning of the word 'betrayal'.

∽

Chapter Seventeen

The Fall

'The Herald, 14th December'

Very Alternative Health!
Cannabis plants found at Clinic

The alternative health clinic known as Yatross was hit by further controversy last night when Police disclosed that cannabis plants have been found growing in the loft space.

Police admitted that the Director, Stephanie Harman, had herself alerted them to the presence of the cannabis as soon as she was told about it by one of her staff.

None of the Yatross staff were prepared to be interviewed, but Robert Dennis is writing a book about the clinic and spoke to the Herald.

"I can assure you that Stephanie Harman knew nothing of this," he asserted.

"Police are looking for a painter fellow who has spent many months up in the loft, doing a painting, or so he said. We now know he had another agenda."

On being asked why the staff hadn't found the cannabis before now, Mr Dennis could only say:

"Who goes up into a loft if they can help it? Certainly not me."

All clinic work has halted while the Police investigation is carried out.

Yatross has been hit by other problems in the past weeks. A fire occurred on Bonfire Night, which destroyed a statue and some gardens. It was thought to have been started deliberately, by a disgruntled patient.

'The Herald, 21st December'

Guns, drugs, fire and death
– Is Yatross jinxed?

The cannabis investigation continues at the ill-starred alternative health clinic. Police refused to confirm the rumour that a gun had been found on the premises, and speculation continues about who owned the gun and why it was there.

A hunt is on for the artist Simon Bevan, who Police now believe to be the instigator of the cannabis farm.

He has not been seen since just before the cannabis was found, and he is believed to have fled to Italy.

The clinic uses a large number of herbs in its practice, and boxes of these were taken away yesterday for testing for the possible presence of cannabis.

Police have now described how the cannabis plants were able to be grown without staff knowledge.

A spokesperson said:

"The artist stole bags of compost from the Yatross sheds, and the gardener believed this to be the work of vandals, so it wasn't taken too seriously. Heating was supplied in the form of several small oil-filled radiators, when he complained about feeling cold up in the loft. He regularly took up water and everything else he needed in his rucksack, and the staff just thought he was a big eater."

On being asked whether the painting Simon Bevan worked on was still up there, the police officer confirmed it was, but that it did not form part of their investigation, so was still in situ.

The Herald's staff have been unable to find any patients willing to admit they were offered cannabis at the clinic, whether as part of their treatment or not.

Meanwhile, local people have spoken to the Herald about their experience of the clinic.

Most of them seem to think it generally does a good job, but there have been a number of casualties recently.

Mr and Mrs Stephens spoke about their daughter, who has an eating disorder.

"She went there for the summer, and managed to put a bit of weight on. But she's lost it all now, and we're really worried about her. It was a complete waste of money."

Mrs Lennox, of Acorn Grove, said:

"I went there, I admit that, but I knew, as soon as I got into that reception place, that something funny was going on. Cannabis, eh? Well, it doesn't surprise me. I left soon after – I never saw any of them doctors, I'm glad to say."

On a sadder note: a relative of Trevor Browning, whose suicide was reported in this newspaper last week, told us that she knew Trevor had been attending the clinic for counselling, following the tragic death of his wife. No clinic staff were prepared to confirm or deny that he was a patient there.

'The Herald, 4th January'

Yatross remains closed – Police investigation continues

The Yatross clinic, which has been hit by a series of damaging revelations over the past weeks, remains closed following the discovery of cannabis plants there in the middle of December.

The artist Simon Bevan is now the only person Police are hunting for in relation to the crime, but they have not yet permitted the clinic to start treating patients again.

No-one on the clinic staff was available for comment.

Chapter Eighteen

Telos

The police finally gave Stephanie permission to re-enter Yatross on 31st January. She was shaking as she took the keys from the inspector's hand, and refused to meet his sardonic gaze. His attitude made his thoughts clear: Yatross had been flouting the law in some way all these years, and it was just luck that they hadn't been found out. But it would only be a matter of time before he caught them. 'In other words: watch your step, Stephanie Harman,' she thought. 'I wonder what happened to the presumption of innocence?' She drove carefully to the clinic, and parked in the visitor car park. As she unfolded herself from the car, the cold air made her skin tingle, adding to her sense of apprehension and anticipation. No snow had fallen yet, but she could sense that it wasn't far away.

Inside the building, she turned off the intruder alarm, and stood for a moment in the dimly lit reception. 'Mine again,' she thought gladly, and allowed herself to feel the relief of it for the first time. But she had a job to do, something that couldn't wait any longer.

She realised that she didn't know where Jim kept his stepladder, but she remembered the incident of Jane catching her costume in the book centre's ladder: 'How long ago that seems!' and so made her way to the book centre's stockroom. With some difficulty she manoeuvred the ladder into place under a trapdoor into the loft space, and flicked the light switch on the corridor wall. A tiny white feather was still caught in the ladder mechanism; it seemed to mock her as she worried about whether she had enough courage for this, and the thought acted like a brace on her resolve. Taking a deep breath: 'Watch your step, Stephanie,' she put one foot on the bottom rung and began to climb.

Her brain told her that this was a crazy thing to do, on her own in the clinic, with her arthritic knee not used to such adventures. Another, more elemental part of her was saying: "Do it, do it now: you have to know, before even another minute passes."

At the loft hatch, she slid the bolt open, and the hatch pushed away to one side on a sliding system of some sort: 'That was easier than I thought it would be.' She clambered awkwardly into the loft space, and looked around. Her first thought was that the loft was so much bigger than she had imagined. Everywhere there were brown speckles of earth from the pots the plants had been grown in. The floor was all boarded, and Stephanie was relieved, as she took her first few steps, that she wasn't going to have to worry about falling through the ceiling of the corridor below. The lights illuminated each of four sections of the loft, which mirrored the layout of the building itself. It was easy to walk upright, provided she stayed in the centre of each section, under the pitched roof.

As she turned a corner, a concertina ladder contraption on the floor puzzled her for a moment, until she realised that that was actually the main entrance to the loft, and would have been a lot easier to use than the stepladder, had she only known about it. She wondered what else there was of the day-to-day workings of Yatross about which she was completely unaware, focussed as she was on the medical side. 'Not any more,' she promised herself, and her eyes alighted on items left over from Simon's occupation of the loft: a box of spent paint tubes, plastic water bottles, a few crisp packets, and a mug from the kitchen. The mug caused a swell of resentment in her chest, which rose up into her head and engulfed her, so that she had to stop walking for a moment. 'Mariella has been feeding him, providing him with tea and cake and everything he could wish, while he sat up here, tending his cannabis plants and planning our downfall. Or was it as cold-blooded as that? Did he expect us to get the blame? Or did he not care one way or another?' Stephanie had asked herself these questions so many times over the past weeks and was still no nearer to knowing the answer.

It had been a big blow to her pride, to realise that she had not seen through Simon Bevan. She thought she understood people well, and could work out what motivated them, and their likely behaviour patterns. 'I did identify a reckless, anti-authority streak in him, but I didn't expect it to be used against Yatross. I always expect the people who work for me to be loyal, and because that expectation is usually realised, I've become complacent. I see that now. One of the saddest things from this whole affair is that I will probably never trust anyone completely, ever again. One thing I am sure of, though. Simon will have finished the painting. His pride wouldn't let him go before he had 'paid his dues' as he put it.'

As she expected, she found the painting on the north side of the loft, where Simon would have taken advantage of the clear light coming through the loft windows. The painting was much bigger than she had expected, and she felt a renewed interest and anticipation as she took the last couple of steps to stand in front of the painting.

Stephanie's first feeling was a mild surprise. She had expected his intellectual conceit to choose an obscure Greek myth that hardly anyone knew of, but no: he had chosen Odysseus, the wanderer. The painting was a story of Odysseus' life, with various aspects of his adventures flowing into each other around the edge of the work, and eventually spiralling into the centre. Here was Odysseus waiting with his fleet at the start of the voyage to Troy, with no wind for the sails and the sea a flat calm; there were battles of the Trojan War, the Trojan horse, and the fall of Troy.

Stephanie then identified aspects of the subsequent Odyssey: twelve jars of wine being given to the sailors by the priest of Apollo; the sailors eating lotus fruit from the African people who made them welcome; the Cyclops, blocking the cave being explored by Odysseus and his men, and the subsequent blinding of the Cyclops with a pointed stick in his only eye. There was the leather bag, which contained strong winds: Simon had painted a small ship spinning round in the gale that ensued when the bag was opened. Circe was there, and the sailors turned into swine; Odysseus bound to the mast of his ship so that he could hear the siren song without going mad. Scylla the sea monster, half woman and half dog, was paired with Charybdis the giant sea swallower: Stephanie saw Odysseus holding on to a fig tree to avoid being swept into her mouth. The beautiful trees and flowers on the island of Calypso surrounded a raft which the nymph helped him build, to try once again to sail home; and finally his arrival in a borrowed ship back home to Ithaca, which Odysseus must have thought he would never see again.

Stephanie stepped back and studied the painting in its entirety. It was an amazing work. In the wrong hands, it would have been a mess, but Simon had artfully drawn the strands of Odysseus' life together in a coherent thread that drew the eyes over the painting in the right way, and did not confuse or irritate. The colours were subtle, but the texture of the painting was not: there was a three-dimensional quality to it that was unexpected. Stephanie looked closer at the many ships, which looked like real wood … they *were* real wood, and so were the masts. How could that be? Tipping her head behind the canvas, she saw that the painting was mounted on an intricate wooden framework, rather than a plain easel, due to its size. Looking at the front again, she realised that Simon had cut the canvas in dozens of small places, to allow wood to protrude just where he needed real wood, which he then painted to fit the scene. The sides of the split canvas must be glued to the same wood, as it stayed taut on the frame. It was a vast, complex piece of work, like nothing she had ever seen. Vast…something about the size of it took Stephanie's thoughts in a new direction. She looked around the loft for something to measure the size of the canvas, and found a ball of garden twine, obviously from Tom's shed, like the compost. She suppressed the resurgent anger at the thought of Simon calmly tying up the cannabis plants, and concentrated on her task. She took her measured length of twine to the loft hatch on the north side, and held it against the hatch door.

It was as she thought. There was not the remotest possibility that this painting would go out through a loft hatch, and there was no other way of getting it out. The canvas could not be rolled, because to remove it from the web of wooden pieces would completely destroy the work. Stephanie walked slowly back to stand in front of the painting, her thoughts racing. 'Why did he do this? Simon is an exhibitionist: he would love people to see and exclaim over his painting. Why did he deliberately create one that would rarely be seen?'

Paintings like this cannot be taken in on first viewing. Stephanie knew it would be one in which she would see something new every time she viewed it. She scanned the painting again carefully, looking for a clue. The first new aspect to claim her attention was the title: Simon had called it 'Telos'.

'Telos. The ends and purposes of life. Yatross is Telos to me; is this painting, probably the best thing he's ever done, Telos to Simon? Certainly the title is appropriate to the painting: Odysseus had twenty years of war and wandering before he reached his goal: his home, his wife, his Ithaca.' Another detail caught her eye. 'What's happening there? I see: Odysseus is having his feet washed by an old woman; I don't know that story. But the brushwork is so beautiful. Oh, Simon, why couldn't you have just stuck to painting?'

Stephanie's attention was diverted by the arrival of snow on the loft windows: the fat smudges of soft white flakes warned her that she could not stay up here much longer, not if she wanted to drive home tonight.

She looked again at the Trojan Horse: a more familiar story. The wooden horse had been a supposed gift, dedicated to Athena. The Trojans had towed it into their city stronghold, thinking the goddess would punish them if they refused it. But it was a trick by the wily Odysseus, who was hiding inside the stomach of the horse with some men. They waited until it was dark, then climbed out of a trapdoor in the stomach, and opened the city gates to their waiting army. The city was burned and looted: the fall of Troy after ten years of war.

So that was it. The lights in the loft appeared to brighten as the answer evolved in her head. The painting was the supposed gift, hiding above the trapdoor of the loft. But it was not a gift at all, as it was never going to hang in the clinic reception, as they'd planned. She had been duped into providing a place for Simon to grow the cannabis plants, and it had led to the fall of Yatross, just as Simon must have known it would. And so Stephanie was back to the same question: did Simon deliberately set out to ruin them, or were they just a convenient cover for his operation? But if that was all it was, why go to so much trouble over this stunning painting?

One thing Stephanie did know. The painting was not going to be destroyed. It could stay up here, always. It would remind her that the gods always punished those who were too proud.

With reluctance, she walked back towards the hatch on the south side of the loft. As she picked her way through the debris again, a memory tugged at her brain: something about a painting in a loft … 'Dorian Gray, of course: that's it.

'And now, it is a new year, and Yatross will thrive again, I know. We will gradually get our patients back, and Yatross will be as perfect as it always should have been. Meanwhile, in the loft space, the painting can perhaps take on all the nasty traits of the humans scurrying around below, and it will spoil and decay, just like the picture in Oscar Wilde's story…' Stephanie laughed out loud at her uncharacteristic piece of fantasy: it was the first genuine amusement she had felt in weeks.

She reached the loft hatch and prepared herself for the difficult descent on to the waiting stepladder. The white feather had completely disappeared from view.

About the Author

Born in Brixton, London, but having lived most of her adult life in Kent, SallyAnne has been writing stories and poems since the age of eleven. This is her first novel.

Sometimes the Healing illustrates her lifelong interest in health, well-being and psychology. In a career involving making and keeping people well, she has enjoyed promoting the alternative health principles that have been effective for her own health.